EVEN PLAYING FIELD

Imogen Pershouse

Published in Australia by Sid Harta Books & Print Pty Ltd,
ABN: 34632585293
23 Stirling Crescent, Glen Waverley, Victoria 3150 Australia
Telephone: +61 3 9560 9920, Facsimile: +61 3 9545 1742
E-mail: author@sidharta.com.au

First published in Australia 2024
This edition published 2024
Copyright © Imogen Pershouse 2024
Cover design, typesetting: WorkingType (www.workingtype.com.au)

ISBN: 978-1-922958-85-3

About the Author

Imogen Pershouse is the pseudonym of a nurse who has worked forty-two years full time in rural and tertiary hospitals in both Queensland and New South Wales. Her experience in general, midwifery and intensive care nursing is being used in this book of biological fiction.

Even Playing Field is her first book.

Even Playing Field is a biological medical fiction book dedicated to the many hardworking nurses, field hands, building labourers and others exploited by unfair, unscientific, draconian, insurance-biased laws, who have been financially compromised by having to fund their own work injuries.

I would like to sincerely thank my sister Viv, husband Keith, and niece SJ for their contributions to this book. I am also indebted to the Sid Harta Publishing team of Kerry Collison, Marie Pietersz, Susan Pierotti, and Luke Harris for making this book so professional.

All members of our family would also like to thank the amazing work of Rare Cancers Australia and Neuroblastoma Australia teams for their support of the vulnerable children with cancer and their families during their crisis.

Disclaimer

The *Even Playing Field* and *Ears Pasted On* stories have been published to raise funds for the cancer prevention relapse drugs required to improve the survival chance of a two-year-old family member with a stage 4 neuroblastoma, who will need lifelong financial support for hearing aids and expensive pharmaceutical drugs to survive and live a quality life. The images included have been selected by the parents of the toddler to convey the importance of infants and children being able to access paediatricians for early diagnosis and treatments rather than having significant signs and symptoms of cancer dismissed by those yet to develop these specialty skills and knowledge.

While these stories are based on real life scenarios, all personal and place names are fictional and any correlation with any real individuals or institutions is purely coincidental.

Contents

Chapter 1

Friday 9 January

Tahlia Bennett

Tahlia Bennett had driven an hour to her favourite beach to get a tan while she slept off her night shift. Blonde, petite and 157 cm tall, Tahlia loved the sand and surf, but only afforded herself this small luxury one day a month, on her first day after coming off night shifts. The rest of the time Tahlia dedicated to her studies. Studying veterinary science kept Tahlia poor, as the university debts spiralled out of control every semester, with the continually rising costs of textbooks, university fees, computer software and higher education taxes. There was little time left after study and work if Tahlia was to finish her degree by the end of the year. Her goal was to be registered as a veterinary doctor by January the following year. To pursue her lifelong dream, Tahlia could afford no failures. Tahlia had been lucky to be offered part-time veterinary nursing work at the Bounty Small Animal Hospital, an opportunity offered to only a few of her classmates. During semester breaks, Tahlia boosted her income significantly with additional waitressing and kitchen work.

Fortunately, thought Tahlia, it was blissfully quiet for school holidays. Today looked ideal for a peaceful sleep and sunbake. A gentle coastal breeze rolled over the swaying grass along the shoreline. Seagulls glided on air currents above and meandered along the sand, looking for food. The beautiful long, white, sandy beach was less populated down the end where she often camped, half concealed behind a small rock wall. Tahlia lay down her towel, peeled her shirt and shorts off down to her bikini, then gazed around at the rolling waves. After unpacking her juice bottle next to her small pillow, Tahlia decided on a quick dip in the refreshingly cool ocean before soaking up the sun on her towel while dozing off. This single day off a month was hers to enjoy guilt free. Several times during the warm day, Tahlia woke up. She sipped her warm orange juice, which seemed to be getting a bit rancid, before rolling over to bake on the other side.

It seemed only a few hours later when the exhausted Tahlia woke up suddenly, totally disorientated in a dark room. Each of her limbs was tied to the end of a bed, with a huge weight holding her down. Her vision and thoughts were muddled. Tahlia attempted to brace her thighs at the searing pain between her legs. When she tried to move and call out, a blow struck her left eye and face, leaving her stunned. Her dry mouth tasted of blood, which trickled unrestrained down the side of her chin and neck. There was a stale smell of garlic on her attacker's breath. He was perspiring profusely, his hair dripping sweat onto her. Panic caused her heart rate to palpitate in her neck. The man was so heavy she could hardly breathe. When all attempts to move her arms and legs failed, Tahlia blacked out. A short time later, a different, lighter weight was pinning her down, uttering filthy obscenities with each thrust. 'I know what you need, bitch. We're taking you in turns.' The husky, menacing voice caused her to panic again. Only able to move her head from side to side, Tahlia looked around at the small dark room, then at the lighter menacing shape looming above her. She wanted to scream. Her wrists and ankles burned when she tried unsuccessfully to get up. With movement confined to lying on her back, her vision blurred and she soon passed out again. When she finally awoke, the room was still dark. Tahlia had no idea where she was, nor who was raping her again. She needed to lie still to stop the waves of nausea and throbbing in her head. Tahlia could only see through her right eye; the left was now swollen shut. Tahlia was ignored when she sobbed loudly, begging him to stop.

Chapter 2

Friday 7 February

Carol Bryant

'Nursing really is the profession of oppression', I say to Cindy, my colleague for over twenty years. 'Here I am at almost 3 am, getting whipped by a confused old lady.'

The combative Connie had removed her oxygen prongs yet again.

'If I was an intelligent lifeform, I wouldn't be here.'

I look at my colleague, frustration oozing from every pore of my being. I have attempted to reapply those oxygen prongs patiently about ten times. Now, I have a double risk situation. If I sedate this cantankerous woman, I might end up reducing her oxygen levels further if she does not comply with keeping her oxygen on. On the other hand, if I don't give Connie the Haloperidol prescribed for her delirium, she is likely to start climbing over the bedrails. God, please grant me patience, damned quick! I am in the wrong job. This deal is meant for those with tolerance that I do not possess at 3 am, especially after working four nights, averaging only five hours sleep a day. I am feeling guilty – I should be counting my blessings.

My buddy, Cindy Ryan, was allocated a strong young male in cocaine withdrawal, who is far more aggressive and agitated. I watch him hallucinating, busily trying to light an imaginary cigarette. Unlike the portly Cindy, I don't have to go home after a twelve-hour night with a sore back and aching feet to prepare lunches for three young children and take them to school or put on a plastic smile of greeting when I pick them up, still feeling like shit on a stick. Cindy always reports that, 'naturally', with an eight-hour window to sleep during the school days, her phone will ring or a retired neighbour will break out their lawnmower.

Tonight is one of those nights where only our sense of humour will get us through. Our other survival strategy will be pulling the bedside curtains around our combined bed spaces to avoid Jenny Marlows.

This provocative supervisor always enters the Intensive Care Unit creating an emotional storm. Jenny's chronic disrespect drains every last grain of mercy we don't possess. Jenny will bounce in here with shit on her liver at any perceived slight. She will expect us to either cower to her or listen supportively while she vents her spleen at anyone possessing the audacity to challenge her explosive outbursts. Knowing our luck, Cindy and I will just get our two patients finally settled before the storm bird arrives. With Jenny pointing her finger and shouting as though berating teenagers, it is a mystery that no cranky shift worker has yet used that digit to impale her brain.

Cindy and I are probably friends because nursing was never a career choice for either of us. At seventeen years old, I ran foul of Queensland law when my father, the last of my surviving parents, died before my eighteenth birthday and I was unable to access my inherited trust funds for university fees to become a laboratory scientist. I applied for the hospital-based nursing training. If being a grieving teenager wasn't stressful enough, landing in the most toxic culture imaginable certainly was anxiety provoking. As novices at the bottom of the pecking order, struggling to adapt to shift work and a steep learning curve, survival required navigating around many superegos, making the least waves possible. Remarkably, when interacting with irritable shift workers, demanding line managers and patients in pain, each shift ended with a hideous inability to please anybody. I hate people. Laboratory equipment, slides and tests would be kinder than dealing with complex humans with irrational behaviours. Unlike Cindy, my career strategy is not to socialise with people who get their sport belittling others. After years of learning medical terminology and professional skills, I have remained profoundly intolerant of leaders treating nurses like glorified handmaidens.

The bubbly Cindy, on the other hand, focuses on building bridges and relationships. Cindy had completed several years of radiological studies in ultrasounds and X-rays before falling pregnant, moving interstate and juggling her parental responsibilities with nursing and shiftwork. Jovial Cindy, now a mother of four, adapts to these challenges by finding the humour in a predicament. Ironically, Cindy's first challenge in nursing arose when Matron Frazer told her to remove the ring that had never been off her hand since her wedding day. To the butch Matron, Cindy's protests about this intrusion into her personal boundaries were unreasonable. Historically, Cindy was informed, wedding rings were slave bands, thus symbols of dominance. Cindy temporarily relinquished the wedding ring to appear subordinate, then pretended to forget when caught wearing it again. While the difficulties of cleaning hands thoroughly while wearing jewelry have validity, the reality is that disposable gloves are worn during all contact with body fluids. However, Cindy hilariously entertained us all with the comedy of the irate matron's stance and English accent, as she demanded the removal of her wedding ring to free herself from oppression. Cindy's best talent is to mimic other's mannerisms and postures to the point of threatening our continence.

I recall that, even as a student nurse, Cindy was not averse to pulling a prank in the right company. In the surgical ward, bedridden young males, in skeletal traction waiting for fractured bones to heal, would often entertain each other with mischief. They would pull stunts like removing items from her dressing trolley, knowing that she was doing a sterile procedure to prevent bone infections. One young male grabbed a syringe full of amber fluid from the bottom shelf of Cindy's dressing trolley when she went to wash her hands. He had threatened to squirt the contents of the syringe out on his top bed sheet unless Cindy bought him a chocolate from the canteen. After the syringe's content was expelled, Cindy cheekily informed the brat that if he wished to spend his day soaking in someone else's urine, she was happy she could accommodate him. This triumph was met with roars of laughter from the other three males sharing the four-bed bay, with him squirming at his predicament. Without considering his vulnerability, the young man continued his antics by having his mates smuggle in a six-pack of beer. The four blokes in that bay knew the game was up when Cindy placed some fizzy indigestion powder into his urinal, with the formula bubbling excessively like froth from a shaken beer when the urinal was used.Cindy's best prank, however, was creating an illusion while I was inside a curtain helping her wash the young man's back.

'Oh,' Cindy exclaimed when she went to change the bed linen, 'you've crapped yourself.'

'What?' exclaimed the embarrassed male. In her gloved hand, Cindy showed him four flattened pebbles that looked like poo. The other three in the bay were ominously silent.

'It must have been those painkillers and sleeping tablets I got last night,' protested the flustered teenager.

'Oh, well,' shrugged Cindy, tossing the flattened chocolate Maltesers into her mouth.

The look on the patient's face was priceless. His facial expressions instantly flashed from utter humiliation to roaring with laughter in appreciation of Cindy's greatest prank yet.

Cindy's humour was often delivered with sexual innuendos to entertain colleagues and lighten the serious ICU atmosphere. Tonight's finding of a $20 note between her young patient's penis and scrotum triggers harmless banter with me about sperm banks and deposits. Her patient, Eric, who is only thirty-five years old, has spent seventeen years of his life in prison. Having been recently released, Eric was assaulted not long after purchasing illicit drugs from a known dealer. Eric arrived in ICU with six fractured ribs on the left side of his chest and a chest drain to remove blood from between the linings of his pleural cavity. For days, the hallucinating Eric had been reluctant to use his physiotherapy spirometer, designed to prevent further lung collapse. So, when Eric suddenly sat up and sucked on the spirometer several times, Cindy had thought his delirium was resolving. Eric was maintaining eye contact and appeared more orientated, right up until he asked, 'Did you put the cone in?'

After Connie has finally settled with her sedation, I tape her oxygen prongs in place to keep the device in her nostrils. With Connie's blood oxygen saturations improving, I wander over to see if Cindy needs a hand or wants to grab a coffee. As I casually saunter to Cindy's bedside in my jade scrubs, returning my pen to my pocket, Eric suddenly calls out to me, believing I am someone called Annie. In a flirty voice with a big smile, he says, 'Annie, I could just imagine you in a G string.'

'God, no wonder you need Intensive Care,' I respond. 'You'd have to be critically ill wanting to see a sixty-year-old, with more corrugations than a tin roof, in a G-string!'

Cindy chuckles, her broad shoulders shaking, as her face lights up in her characteristic grin. In our worst possible moments, Cindy's personality has taught me to maintain my grace by using humour as a coping mechanism. Trying to give Eric less attention in the hope that he will fall asleep while Cindy is away, I stroll over to look through the window at the car park below. A strange van has jumped the curb and is being driven diagonally towards the Emergency Department to conceal its number plates from the security cameras. As I alert security to this suspicious activity, I watch on as they arrive in the parking lot below, only to discover a nurse's antique car has been jacked up on bricks with all four wheels stolen. Rather than sleeping after her night shift, poor Emma from the children's ward will be shopping for wheels and tyres before returning tonight. Since Bounty Hospital never accepts any liability for personal property, Emma is now left with more debts than when she began her night rotation.

Cindy returns from her break with an amused facial expression, undoubtedly thoroughly entertained by new hospital gossip. 'What's so funny?' I ask.

'Jayney Whyte,' Cindy says, 'she's livid!'

'What's happened?'

When we had arrived on duty, Jayney, our normally placid new grad, had been instructed to transfer her allocated patient to the ward, then clean and restock her bay for a new arrival. After listening to a verbal handover on her new admission's age, medications and social history, Jayney was still unclear on what exactly the patient's overdose was. Frustrated that the Emergency novice, Ellen Hendricks, was also unsure on what her patient, Joan, had taken or the antidote to the poison, Jayney proceeded to attach the monitor leads and record her preliminary observations.

With the stress of the unknown outweighing the risk of humiliation, Jayne rang Emergency to make enquiries from the admitting doctor, since it would be a while before the ICU doctor returned from the ward emergency he was attending. While waiting for Dr Simon Lake to come to the phone, Jayney read the perplexing notes again. The medical records said, 'had KFC with Coke, vomiting ever since'. Jayney's extensive search found no mention of KFC anywhere in either the pharmacy or toxicology manual, and no antidote information was available either. In her handover, Ellen had shown Jayne the prescribed intravenous fluids and anti-nausea medications, but the overdose substance remained a mystery to both. Although Jayney assumed that 'KFC' must not be extremely toxic, unprepared to risk her newly acquired registration or her patient's life, she rang the Emergency doctor to declare her ignorance.

Jayney wanted to know what adverse reactions she was supposed to be observing this patient for, and what interventions like dialysis or respiratory support might be required should deterioration occur. To her horror, Dr Simon Lake's response to her questions left her acutely mortified.

'KFC is not a drug; it's Kentucky Fried Chicken,' replied the caustic Simon. 'What the hell is she doing admitted to ICU? Joan was supposed to be admitted to the surgical ward with probable appendicitis until her blood results are processed. Don't tell me it was that idiot supervisor again!'

'Oh … I'll ring Jenny to see if there are any surgical beds available,' Jayney replied, keen to get off the phone.

'Those bloody doctors need to comply with the hospital abbreviation guidelines,' shrieked Jenny down the phone. 'Now we have to either leave Joan in an ICU bed overnight if I can't find a female surgical bed or disturb the whole bloody ward.''So, Jenny is already at pre-ignition,' reports Cindy, giggling to herself. Cindy was smirking about the war drama playing out between Jenny and Simon. 'Anything that keeps Jenny fuming for the night will surely keep the novices safe from her nitpicking.'

I looked over at Jayney finalising both the admission and discharge paperwork just as the orderly arrived for the transfer out.

Naturally, it was not beyond either Cindy or me to use Jenny's authoritative attitude for amusement. On one occasion, a patient's wife was asked to wait outside the curtain while Cindy was removing her husband's urinary catheter. The irate wife marched abruptly to the nursing station, demanding to file an official complaint with the hospital manager. After Jenny was notified, she immediately arrived in the busy ICU where an aeromedical retrieval was occurring, keen to display her managerial skills to the enraged relative.

When Jenny meekly offered to help, the wife pointed to Cindy, saying, 'That nurse has stolen my husband's testicles!'

At handover for the oncoming shift, Cindy had delighted the new shift by reading out Jenny's elaborate documentation of the robbery. Cindy had marched on the spot, describing how Jenny had attended the husband's bedside, procuring the wife as a witness. After rolling the patient onto his side, both had confirmed that the missing gonads had been found, Cindy loudly declared with a victorious hand pump gesture. Cindy had miraculously turned an intimidating situation into a comedy yet again.

'What's happening around the rest of the unit?' I ask Cindy, watching a ventilator and infusions being prepared in bay six.

Although we receive a broad summary of the ICU's existing patients on a diagnosis sheet at the start of each shift, we only get full bedside handovers on the specific patient we are allocated.

'Steve Jacobsen is getting a ventilated overdose who has aspirated, a young male testing positive for narcotics ...'

We both watched as Team Leader Lauren Poulsen, just returning with Dr Sam Lee from the ward Medical Emergency Team (MET) call, saunters over to offer Steve a meal break before his admission arrives. Sam rings Ray Fischer, the intensivist on call, to discuss what lines and tubes should be inserted into Peter Robinson, the new arrival. He records Ray's sedation preference, the ventilator settings and his recommendations for emergency responses should deterioration occur.

Steve returns from his break to a flurry of activity. The Emergency stretcher had arrived, and the orderlies are transferring the unconscious patient onto the ICU bed. Sam is at the top of the bed, supporting the breathing tube. Lauren connects the new arrival to the ICU ventilator before moving to the other side of the bed to attach the monitor leads. Steve is receiving a verbal handover from Linda Hendricks, the Emergency nurse. Jayney, just returning from her surgical ward transfer, has helped with the bed transfer before recording the initial observations on the patient's flow chart.

Next moment, the ventilator high pressure alarm sounds loudly, at the same time as the high-pitched low blood pressure alarm flashes red on the ceiling-mounted monitor. With Cindy offering to keep an eye on both our patients, I rush over to help. The new admission's neck veins are grossly distended. I temporarily silence the alarms. As Sam detaches the ventilator to connect the breathing tube to a manual inflation bag, a huge audible gush of air escaped the breathing tube. Sam begins manually ventilating the patient to ensure the breathing tube is open, to check that both sides of Peter's chest are rising evenly with each breath. The grossly distended neck veins begin to collapse, no longer visible. I hold Sam's stethoscope for him, moving the diaphragm end around Peter's chest. Sam hand-ventilates the patient, synchronising his actions to listen for air entry.

The arterial waveform recording the blood pressure rises to normal parameters as if the ventilator were the problem. I look over in shock at the ventilator. Someone had set the Positive End Expiratory Pressure (PEEP) to fifteen centimetres of water instead of three to five, the normal range. A small amount of PEEP is usually set to stop alveolar collapse, as ventilator gas entering the lungs always follows the path of least resistance. A setting of around three to five centimetres of water keeps extra air in the lungs to prevent collapse and recruit alveoli. However, an extremely high setting of fifteen had caused air to become trapped in Peter's lungs, making him unable to breathe out. The rising pressure of the air trapped in Peter's lungs had squashed his heart, causing the neck veins to distend and the blood pressure to drop when the heart chambers could not fill.

I stared at the ventilator before pointing to the setting in disbelief.

Chapter 3

Monday 10 February

Steve Jacobsen

All the ICU teams involved have been invited to the incident analysis room to review this Peter Robinson event with the clinical governance risk analysis team. I am sitting in this meeting wondering how the PEEP ended up dialled at fifteen centimetres when I know I set it at five. Although it was 4.10 am, Lauren had fortunately double-checked my ventilator settings with the phone order Sam had written down before I left for my meal break. Even the first set of observations recorded by Jayney had documented the ventilator PEEP setting at five.

Unfortunately, the ventilator dial is not a flat screen button that makes a noise when you enter a value; it is a knob.

I have not slept. I am alarmed that this near miss was not an accident. I am concerned that someone has tried to kill Peter Robinson, both before and after his ICU admission. A chill creeps down my spine, making me paranoid and wary. I find myself constantly observing everyone and everything around me. Had Peter taken a narcotic overdose prior to admission, or was the ventilator sabotage a second attempt on his life? Most of the nurses not on duty are present at this human error and patient safety (HEAPS) analysis, but not the orderlies, who would not usually be expected to attend. The ICU nurse manager is present to protect her staff from the stern-faced suits migrating out of their offices for the sentinel event review. No matter what the outcome, the Nursing Director for ICU Marcus Maitland, the Executive Director of Nursing and the Operational Services Manager can be relied upon to exclusively protect their own reputations and budget integrity.

There is a distinct lack of friendly interaction between the clustered bureaucrats saturated with their own self-importance sitting at the back of the room and their workforce who look forward to avoid the gaze of their 'kiss up, kick down' line managers.

Police officers Julie Wright and Vivienne Hales are observing the HEAPS analysis process. Vivienne brushes a hair of her nutbrown stylish bob behind her ear as she takes out her notepad and pen. Both seem keen to listen to Peter's case review to determine whether any participants can provide a legitimate medical explanation for the PEEP incidence. Julie's sandy blonde hair is swept into a bun, drawing attention to her sapphire blue eyes keenly observing the power dynamics. As an avid jogger, Julie, at 173 centimetres tall, has an athletic physique and sleek posture. Julie looks across to her colleague, acknowledging the silent, tense atmosphere that has not escaped Vivienne's attention. Fine boned Vivienne, at 155 centimetres tall, has a heart-shaped face that portrays her intrinsic sensitivity and astute ability to interpret body language. Her slightly elevated eyebrows and slow, subtle nod perceptively communicates agreement. The deafening silence and plummeting mood in the room has alerted all to the arrival of the leadership.

To lighten the mood, Julie leans over and whispers to Vivienne, 'I think I've just developed a fetish for black hair, blue eyes and black leather ties', diverting Vivienne's gaze subtly towards the handsome Ray. Vivienne smirks, before taking a second look at the charismatic doctor's profile. Though neither officer was currently dating, when they did, both had a preference for intelligent men with clever humour and stimulating conversation.

Tall, handsome Ray Fischer is keen to get the proceedings

underway; since he is not on call for this evening, beginning this one-hour meeting on schedule will allow him time to surf a few waves. Ray rakes his black, wavy hair and trimmed full beard and scans the room to ensure his interns have arrived. Taking advantage of the frosty silence that has just enveloped the room, Ray begins the HEAPS process by explaining the concept of the PEEP valve to the clinical governance team, as being 'positive end expiratory pressure used to increase the amount of gas remaining in the lung at the end of expiration'. He elaborates: 'In the lung, the blood gets shunted away from alveolar that are collapsed, so the PEEP helps alveolar recruitment. When you can get air into the lung alveoli, the blood does not shunt past collapsed areas, so oxygen transfer between the lung and alveoli improves.'

Mentally, I make a list of who was at the bed area:

Sam Lee, ICU resident doctor

Simon Lake, Emergency resident

Linda Hendricks, Emergency nurse

Lauren Poulsen, ICU team leader

Mandie Lane, ICU orderly helping with the transfer

John Simpson, Emergency orderly

Carol Bryant, ICU Registered Nurse

Jenny Marlow, night supervisor.

The woman from clinical governance goes through the HEAPS analysis format. Those present make suggestions to identify what potential environment factors like workloads, night shift and staffing issues could have contributed to this serious event. Little is achieved other than to complete a paperwork process that places everyone at Peter's bedside under a cloud of suspicion.

Jenny and Carol had both arrived after the emergency. Carol had not been on the side of the bed where the ventilator was located. I had not seen where Paula was before I arrived, so I could not eliminate her as a suspect – that is, if this PEEP incident was not accidental. Since I don't believe the PEEP dial was accidently bumped to be turned around such a distance, there are six staff members I intend to watch in case anything like this happens again. Ventilator settings do not just adjust themselves. Why is someone trying to harm Peter Robinson? Who is he, and how did he attract his enemies?

Before I leave work that morning, I report my concerns to Gail Tontine, the ICU nurse unit manager. Together we ring the hospital security to officially report and document our concerns. I have been working with this ICU team for over two years. While there is always the occasional episode of shiftworker bickering, nothing like this has occurred before.

Will my colleagues consider *me incompetent*? I wonder.

Chapter 4

Peter Robinson police check

Peter does not seem to be the typical, depressed, overdosed patient at all, yet he has remained unconscious since his admission two days ago. According to his family and police records, Peter has no prior history of illicit drug use and no suicidal triggers like recent conflicts or relationship breakdowns. So, how did the drugs get into his system?

Peter's concerned parents have visited the ICU every day, getting progress updates from the intensivist, Ray Fischer. Although both brothers were known to drink a few rums at footy barbecues and at the pub, even Craig was shocked about the narcotics discovered in his brother's drug screen. Since drug screens only identify broad drug classifications, the narcotics could be anything from heroin to prescribed painkillers. However, no recent sporting or farming injuries were on file with either Peter's general practitioner or the Emergency Department. The possibility of a heroin dealer's hot shot of pure product intended to kill was eliminated in the absence of any detectible puncture marks or needle tracks on Peter's body. The positive drug screen results have been scientifically validated twice. With hair growing at a predictable one centimetre a month, the family's testimonies of Peter's clean lifestyle have been verified by hair analysis. With no history of prior drug abuse or warrants for arrests for deviant behaviour, the positive narcotic screen is perturbing.

A police officer has been stationed at Peter's bedside until he wakes up and is able to confirm foul play. Should Peter die, the police advice is that the bed area is to remain untouched to preserve the crime scene until investigators arrive. Nothing is to be removed, unless equipment (such as a ventilator) is required for other patients. Nurses are to follow the usual procedure for a coroner's case by arranging for a family member to identify the body in the presence of the police, and the police will escort the body to the morgue. The police have collected swabs from Peter's rings, nail clippings, hair follicles, gastric and lung secretions, as well as blood and urine for forensic analysis. Visitors and information about Peter's condition have been restricted to his immediate family.

When questioned by police officers Julie Wright and Vivienne Hale, Sandy and Brad Robinson said their son Peter lived at Gynter on an isolated, 160-hectare, rural property twenty kilometres south of Bounty. Peter and his brother, Craig, are co-owners of the property they have purchased with a bank mortgage. To guarantee their mortgage repayments, twenty-eight-year-old Peter was employed as a full-time rural insurance salesman to offset any income fluctuations caused by unpredictable weather events. Thirty-year-old Craig managed the cattle as the primary farm manager responsible for feeding, tagging, tracking and marketing the cattle; Peter helped out with fencing and mustering when required. Sandy mentioned that Craig and Peter were supportive of each other and lived harmoniously on their property after they'd moved out from home.

Despite Sandy and Brad describing both their sons as hardworking, it was odd that neither of these tall, olive-skinned men were in a current or full-time relationship. With only a two-year age difference, the brothers were described as being 'close'.

Although parents will usually boast of their children's achievements or provide entertaining memories from their childhood, it was noticeable that neither Brad nor Sandy commented on Peter's personality at all. Both Brad and Sandy described their sons' generic interests like sport but with no intimate comments attached.

Both brothers played football on weekends. Peter's football

team manager, Simon Dunlop, sent flowers to the family and made enquiries to monitor Peter's condition, through Sandy and Brad, to update the team. Keith Salzman, Peter's boss, described him as reliable and efficient, but again used non-specific language to describe the footballer he had been acquainted with for over ten years. Keith mentioned that Peter processed insurance claims and sold policies for the rural industry, working variable hours on a salary. As for most farming communities, the salary conditions allowed Peter to make up his hours when the brothers needed to work together to brand or muster cattle. When asked about Peter's social and family life, Keith reflected that Peter's commitments had left little time for socialising. It was noticeable that all employees used words that were distinctly lacking personality traits, like 'friendly', in their conversations. Keith had reported no conflicts between Peter and other staff.

Other employees, working alongside Peter in the shared office, had also experienced limited personal interaction with him. Both Sarah and Lucy stated Peter tended to use his mobile during breaks to order farm supplies rather than conversing with them in the tearoom. Since Lucy and Sarah described themselves as wives and mothers of small toddlers and children, both had rationalised that their 'baby talk' may have discouraged Peter from engaging in conversations with them.

After finalising these interviews, both Julie and Vivienne walked away with a sense that while their questions had been cautiously answered, a lot had been left unsaid. Nothing about this bizarre case was adding up.

Next, Julie and Vivienne's appearances in uniform and attempted questions provoked endless distractions for the footballers before the team's practice sessions began. Most of the players described Peter and Craig as 'highly competitive' or 'aggressive' on the football field. When questioned about any conflicts, both brothers were described as keeping mostly to themselves. Again, every interviewee had conspicuously discussed the brothers as interacting with each other rather than teammates. The brothers did not usually travel on the bus to sporting events, but instead flew or took their own vehicles to cope with the farm's heavy workloads. On the few occasions the brothers did socialise with their teammates, both Peter and Craig had sat together and drunk rum, then stayed overnight at the nearby Bounty Hotel.

The Brumbie Football Club's kitchen, waitressing and bar staff also reported no conflicts from the brothers. However, like the employees from Gynter Rural, the female staff appeared more wary of the brothers than their male teammates. Most of the ladies were looking around during conversations as though on alert.

When casually asked their opinions as to why these two buffed, handsome brothers were still single, a sassy, unfiltered bar attendant made an offhand remark about the brothers treating women like 'meat on a sheet'. No one could remember either Peter or Craig socialising with partners, girlfriends or even family members. The majority of the females who were questioned displayed a subconscious defensive wariness of both siblings.

At the daily case briefings, Police Officer Mike Mahoney, who had been interviewing neighbours, had also detected a distinct pattern of subliminal social withdrawal being reported when the brothers were discussed. Most questions about Peter's mannerisms led to responses describing both brothers as though they were inseparable. One farmer, interviewed from the neighbouring property on the town side, said that in the eight years since the brothers had purchased their farm, neither Craig nor Peter had engaged him in a single conversation about meat prices, rural supplies or anything. Although there were no conflicts or disturbances, the farmer and his family kept their distance from both brothers, with the most contact being a brief wave from a distance.

The long-term history of a lack of relationships and social

distancing was beginning to alert the police to the possibility that these two brothers could be psychopaths. Many of the characteristics described, like the lack of empathy, emotion and antisocial behaviours, were ticking the boxes. With these red flags raised, Julie and Vivienne were still considering whether there were any benefits to be gained from talking to their teachers at the local school. The social alienation described in so many testimonies suggested there was something pathological about these brothers.

*

Craig was using a tractor to unload bales of hay that had been just delivered to a shed, when Julie and Vivienne arrived. There was no warm welcome nor invitation into the homestead for a coffee. Craig actually looked reluctant to turn off the tractor, and appeared frustrated that he was unable to ignore them. When interviewed, Craig Robinson appeared distant and unemotional for a sibling whose brother was in an ICU, ventilated and critically ill. Julie, a thin, tanned, tall, leggy blonde, was often greeted with flirty responses from men, even in her bulky navy uniform – Craig's menacing demeanor exhibited more contempt than signs of respect or attraction. While the sensitive Vivienne suggested Craig could be distressed by his brother's serious condition, his cold, predatory gaze prickled the back of their necks. Julie's discomfort rose to the point that she instinctively unclipped her gun holster button, despite Craig's behaviour giving no direct signs of malice.

Julie had maintained an open stance, with both hands flexed on her hips, as she glared and challenged Craig to provide explanations for the positive urinary drug screen. After Craig had denied Peter had used any illicit drugs, Julie had brazenly stepped closer. She crowded his personal space, asserting the presence of narcotics in Peter's system was unquestionable.

'That bitch needs to be taught a lesson,' Craig swore under his breath through clenched teeth.

Yes, Vivienne and Julie agreed, something was 'off' about these brothers. Both officers looked around intuitively searching for firearms as they returned to their vehicle, but none were visible. Both officers intended to dig more deeply into these sibling's backgrounds. The more they investigated, the more suspicious the lifestyles of these brothers became.

Chapter 5

Monday 10 February

Julie Wright

'm walking my pale yellow labrador, Rosie, along the sandy beach, revitalised by the cool evening breeze. Being in nature is so refreshing and soothing, I contemplate, as I inhale the salty air and step barefooted in the firm sand and incoming shallow waves. The exuberant Rosie barks, then splashes and shakes, chasing the waves as far as her leash permits. I am casually dressed in a denim skirt and candy pink shirt after escaping the heavy human dramas that occupy my days. *This twenty-kilogram puppy is the best therapy ever, I think, stroking Rosie's pretty face. I smile at my excited Rosie* as she takes off, chasing seagulls that take flight for their own preservation. The gulls cry out in defeat at having to relinquish their dinner temporarily to the playful pup. Surfers are catching waves and paddling out on waxed boards that glisten in the sun as it reflects off the ocean. The sun is still radiating enough warmth to make my stroll remarkably pleasant. My untied hair is drifting across my face and sweeping upwards in the gentle breeze.

I am just returning to my car, beginning to navigate the final rocky incline up to the lawn near the car park, when the sight of a tall surfer with a six-pack abdomen, broad shoulders and trim hips distracts me. Dressed in board shorts, he is rinsing off and combing back his black wavy hair as the water streams down his tanned, toned physique. I am ogling the virile movements of this enticing male showering when something familiar about his mannerisms piques my attention. The surfer combs his fingers distractedly through his full facial beard, extending his chin towards the water spray as though experiencing a delirious pleasure from the cool water bathing him. I'm almost a metre away from the lawn when Rosie abruptly dashes towards another seagull landing on a rock to her left.

I cry out in surprise as I am suddenly propelled head first into the side of a rock, losing my footing on the hilly incline. My hands explore a cut on my forehead as it begins bleeding into my eyes. I am so shaken from the sharp pain that I fail to realise I've let go of Rosie's lead. Rosie has bounced up towards the surfer to play in the water. Attempting to get up too quickly on the rocky slope, I lose my footing, overbalancing again, grazing both hands on small rocks as I land. Rosie returns about two metres out of reach, barking loudly and pawing at the ground as I shake my head, trying to regain my balance. A wave of dizziness is temporarily immobilising me.

Water drips onto me from above, out of the surfer's hair, as his soft hands grip my shoulders, holding me steady on my third attempt to stand. The rocks and sand are swirling around in front of me as I blink to uncloud my vision. Wiping the blood out of my eyes with sticky fingers, I sway in an uncoordinated fashion, stumbling, still struggling to focus. I am being guided up to the grass, my unsteady legs functioning independently of my brain. I hold the picnic bench for support to sit down. Rosie's front paws land on my knee as she begins licking drops of blood off the side of my skirt. Feeling clammy, I hold my head to dispel the nausea. My forehead is throbbing, and my neck muscles feel jarred. Rosie's tail is wagging furiously in anxiety.

The familiar face of Dr Ray Fischer crouches in front of me, asking a myriad of medical questions I can't keep track of. My single thought is that he needs to move in case I vomit. I sit still for another ten minutes, batting off his questions with a repetitious

'I'm okay', even though clearly I am not. When I stand, attempting to get out my car keys, he takes them from me.

'You can't drive so soon after a whack like that,' Ray says. 'Come over the road to my house and let me take a better look at you. Let's see how you are after a little rest.'

I make it across the road, with Ray steering my shoulders, his arm around me. Ray sits me down on his balcony in a sun lounge. Rosie is watching me, with her tail wagging and a shoe in her mouth. Ray checks with a small torch that my pupils are equal and reacting. Ray instructs me to look at his nose but I find my gaze is drawn to those mesmerising blue eyes and the genuine tenderness there. He brings me a glass of water, two paracetamol and an ice pack. Ray fills a water dish for Rosie and places it on the patio beside me with a blanket for her to lie on. Then he returns with a slice of roast meat, trading Rosie to retrieve his shoe. Rosie accepts the bribe, relinquishing her treasure, then lies with her head on her outstretched front legs, looking up at us.

Lying still, I begin to feel a little better until my skin starts stinging, making my left eye water. Ray is putting iodine antiseptic on my forehead cut and using butterfly bandaids to secure the edges of the cut skin together.

Ray puts the icepack wrapped in a pillowcase on the left side of my face. After dressing the abrasions on my hands, he uses a warm soapy cloth to remove the blood from my sticky fingers.

I doze briefly. When I wake up, the sun has gone down. Ray is reading a journal in a nearby sun lounge. I apologise profusely for my intrusion and stand up, checking my pockets for my car keys. Ray is hesitant about letting me drive or even being at home alone, after what he describes as a minor concussion.

Ray encourages Rosie and me to stay the night in his spare room. Still feeling headachy and a bit queasy, I gratefully accept. I take a warm shower to remove the blood from my matted hair and fingernails. I inhale the pleasant, citrusy fragrance of Ray's cologne that lingers in the bathroom. I emerge from the bathroom wearing the draw-string shorts and T-shirt Ray has offered. Ray does a precautionary check of my pupils again before putting my car in his driveway overnight. Ray's guest room has a single, dark timber-framed bed and matching bedside table. The bed is made up with navy sheets covered with a navy and gold-striped doona.

With the nausea still coming and going, I decline Ray's offer of a homemade burger, accepting more paracetamol instead. I am feeling much steadier on my feet, but the spongy bruise at the side of my left brow remains quite tender. Ray takes Rosie outside for a bathroom break before leaving more painkillers and water for me for overnight.

In the morning, Ray drives us home in his Honda Accord after I decline his offer of cereal and toast. I have never really been a breakfast eater, so I settle for an apple juice instead. I call in sick for work. Ray informs me that he will check in on me again around 5 pm when he finishes work in case I want to retrieve my car. I take more analgesia when the pounding headache returns. My left eye is crusted, the cheek is swollen, and I am feeling irritable and agitated.

It seems as though I had not long dozed off when there is a knocking at my front door. Rosie is madly pacing and barking. I wake up feeling, still sleepy and sore. I open the door, squinting at the outside daylight, when I suddenly realise that I am only wearing my light pink cotton shorts and a matching pyjama top.

'Come in,' I say, welcoming Ray into my small unit. My attire is a hideous contrast to Ray's immaculately tailored white shirt, black trousers and black leather tie. Acutely embarrassed to realise that the whole day has slipped away, I excuse myself to quickly grab a dressing gown. As we sit at the kitchen table, drinking coffee, Ray's magnetic blue eyes scan my facial bruise.

'Headache any better?' he enquires.

'Not as pounding,' I reply, feeling sorry for myself.

'If you need a certificate for tomorrow, let me know and I'll sort it for you,' Ray kindly offers.

'I really need to get back to work tomorrow', I tactfully reply, feeling frustrated. I grimace. 'I have so much to do. I'll let Vivienne do the driving, though,' I assure him.

'How about we leave your car where it is for now? I could pick you up in the morning at 7 am if you want,' Ray offers.

'No, it should be fine. I'll catch a ride with Viv. She's just a block away. I feel terrible. You have such heavy responsibilities in the ICU. I should not be burdening you with my clumsiness,' I say apologetically. 'Thank you for the kind offer, though.'

'Hey, it's no problem. I just hope you're feeling better tomorrow. Have you got enough paracetamol? You may need to keep taking them every four to six hours for a few days.' Ray frowns. 'You're still quite pale … any more nausea?'

'No. I've just been drinking water and weak apple juice. This is my first coffee,' I say, wrapping both hands around the cup, as though suffering from addiction.

Ray pushes up to leave. 'Well, I'll leave you to go back and lie down again. How about we leave your car where it is until Saturday then?'

'Yeah, that would be great, thanks.' I sigh. 'I am sorry for being a bother.'

Rosie places a paw on Ray's thigh, moving her head in for a cuddle. Ray combs her short hair back from her face, admiring her chocolate puppy eyes.

'She's adorable,' he says.

Before Ray can get to the door, Rosie has grabbed her ball for a quick game.

'Come on, girl, we'll have a quick toss.'

Ray steps outside and throws the ball a few times. Rosie catches the tennis ball in her gob before returning to drop it, covered in saliva, at his feet.

'Good girl, Rosie,' Ray claps. 'I will see you tomorrow too, Julie.'

Ray smiles, adding another pat. 'Will you be home around 5 pm? I'd just like to check you're still going okay on my way home.'

'Yes, I work mainly 8 am to 4.30 pm, so usually I'm home by 5 pm. Thank you so much.'

'See you then.'

Ray leaves, closing the groaning gate, left intentionally unoiled for security measures.

I wave and go inside, closing the door.

'Yes, you got all the pats,' I remind Rosie, not disguising my jealousy.

*

Vivienne picks me up Wednesday morning.

'What's happened to your face?' Vivienne zooms in, looking at the deepening bruise barely concealed by makeup.

'Perving,' I confess. 'I tripped over Rosie when she crossed in front of me. I was looking up, instead of where I was going.'

'Perving at?' Vivienne smirks, lifting an eyebrow in interest as she turns on her indicators and checks the side mirrors before driving off.

'Mr black hair, blue eyes and black leather ties,' I smile. 'So totally worth it ... seeing those rippling abs showering at the beach. And he's totally drop dead gorgeous, I might add.'

'Well, good luck to you,' Vivienne smiles, looking up at the traffic lights. 'You're one smitten kitten by the sounds of it. I do hope he's single,' she concedes, laughing.

'From your lips to God's ears,' I beg, placing my hands in the prayer position, while simultaneously visualising Ray under that beach shower.

Chapter 6

Wednesday 12 February

Carol Bryant

arrive on duty just as Cindy returns from a MET call with a red mottled rash climbing up her neck. Cindy had been relieving Steve's meal break by covering the MET pager. When Cindy suggested to Steve that she needed a ten-minute break, I am intrigued at what could have transpired to leave her so acutely uncomfortable. I am busting with curiosity since my friend is not easily flustered. With fifteen minutes before my shift officially begins, I decide to accept Cindy's offer to join her for a coffee.

'Cindy! What's happened? There's a beetroot red rash all over your neck, right up to your ears.'

'I just went to a surgical ward MET call,' begins Cindy. 'A young twenty-six-year-old female had a clot blocking off the circulation to her right arm. So, while the surgical nurses were getting her prepared for theatre with consents and check lists, I got a dressing trolley and put a urinary catheter in her bladder.'

'Couldn't you get the catheter in?'

'The catheter went in easy; that wasn't the problem. I was wheeling the trolley backwards, exiting from the bed area, when I accidentally stepped on someone's cotton theatre boots.'

'Did you hurt them? Lose your balance?'

'No, no! I put my hand back behind me with my palm out to apologise.'

'And what happened?'

'Carol, we'll just say that sometimes I forget how short I am,' Cindy says, dropping her head in embarrassment.

My buddy Cindy is mortified. Whatever happened was totally out of her comfort zone. Now, I am truly busting with anticipation, sitting on the edge of my chair.

'So, what happened?' I press onwards, trying to get the dirt.

'Well ... my hand went backwards with my palm outwards just as Suzie's boyfriend, Jake, the surgical resident, went to step around me. My hand was out at the right height, and I accidently grabbed his package!'

'Oh, you didn't!' I laugh, tears spilling from my eye. Try as I might, I just can't stop giggling.

'Yes, I'm afraid I did,' replies the blushing Cindy. 'And it was too much information! We'll just say that Suzi is blessed.'

I scream with laughter, wiping tears from my eyes. My hand covers my mouth to muffle the amusement, magnified by the horror displayed on poor Cindy's face.

'Then,' continues Cindy, 'just when I wanted to escape so that he would not remember this face, the same lady crashed in theatre about three minutes later, as soon as she arrived. So, I had to attend a second MET call, with him there trying to avoid this handy nurse.'

'Hell's bells, is she okay?'

'Yes, *she's fine,*' moans Cindy. '*The clot's been removed. Her arm has a good colour and has a sturdy pulse. I just wanted the floor to open up and hide me.*'

'*That's too funny!*' *I try to stifle my laugh, looking over at the still profusely red-faced Cindy. She is beginning to rally at the humour of her situation.*

'*How am I going to look Suzie in the eye after that little misadventure?*' *queries Cindy in a fatalistic tone.*

'*I'd probably be more worried about running into Jake,*' *I giggle.*

I look at my watch. '*I better get in there for handover – if you can control yourself now!*'

Chapter 7

Wednesday 12 February

Carol Bryant

A fter my two days off, Peter Robinson is still ventilated. He has been allocated to me as my patient for this twelve-hour day shift. I get my handover from Charlie Boyce, who states that Peter's vital signs are stable.

Ray's instructions are that Peter is to continue being weaned off the noradrenaline infusion that has been propping up his blood pressure as his recovery from septic shock improves with the antibiotics. With Peter's parameters looking normal on both the ventilator and cardiac monitor, I proceed to reduce the noradrenaline by one down to five micrograms per minute for this hour.

Ray has just done group rounds with the pharmacist, physiotherapist, dietician and the ICU resident, Holly Chambers. Ray considered that the hazy area, visible on the X-ray, in Peter's left lower lung lobe remains at risk of collapsing. Since the ventilator gas follows the path of least resistance, gas is less likely to flow to the left lower base due to the sharp angle at this zone of the lung. The physio suggests that Peter needs to be turned onto his side, with his left lung uppermost, to optimise air entry and recruitment of these alveoli.

Peter is only requiring thirty per cent oxygen and a PEEP pressure of five. I am so paranoid after Friday night's event that I intend to watch the PEEP more often than the usual hourly observations inscribed on the flow chart. I call the orderlies to help me turn Peter onto his side. Soon after, John and Mandie arrive to assist with his turn and linen change. I hold the breathing tube to prevent it migrating too far up the airway where it can damage the vocal cords or migrating downwards where it could cause only one lung to be inflated. The ventilator is turned slightly diagonally so that I can watch Peter's ventilator pressures as well as the cardiac and oxygenation waveforms on the monitor. Sometimes putting the worst lung upright can cause the patient to become unstable, particularly if adequate oxygen cannot transfer from the affected lung into the bloodstream.

Lauren, our team leader, washes Peter's back and changes his bed linen. All is progressing smoothly until the monitor alarm sounds with a red flashing, warning that Peter's heart rate is two hundred per minute, and the rhythm has changed to a broad complex, potentially lethal rhythm called 'ventricular tachycardia'. I instruct the team to help me return Peter onto his back again, ready for defibrillation. Rather than improve the situation, Peter looks flushed, with hot clammy skin. With Peter already heavily sedated with a fentanyl and midazolam infusion, Lauren places the defibrillation gel pads onto his chest.

'Stand clear. Charging,' Lauren announces.

Lauren does a visual sweep to check everyone is away from the bed and the central line infusing electrolytes before discharging the two hundred joules of synchronised electricity from the defibrillator.

'Okay, back in sinus rhythm. Let's get a heart tracing and bloods to check for damage and the electrolyte balance.'

With Peter's monitor back in a normal rhythm but at a faster rate – a sinus tachycardia – the blood pressure emergency alarm sounds and flashes red. Peter's blood pressure has practically doubled to 240/100. I ask our resident, Dr Suzie Murtagh, standing next to the noradrenaline pump, to put the program on hold so that no further noradrenaline is infused, to prevent Peter having a stroke or heart attack.

'Good God,' Suzie cries, 'the bloody noradrenaline is on thirty-five micrograms a minute!'

With Suzie stopping the infusion immediately, the blood pressure drops rapidly to 160/90 and the arterial waveform on the monitor trends down. There is no way that inotrope was on thirty-five micrograms a minute; the heart rate and blood pressure would have shot up sooner. Someone has done this. I look at Peter's chest rising, the ventilator pressures and the monitor to ensure that the vital signs are trending in the right direction. Then I observe all those present at the bedside. Most have their eyes fixated on the cardiac monitor. I'm staring at my colleagues, wondering who did this.

The bedside policeman, Constable Anthony Badke, who had a reputation for gagging and retching when a patient's airway was suctioned, had just stepped out of the curtain while we performed the procedure. I had stopped Peter's feeds, ready for repositioning. Someone saw this as an opportunity to move the noradrenaline dial from zero to three, changing the infusion from five micrograms per minute to a dangerous thirty-five micrograms a minute.

Anthony radios his station, reporting the latest medical sabotage to his superiors. His sergeant, Michael, wants a list of the suspects in attendance to be compiled. Besides me, they are:

Mark Shultz, physio

Suzie Murtagh, ICU resident

Carol Bryant, bedside Registered Nurse

Lauren Poulsen, team leader

John Simpson, orderly

Mandie Lane, orderly.

Police background checks later show that no one has a criminal record or large amounts of cash recently deposited into their bank accounts. There are no gambling debts and no traffic violations, except for Suzie Murtagh who was pulled over and fined for not wearing a seat belt at 8 am, most likely after a night shift. Yet, it seems obvious that someone has intentions to kill this patient.

The infusion pump was a dial that had to have been deliberately clicked three times to get from zero to three. With the two-minute half-life of noradrenaline, I was at the head of the bed for ten minutes before the alarms had sounded, so this was not my error. However, most of the other staff had rotated from one side of the bed to the other. Why was Peter being targeted, and what was to be gained from his death?

Who is trying to kill this patient and why? Someone used our distraction as an opportunity. Everyone will need to be questioned again to determine who had a motive while the police search deeper into Peter's background.

Chapter 8

Friday 14 February

Interview with Lauren Poulsen

auren Poulsen, as the most experienced professional present on both occasions when adverse incidences had occurred, was a primary suspect. At fifty-two-year-old, this team leader was well qualified, possessing extensive medical knowledge and experience. If so inclined, Lauren would undoubtedly be skilled enough to manipulate most of the ICU's medical devices if she chose to inflict a lethal act. Lauren's thirty years of nursing experience included twenty-five years of experience in the management of critically ill ICU patients. Lauren had also achieved a Masters in Clinical Practice in Nursing and had Melbourne tertiary hospital ICU and midwifery qualifications.

Her finances are strained. With a $300,000 mortgage debt that has increased by $20,000 in the last six months, Lauren's banking arrangements have changed to paying the interest only on her mortgage rather than reducing her balance. Lauren's credit card is maxed.

Lauren's frown lines deepen as we approach her, giving us the impression that she is stressed. At 170 cm tall, Lauren had a medium build, a fair complexion, hazel green eyes and walnut coloured long hair tied in a loose ponytail. Today she is wearing jade scrubs and walks with a stiff cautious gait, drawing attention to her black trainer shoes.

'Hi, Lauren, I am Sergeant Julie Wright and this is Constable

Vivienne Hales. We are hoping you might be free for a quick chat in the tearoom. Is that okay?'

'Yeah, sure.'

Lauren looks around the glass-partitioned ICU bays congested with medical equipment attached to unconscious patients, looking for someone to notify that she is intending to temporarily leave the unit.

'I'll have to take the Medical Emergency Team pager with me and leave if there is a MET call,' Lauren warns and, looking at one of the wall clocks situated in each bay for orientating patients, 'I've only got about thirty minutes, before I have to start meal reliefs.'

'Yeah, that's fine. If we don't finish, we can reschedule for another day. The unit looks busier today.'

'Yes, there's been two aeromedical transfers to Brisbane and three admissions already this shift, so we're still cleaning up and restocking.'

In the small tearoom that overlooks the murky water and mangroves on the riverbank, a large television screen is mounted in a far corner of the tearoom. The circular placement of chairs around the periphery suggests the tearoom is also used for education and teleconferencing. Lauren drops the MET pager on the coffee table and places the bulky resuscitation equipment bag on the floor next to it. Her eyes subconsciously wander over to the coffee machine as though the temptation is too much to resist. The gaze suggests that this could be the only break she gets until home time. Although Vivienne and I have just had a drink, we join Lauren in another tasteless hospital beverage.

'So, Lauren, you've been present when the two incidences of the PEEP and noradrenaline tampering occurred.' Julie intentionally confronts Lauren, aiming to put her off kilter.

'I couldn't believe it the first time! Now I am just constantly worrying whether it could happen again.'

'How do you think those dangerous settings came about? Did you see anything or have any suggestions about who may be responsible?'

'No, I honestly can't explain either of those events. I remember checking all the ventilator settings, including that PEEP dial, with Sam's written orders before Steve left for his break. I checked the settings again after I had connected Peter from the portable ventilator on to the ICU ventilator, while Sam checked the breathing tube was secure and listened to his chest. The breath tidal volumes, pressures and everything were fine. I know the needle on the gauge was going back to the dialled-in PEEP setting of five because I checked for air trapping. Satisfied that everything was okay, I went around the other side of the bed to unplug his leads from the transport monitor to connect Peter onto the ICU monitor. Jayney Whyte started unclamping the infusion pumps from the transport trolley and mounting them onto the bedside infusion pump stands. Steve returned and took a verbal handover from Linda, the Emergency nurse.'

'So, you're saying that you saw nothing suspicious at any time Friday night?'

'No. I had my back to everyone after that. I was focused on plugging in the leads and checking the alarm parameters and waveforms on the cardiac monitor.'

'When did the extra help arrive?'

'Jayney was transferring her patient to the surgical ward, so she came to help with the admission before she cleaned up her bay. After Jayney helped push Peter onto the ICU bed from the trolley side, I asked her to sort the infusions. I don't think Jenny, the supervisor, came in until the ventilator alarmed. I suspect that was when Carol left her patient to help too.'

'And you did not see anyone touch the ventilator?'

'Once I left the ventilator, I didn't really look over there again. Sam was at the head of the bed and the ventilator was turned towards him so that he could silence any alarms. I was adjusting the monitor alarms on the other side of the bed then, so I was focused on that task. Nothing was alarming, so I don't recall having any reason to look. After that horrendous PEEP setting was discovered, I did check the flowchart out of curiosity. I wanted to see what PEEP measurement Jayney had recorded, because she had arrived at the ventilator as I was walking around the bed to the monitor. Jayney had written five, and she had taken all the measurements she recorded on the flowchart off the ventilator.'

'That narrows the timeline, then. So, Jayney could not have just recorded the PEEP setting from Sam's prescription?'

'No. The observation measurements are usually recorded in real time from the ventilators. The monitors allow retrospective measurements from alarms to be reviewed as a snapshot and recorded after emergencies. However, the software programs were not purchased for the ventilators, so all those measurements are not stored. We have to record the ventilator data hourly. The phone instructions that Sam had received from Ray were still on a piece of paper in my scrub shirt pocket. I put them there to double-check the settings after the patient was attached.'

'Then, Wednesday, you were washing Peter's back and changing the linen, is that right?

'Hmm ... yes, that's right,' Lauren purses her lips and nods her head. 'Carol knocked the noradrenaline rate down to five during Ray's rounds, then recorded the hourly observations. I rang for the orderlies to help us turn Peter. Carol got her plastic gown, gloves and googles on to suction Peter's airway and temporarily stopped the feeds. I grabbed some fresh linen, donned my gown and gloves, then dragged the dirty linen carrier into the bay just as John and Mandie arrived. Everything was normal.'

'So, what did you think when the heart rate and blood pressure alarms went off?'

'Well, normally, when you turn someone, putting the collapsed lung uppermost, you would suspect low oxygen levels could be causing the arrhythmia. But the oxygen saturations showed enough oxygen was getting from the lungs into the blood stream. However, in an emergency, we go temporarily up to one hundred per cent as the higher metabolic demand of the fast heart rate can increase oxygen requirements. If they are in pain or waking up, the blood pressure can rise in someone with a low blood pressure needing noradrenaline. But the blood pressure measurements were extreme from the toxic noradrenaline dose being delivered. Honestly, that is not something you would routinely even think to look for.'

'And you saw no one near the infusion pumps?'

'Not really. All the pumps were moved back to make room for the orderlies turning Peter, then moved closer to the bed again to prevent the intravenous lines getting stretched or pulled out.'

'So how far was the noradrenaline from you?'

'Well, initially, I was on the right side of the bed where the infusions were while I was washing Peter's back and changing the linen. Then, I was on Peter's left side because we were intending to leave him onto that side with the left lung up for alveolar recruitment.'

'How far was Carol from the infusion pump?'

'About a metre away. She was at the head of the bed, guarding the breathing tube and supporting the ventilator tubing, so both her hands were full.'

'So ...' Julie pauses for effect, 'you are saying that you, John and Mandie were the ones moving the pumps closer to the bed to get in and out during the turn?'

'Yes, but I did not see anyone playing with the rate.'

'And it would not have taken long for the signs to appear on the monitor. Ray said, about two minutes. So, if you were turning Peter onto his left side, and the infusion was being delivered in a line that was attached, on the right side of his neck, you were on Peter's left side of the bed when the monitors alarmed, yes?'

'Yes. Both John and Mandie may have had to move the infusion pumps to get closer to the bed after I left to swap sides.'

Both officers milk the awkward moment of silence to see if Lauren has anything else to add.

'I wasn't looking when I left that side. I was taking the sponge bowl around to the other side, trying not to spill the water. I have never seen either of the orderlies tampering with settings. They are both a pleasure to work with. I just cannot imagine how this happened.'

Lauren shakes her head and shrugs, gesturing with open hands.

'How long have you worked here, Lauren?'

Lauren's frown and the tightening of her jaw are uninhibited. 'Thirty bloody years!' Her eyelids close slightly in an angry squint.

'So, you don't like working here?' Julie questions.

'Not at all. The line managers are criminals!'

'Criminals?' repeats Julie, raising her eyebrows in surprise, before her face resets into a blank passive canvas.

'Yep. Bounty Hospital is defrauding its staff by making them pay for work injuries. The managers and hospital insurers claim that injuries are "personal and degenerative". As a student nurse, I was taught to use the "Australian lift", where a patient's arm is placed down a nurse's back for upright positioning of the patient. That technique maimed a lot of nurses because it created the dual danger of lifting with a bent back and a hazardous disc loading. For health workers, back injuries should be compensated as "repetitive strain", as they are the result of chronic mechanical forces of bending, lifting and twisting. Bounty Hospital colludes with its insurers, as no safety needs to be improved if you can dismiss injuries as "personal or degenerative". Truthfully, the only personal aspect of our injuries is the cost! Due to this negligence and fraud, injured workers keep returning to the same hazards with no compensation, rehabilitation support or risk mitigation until left with chronic pain and permanent disability!'

Lauren's tone is raised, with clenched teeth visible between her lips.

'The administration doesn't believe there is a need to provide ergonomic workplace designs, products, equipment or policies for an aging workforce, one that the government wants to keep working longer. Any medical equipment purchased just needs to be Therapeutic Goods Act approved as "fit for purpose" under the law. Those cheap ventilators have humidifiers and humidifier alarms only thirty centimetres from the floor. Their design is a risk, causing repetitive strain injuries for aging nurses as it forces them to unnecessarily bend very low.'

Julie's eyes widen in surprise, 'So you're implying Bounty Hospital is defrauding and intentionally maiming their workforce. How could they do that?'

'Very easily, I'm afraid. The nursing directors instruct junior doctors to override the consultant's opinions by issuing different medical certificates "to satisfy funding arrangements". Then the consultant's instructions and MRI evidence are separated from the compensation application forms, before the rehabilitation officer submits them to the insurer, to make sure compensation claims do not satisfy the onus of proof law. Under the rehabilitation standard, an employer is supposed to provide early contact to support injured employees, paperwork assistance, suitable duties plans, coordinate employees transitioning back to work on reduced hours and provide a workplace investigation after a serious injury. However, if the Rehabilitation Officer removes the evidence, Bounty can deflect all rehabilitation costs back onto the injured workers.

'What would that achieve?'

'Well, firstly, if you can dismiss injuries as "personal or degenerative", you don't have to improve safety,' replies Lauren, her tone dripping with sarcasm, 'so non-ergonomic workplace designs are never changed. Everyone stretches over the tall wide infusion pumps stations that are always in front of the monitors to silence the ceiling mounted monitor alarms. The nurses then twist and bend excessively behind the beds to change the floor-level suction bags daily. Injured workers have fewer rights than criminals, who are presumed innocent until proven guilty under common law. The injured who are sleep-deprived and suffering from pain and disability must impossibly prove their repetitive strain injuries are work related. So, the insurer's doctors generate and accept fictitious misdiagnoses in collusive activities that are mutually beneficial to both parties. The insurer saves money when they reject compensation claims, while the employer denies rehabilitation entitlements to financially strain the injured. If you cannot satisfy the onus of proof with magnetic resonance imaging and three consultants' opinions validating a disc tear, then how is satisfying onus of proof possible? MRIs have been considered definitive evidence since 1988!'

'Oh, so that happened to you?'

'No, it didn't happen to me – they strategically defrauded me! Bounty Hospital is exploiting a lot of us,' Lauren raises her voice in anger. 'In my case, the deliberate grievous bodily harm was retaliation for testifying at an inquiry, without whistleblower protection, about a rogue doctor. When asked my impression of that surgeon, I said under oath that since I did not work in theatre, I could not testify about his surgical skills. However, having worked in tertiary hospitals in Sydney and Melbourne, I knew that Bounty Hospital was performing complex surgery on high-risk patients that was beyond the scope of practice for this small rural hospital.'

Julie's interest sharpens. 'How did your line managers retaliate?'

'The nursing director refused my human right to go to Emergency with an MRI-diagnosed disc tear to access the only spinal surgeon in town on staff. He intentionally left me on twelve-hour rotating shifts and on the spinal surgeon's three-month waiting list. Neuropathic foot pain characteristically gets worse at night, so I was left on the night shifts, unable to take painkillers. My feet were burning severely, but I could not take the pregabalin tablets, as they cause drowsiness and affect memory. I only lasted six weeks until the pain got so severe I could no longer walk.'

'Seriously?' Vivienne says in a raised tone, glancing towards Julie.

'Yes. I testified under subpoena that Bounty Hospital was doing complex procedures that were beyond the scope of a rural hospital, one that did not have a twenty-four-hour laboratory, X-ray services or relevant specialists. I felt the adverse outcomes occurring were the consequence of doing those complex surgeries on elderly patients with conditions like renal failure.

'Why would the executives permit that?'

'It's all about funding arrangements. The revenue stays with the patient. Ship them off to the city and you lose revenue. All the patient complications and adverse outcomes created a huge bed crisis when patients required a longer stay than was planned or funded for. The operating theatre was overloaded from repeated surgeries on the same patients returning to theatre for wound dehiscence (ones that burst open), haemorrhages or abscesses. The ICU was chronically functioning over capacity, because the high-risk patients operated on were getting complications. The ICU had to open more beds than they were funded for when ward emergencies and casualty admissions also needed a bed. The clinical nurses and doctors were overwhelmed with excessive overtime and heavy workloads.'

Vivienne listens intently with a puzzled expression, her right pointer finger picking absentmindedly at her front teeth. 'Sorry, I'm still stuck on your previous comment about foot pain. How did you get foot pain if the disc tear was in your back?'

'Part or all of the gelatinous material in the disc gets forced through the disc tear and leaks onto the sinuvertebral nerve. The disc fluid irritates the sinuvertebral nerve, causing severe burning on the top of the foot and sharp pain like a razor blade under your feet,' explains Lauren.

'So, you are saying they deliberately left you on a three-month staff spinal surgeon's waiting list to make you suffer and to exacerbate the disc tear injury?' Julie clarifies.

'Absolutely. It was retaliation after my testimony was perceived to be against the Bounty Hospital rather than the surgeon. The nursing director said he was instructed to "keep the ICU staff in line" after the adverse media attention that surrounded the inquiry. A disc tear should be treated with conservative management, like bed rest, but I could not get a medical certificate or access the only spinal surgeon in town.'

'Couldn't your GP write a certificate?'

'I had been to my doctor thirteen times because I was struggling to work on burning feet for twelve-hour shifts. The GP kept telling me that "osteoarthritis does not hurt that bad" and sent me for podiatry and orthotics. The GP thought I had a Morton's neuroma nerve tumour in my foot. My arthritic back pain from a previously witnessed nursing hyperextension injury twenty years ago was unchanged, but the foot pain was killing me,' emphasises Lauren.

'So, your GP would not provide a medical certificate?'

'No. My GP wanted me to see the spinal surgeon first, because she was confused about the source of the foot pain. The GP wrongly thought my back pain should have been worse if the pain was caused by a back issue. I was on three anti-inflammatory drugs that had little effect on the neuropathic pain. The disc was probably just bulging originally, but I kept getting misdiagnosed because the back pain was unchanged. Then, one day, the staff rheumatologist, Dr Berry, was walking behind me, returning to his rooms, when I was trying to transfer an ICU patient over to the rehab unit for palliation. I began limping so badly I had to ask the orderly to stop the trolley. Dr Berry stopped to help me. He rang my GP, asking her to order a lumbar MRI because he believed my pain was neuropathic. When I took the MRI results up to Dr Berry's office, he told me to present down to Emergency to show Dr Hunter, the spinal surgeon. On my way to Emergency, I stopped in to let Gail Tontine, know that I was going to need sick leave. Before I could leave her office, the nursing director, Marcus Maitland, arrived. When Marcus overheard my comment about needing sick leave, he said I had to make an outpatient appointment because "neuropathic pain is not an emergency".'

'And did you make the appointment?'

'Yeah ...' said Lauren, not hiding her disgust. 'Marcus saw the MRI, so he was aware the disc tear was confirmed. Gail had an argument with him about the earliest spinal surgeon outpatient appointment being three months away. Gail had insisted that if I could not see Dr Hunter sooner, I should be taken off line on sick leave immediately to prevent the disc herniating. Marcus angrily retorted that "staff must not be seen to get preferential treatment". Gail asserted that the conservative management of a disc tear, with bed rest, was basic, not preferential, treatment. Marcus began ranting about clinical indicators like Emergency waiting times, absent days and compensation claims needed priority over my safety. Even when I saw Dr Hunter six weeks later as an emergency after the disc tear injury had been extended by Bounty's negligence, the spinal surgeon's directions for sedentary duties and transitioning on shorter hours were overridden. Marcus insisted that the ICU resident write a different certificate. Sick leave is funded and budgeted for. However, Marcus claimed that transitioning was offered only when the cost was covered by the hospital's insurer or a worker's superannuation fund. '

'They can't do that!' exclaimed Julie, perturbed that Bounty Hospital was capable of maiming their employees intentionally.

Lauren's mocking laugh was almost hostile. 'I assure you that they do with monotonous regularity and profound success. I had to pay $550 for flights and taxis to go to Brisbane to see the hospital's insurance doctor for the compensation claim to get "processed". The compensation claim was rejected with the doctor not even examining me, and I can prove it. The gluteal muscle wasting present from my 1987 injury was not recorded on his report. The insurer's doctor claimed I had an entirely benign over-medicalised Morton's neuroma. This fictitious misdiagnosis was accepted by Bounty Hospital and their insurer, despite no Morton's neuroma ever being found on two ultrasounds or MRI. Bounty Hospital then used the Morton's misdiagnosis to deny all the risk mitigation and rehab support requested in over seven medical letters.'

'But that's dangerous, surely?'

'Yes. I ended up with four permanent injuries, a significant risk of quadriplegia, two chronic neuropathic pains and needing twenty-seven surgical procedures. They are bloody dangerous!' exclaimed Lauren.

'Do you have proof? These are startling allegations! I've heard this hospital had a bad reputation but that sounds like blatant fraud, negligence and grievous bodily harm.'

'Yes, it is. I tried to fight it, but with 1485 hours of sick leave worth over $75,000 accrued, I could only transition back to work after spinal rods were inserted, using "annual leave offered as flexible working arrangements". These tactics permit Bounty Hospital to skillfully navigate the clinical indicators monitored by Work Safety.'

'What? Wasn't the union representing you?'

'I paid union membership fees for thirty years, and then they aligned themselves with the Nursing executives – who are also members of the same union! The union tells us that we need counselling to accept this fraud and maiming, when we thought we worked in a supposed *health industry! The hospital deflected $20,000 medical gap fees to me and then,* during my three weeks' absence for the insertion of spinal rods, they advertised the education and auditing duties I had been doing for two years. After it had taken me eight years and seven medical certificates to get the education role that I was qualified for, Bounty Hospital deliberately returned me to more physically demanding workloads on full eight-hour shifts.'

'That is shocking! Can you bring us that evidence? Are you here tomorrow?' an animated Vivienne replies.

'I'm on day shift again. I have loads of pay slips, MRI and medical evidence in a folder at home. I will probably be forcibly medically retired anyway, so I have nothing to lose. Bounty Hospital operates with the ethics of an alley cat. I'll be impressed if anyone can stop them. They have already threatened me with a "physical fitness test that no one ever passes" for asking for a Health and Safety workplace investigation, that is supposed to be the right of any worker sustaining serious work injuries, according to the Rehabilitation Standard.'

'There must be ways to stop this.' Julie is blatantly shocked, leaning forward, conveying her desire to help.

'The Executive have already weaponised the Public Service Act, directing two assaults upon me. The insurer's doctors were instructed that "our employee is not required to consent to your medical examination ... your examination should proceed irrespective of consent".'

'Hell, that is assault!' Julie exclaims.

'Yes, assault using the Public Service Act in the rehabilitation standard is only legal if they can claim you have a "personal" injury. Even if Bounty claims the mechanism of injury for the disc tear was personal, they exacerbated the injury by leaving me on twelve-hour shifts with full clinical duties. Therefore, Bounty insists I have a Morton's neuroma because it gives them more power to abuse. Another hideous aspect of these Public Service Act assaults is that the Chief Executive Officer justified this victimisation by alleging "concern for safety". What "concern for safety" is evident when seven medical requests were ignored, no suitable duties plans were provided for twelve years and the education duties were removed from my role after the insertion of spinal rods? The CEO further justified the weaponising of the Public Service Act to direct assault by claiming that I was "not working a roster schedule that matched my contractual hours", as though I can control the rate of spinal nerve regeneration which, at one millimetre a month, requires a four-year recovery!'

'And you say others have been injured too?'

'Deb paid for her bulging disc to be shaved about eighteen months ago. Toby and Lina have had hip tendon repair surgery, most likely from the bed-to-bed transfers. When Carly got shoulder pain after a lift and reported it immediately, she got no ultrasounds for six weeks after presenting to Emergency in pain and was accused of diminished performance for not being able to lift. Then, after an ultrasound had identified that her shoulder nerve had actually been ripped out of her spine at axonal level, nerve damage needing six weeks of light duties to heal, the rehab officer returned her to full duties because the "shoulder joint was intact". Desley paid for a knee replacement after the 220 kg hydraulic trolleys were loaded onto her knee joint whenever the trolley height was adjusted for the theatre or X-ray tables. Instead of safer policies like admitting patients into the electric battery-powered beds from Emergency and stopping the unnecessary bed-to-bed transfers and use of hydraulic trolleys, no safety has improved for twenty years.'

Lauren's eyes look up towards the ceiling, recalling other injuries. 'Oh, yes, and David got scaffolding spinal rods too. David is only about 157 centimetres tall, so leaning over two beds to transfer patients from ward to ICU beds was high risk for him. There are too many injuries for me to recall them all off the top of my head …'

'Lauren,' Vivienne interrupts, 'we're not medically trained, so I still don't really get how you end up with twenty-seven surgical procedures from one disc tear.'

Julie raised her eyebrows, indicating that she is curious too. On the one hand, Lauren seemed genuinely prepared to bring in evidence, but with only three staff being present at both potential murder attempts, was this a distraction?

'Let me see ... There were ten rhizotomies, where they cut the pain nerves exiting the spine at lumbar level. The nerves regenerate between nine months and two years. So, you have to keep having general anaesthetics to get the probes put in to heat the pain nerves to sixty degrees to cut them; otherwise, you can't walk. Then as the disc kept deflating, I had spinal rods and screws put in; that's called decompression, fusion and fixation surgery. I fractured six crown teeth needing crown restoration from bruxism when the neuropathic pain was constantly disrupting my sleep. The masseter muscles in your cheeks are one of the strongest muscles in your body, so I was clenching my jaw, fracturing the cusps, when I went to sleep.'

Lauren pauses, counting before continuing. 'When I was returned to full twelve-hour rotating shifts against medical advice, with neuropathic pain worse at night, I could not take the pregabalin for pain on duty. Unfortunately, while limping a lot on the twelve-hour shifts, I sustained a right foot bursa which had to be aspirated. As the disc deflated, the lumbar 4 vertebrae moved forward onto my hip and bladder nerves, causing a hip bursa and effusion, also needing aspiration. When I tried to maximise the dose of anti-inflammatory medications, to cope with the twelve-hour shifts, and being still required to attend MET calls, I ended up needing an endoscopy and colonoscopy after vomiting blood. I cashed in all my long service leave to get a botox cystoscopy so the bladder spasms would not keep waking me up with the hourly urge to pee day and night, but that money had to go to lawyers to protect me from the Public Service Act assaults.'

'I am in disbelief. That's a lot of surgical procedures!'

'Yes, yet, despite being managed by seven consultants – a

cardiologist, urologist, neurologist, general surgeon, orthopaedic surgeon, dental surgeon and spinal surgeon – I was not permitted to use 1485 hours of accrued sick leave!'

'A neurologist?'

'When the spinal rods were going into my lumbar area, my head was rotated laterally for mechanical ventilation during the surgery. The sustained rotation of my head for hours caused an additional cervical 7 disc tear in my neck. My fingers were numb in my left hand after the surgery. The neck MRI found a cervical 7 disc tear, with a congenital mass of blood vessels called a central haemangioma, above the disc tear around the spinal cord, at the cervical 4 vertebrae level. I was therefore left with lifelong permanent restrictions, with a risk of becoming paralysed from the neck down should the haemangioma vessels bleed from the cervical 7 disc tear below, affecting the stability of the neck vertebrae. I am left with permanent ten-kilogram lifting restrictions and I'm not supposed to do cardiac compressions, but as you see,' Lauren says, gesturing at her pager, 'with impaired mobility as well, I am responsible for MET calls.

To manage the neck disc tear causing muscle spasms in my face, neck and shoulder muscles, the neurologist had to inject the muscles with botox, so I had botox laboratory fees to pay too. I was managed by seven consultants but get no suitable duties plan for twelve years, because the hospital insurer and employer fraudulently insist I have a Morton's neuroma. I can't sleep for the neck and feet pain.'

Lauren declares in frustration, 'And even though I am peeing hourly day and night, I can't access my sick leave! To reduce the hours I work, despite 1485 hours of sick leave accrued, I am only permitted to use "single days of annual leave" for one day off a week rather than return to work for only four to six hours a day, using sick leave, which is an entitlement in the Rehab Standard. However, with disc tears taking up to two years to heal, and spinal nerves regenerating at one millimetre a month, requiring a four-year recovery period, I had to work full shifts for those six years. You have no idea how exhausting it was having only single days of annual leave off weekly for four years after spinal surgery!'

Lauren's eyelids rimmed with tears.

'This was very all entertaining for the executive, who enjoyed their retaliation of subjecting me to this never-ending circus of needles and knives. Disc pressures rise to five hundred per cent when leaning forward pulling unconscious patients onto ICU beds, so they left me doing this with a MRI diagnosed disc tear, with an intention to harm me. The executive are confident that no worker paid $30 an hour can challenge this fraud, with lawyers costing $690 an hour, especially when you have to pay for your own private health cover, medical gap fees, pain management and get no access to Legal Aid or accrued sick leave. The onus of proof law has exploited nurses since 1995. Despite nurses spending eighty per cent of their shifts lifting, bending and twisting around medical equipment, these draconian, unscientific laws are so effective that statistically seventy-four per cent of injured workers are financially strained funding work injuries.'

'That is dreadful!'

'Unfortunately, my case is only skimming the surface of the extensive Bounty Hospital fraud and negligence. Budgets are the priority here, not safety!'

'So, you have tried the union, the lawyers and the Industrial Relations Commission?'

'Yeah, but there is no even playing field, just a huge disparity between the law and justice. This fraud is possible because the legal system misuses the medical term "degenerative". Degenerative means that deposits are visible to radiologists on medical imaging equipment. Insurers exploit the "degenerative" comment that appears on medical imaging reports to imply that work injures are age-related wear and tear. Crucially, the medical definition of "degenerative" covers the scientifically proven phenomenon of post-traumatic arthritis, which occurs after injuries when inflammatory mediators flood to trauma sites. I sustained post-traumatic facet joint arthritis from a 1987 witnessed hyperextension work injury that caused the disc tear in the same location twenty years later, because the post-traumatic arthritis had altered the mechanical loading of my facet joints. Yet, I got no compensation for the facet joint arthritis, the torn disc or the spinal rod surgery that all resulted from work injuries. Sorry, Julie, you shouldn't have started me! The truth is – I just work in a dangerous place.'

A blotchy red rash floods Lauren's neck to her jaw as she becomes more agitated. 'All the legislation surrounding work injuries is insurer biased. For example, a jockey who came off a horse at work, injuring his hip, was left funding his post-traumatic arthritis deemed "degenerative" by legal teams, misusing that medical term. Unfortunately, that unscientific legal precedent has exploited injured workers ever since.'

Vivienne asks, 'And you can't work anywhere else?'

'All my experience and qualifications are exclusively in ICU, and this is the only ICU for 300 kilometres. This victimisation continued for twelve years after my testimony without whistleblower protection. That's why, at the last inquiry held in this hospital, no staff members voluntarily testified. There is no benefit to anyone compromising the financial stability of their family in this toxic culture when nothing changes. Every government authority permits these criminals to investigate themselves. Bounty Hospital constantly threatens staff with "codes of conduct" or makes accusations of "diminished performance" to intimidate their clinicians. Two sacked doctors had to be reinstated when their dismissals were deemed "unfair, unjust and unreasonable" by the Industrial Relations Commission. However, on less income, nurses cannot challenge this exploitation.'

'I am stunned!'

'I did not harm Peter. I would never take my anger out on a patient. I am telling you this because I will be forcibly medically retired soon. Anyone testifying in court against this hospital will be victimised relentlessly. So, please make sure every staff member issued a subpoena gets whistleblower protection for any legal proceedings.'

The pager light flashes red and beeps as Lauren grabs the bag.

'See you tomorrow. I'm here till 7.30 pm.'

'Yeah ... sure. Oh, and Gail will roster you off to come to the station at some stage so we can get a statement from you,' Vivienne hurriedly advises.

Lauren nods en route to the surgical MET call.

Julie looks at Vivienne. 'No wonder the others say she is serious and no longer jokes around. I'd be livid, too. I was expecting Lauren to be angry, but she is just devastated by this ordeal.'

'But what can we do?' Vivienne asks.

Both enter the ICU again to look at the equipment surrounding Peter in bay six.

'I'm not sure ... Let's see what she brings in tomorrow.'

Vivienne ponders. 'Assuming these two incidents weren't accidents and someone was out to murder Peter Robinson, it seems like it was just the three staff on for both events. There was only Lauren and two orderlies ... unless there is more than one person with a murderous agenda?'

Julie looks at the list. 'Of the three, Lauren would probably be the only one most familiar with the ventilator modes and potent drugs.'

'I must say, I found her emotions honest and raw,' Vivienne comments.

Chapter 9

Friday 14 February

Interview with Carol Bryant

'Carol? Hi, I'm Vivienne Hales and this is my sergeant, Julie Wright. Did Gail tell you we are interviewing staff and getting statements about the suspicious PEEP and noradrenaline incidents?'

'Yeah. You want me to come with you now?'

Julie nods and smiles. 'Yes, that would be great, thanks.'

Carol is sixty years old. Her straw-blonde, dyed hair is cut with a fringe and secured in a shoulder-length ponytail. Carol wears mauve glasses and jade coloured scrubs that reveal a slight middle-aged spread around her waistline. Carol's pockets are bulked up with eye torches, scissors, clamps and pens on her right-hand side and a cordless phone, identity badge and tapes on the left.

They enter the tearoom shortly afterwards. 'So, Carol, Gail says that your patient allocation on Friday was Connie. Is that right?'

'Yes, Cindy and I had two patients side by side, so we were relieving each other for meal breaks. Cindy was just returned from her break of about ten minutes when the new patient, Peter Robinson, arrived. When the alarms went off, Cindy kept an eye on Connie and Eric at bays two and three while I raced over to see if they needed a hand.'

'What did you see?'

'Peter's neck veins were all engorged and he was flushed. The ventilator was unable to push a breath in. When Sam disconnected him from the ventilator to manually squeeze a breath in, there was a huge exhalation as excessive air escaped from Peter's lungs under pressure. That meant that Peter was air trapping. The ventilator couldn't push in a breath, since not enough expired air was being removed. The moment Sam took Peter off the ventilator, his blood pressure improved on the arterial waveform. The arterial waveform gives a blood pressure with every heartbeat, so within seconds Peter was instantly improving. I helped Sam by moving the diaphragm of his stethoscope over Peter's chest for him to listen. Sam was holding the breathing tube and squeezing the manual inflation bag to breathe for Peter. Sometimes ventilated patients can get what we call a tension pneumothorax, where a hole pops in the lung lining, causing a pocket of air to form between the visceral and parietal pleura, so Sam was checking for that.'

'Then what did you do?'

'Well, I was looking for the cause for the air trapping, wondering if the breath size was set was too large. I peered over at the ventilator, which was rotated towards us. I was on the monitor side of the bed. I was shocked when I saw that the PEEP setting was fifteen. It is rare to set the PEEP setting above seven point five, so fifteen was double the normal range. This meant that the amount of gas remaining in the patient's lungs at the end of expiration was huge and dangerous. With both lungs hyperinflated, the lungs were squashing the heart, not letting the heart chambers fill. The blood flow from the compressed heart was backing up Peter's neck, causing the distended neck veins.'

'Yes, the intensivist, Ray, said it would not have been like that for long.'

'No, I can't imagine it was.'

'Did you see anything suspicious, like anyone near the ventilator?' Julie persists.

'Not really. There was no one present who I did not know, so I assumed it was accidental. Mandie and John had been pulling Peter off the trolley onto the bed using the trolley sheet when

Cindy and I had glanced over from our bays two and three. Then with Peter in the middle of the bed, they turned him slightly side to side to get the crumpled sheet out.'

'Who was closest to the ventilator?'

'Initially, Mandie was closest, lifting his chest and John had his hips when they first pulled Peter across onto the bed from the ventilator side of the bed. Lauren tucked the trolley sheet across to the middle of the bed from the monitor side when they tipped Peter on his left side. Then Mandie and John swapped sides to turn Peter and get the sheet out from the middle of his back from the other side. As they came around to the monitor side of the bed, I believe John was at the chest and Mandie came around last to take the hips. Lauren was then on the ventilator side, getting the trolley sheet out. Simon was holding the transport monitor at the foot of the bed. Linda was standing at the head of the bed just under the monitor, making sure the transport ventilator and tubing reached during the transfer onto the bed. When Jayney walked in, she stayed on the outside of the trolley, helping to push Peter over towards Mandie and John. Next, Jayney and Linda unlocked the brakes on the trolley to move it out of the bay, as John and Mandie swapped sides.'

'So, Mandie was closest to the ventilator when Peter was slid onto the bed, using the laminated panel and sheet?'

'Yes, the ventilator was on her right-hand side. The curtains were only partially closed, but she was facing the trolley, not the ventilator, when I glanced over.'

'So, you did not see Jayney, Simon, Linda or Jenny Marlows near the ventilator?'

'No, Linda helped Sam at the head of the bed, from the monitor side of the bed, by disconnecting the transport ventilator while Lauren attached the ICU ventilator from the other side after Peter landed in the bed. Simon stayed at the foot of the bed. Jayney then started recording the baseline observations onto the flowchart from the monitor and ventilator. The curtain was half pulled across the glass panel on that side, and I had to keep a watch on my patient. I am not sure how close Jayney got to the ventilator when she was documenting those settings. Cindy and I were just looking over in case they needed help. We both had confused patients, so we were also watching that our patients did not remove their oxygen tubes and catheters.'

'And you were on duty Wednesday when the noradrenalin infusion was found at a rate of thirty-five?'

'Yes, I'm afraid so.' Carol grimaces.

'You told Gail that you believed the infusion pump was tampered with after you had reduced the rate to five micrograms per minute. Where were you when that happened?'

'I was at the head of the bed, managing the airway and coordinating for Peter to be turned onto his side, making sure that none of the drips or the breathing tube got dislodged.'

'So, the noradrenaline pump was not within your reach?'

'No, the noradrenaline pump was over a metre away.'

'Mm ... did you see anyone touch the pump?'

'Not changing the settings, no. I was holding Peter's chin and the breathing tube, watching both the monitor and ventilator. It would be usual for the orderlies or other staff to move the infusion pumps closer to turn the patient. You always need to check there is enough length in lines and tubes so that nothing gets pulled out or disconnected. I was totally focused on the ventilator and the monitor, with my right finger and thumb holding Peter's breathing tube and chin. My left hand was threaded through the Y in the ventilator tubing to support Peter's head. I had to watch the ventilator pressures and monitor in case the oxygen levels dropped when the bad lung was placed uppermost to improve air entry. You have to watch the monitor screen for cardiac rhythm disturbances and the oxygen saturation levels as well.'

'Which alarms sounded?' Julie enquires

'The heart rate was first, then the blood pressure. The heart rhythm changed to ventricular tachycardia, a lethal rhythm, so we had to return Peter onto his back to administer a shock. The defibrillation pads were placed on Peter's chest and a shock was administered by Lauren to get the heart rhythm back to normal.'

'Then what happened?'

'The blood pressure went really high. Suzie was standing next to the pump, so I asked her to put the noradrenaline infusion program on hold. There was no point administering a drug to increase the blood pressure when it was now too high. Initially, I was wondering if pain was the cause of the blood pressure. Then Suzie gasped when she saw the rate.'

'And you saw no one near the infusion pump?'

'Maybe one of the orderlies might have shifted the infusion pole to stand closer to the bed and then moved the pump back closer again, to ensure the intravenous lines weren't overstretched.'

'Which orderly was at Peter's chest?'

'I'm not sure. They swap over all the time ... Maybe Mandie?'

'You didn't see anyone moving the dial on the noradrenaline?'

'No, we were all doing the turn, I thought.'

'Yet Ray says it would have only been like that for a few minutes.'

'Yes, that's true. After ringing the orderlies on the cordless to help me to turn Peter, I had asked Lauren, as team leader, to help too. I went to the head of the bed to suction any secretions from Peter's mouth and breathing tube with a suction catheter. I also had to stop the feeds before laying the bed flat. I had just done a set of observations on the flow chart, so I know I had reduced the rate to five. There is no way that infusion was on thirty-five for those ten minutes. Only in severe shock would someone tolerate that rate. I cannot explain how the rate got to be thirty-five. Everything about this Peter Robinson case is dodgy.'

'What do you mean?'

'Well, why did he come in unconscious and ventilated with a

drug screen positive for narcotics when his brother, who lives with him, and his parents say he did not take painkillers or use illicit drugs? His GP had not prescribed any painkillers for Peter, and there is no record of fractures or injuries on any emergency notes to warrant a narcotics prescription. When found by the paramedics, Peter was so deeply unconscious that he did not even need sedating to prevent gagging for the insertion of the breathing tube. I checked Peter's notes for the time of the drug screen, to double-check the sample was collected well before the fentanyl and midazolam infusions were started, and of course it was. Then the PEEP incident … there are too many coincidences.'

'Yes, that is why we are here. And there was no one in that bed space that you did not know?'

'No. Peter's parents had just gone home.'

'Do you like working here?'

Carols laughs. 'No one likes the chaos and fatigue of shift work – I'm sure you know that!'

'Have you ever seen any unusual events like this before since working here?'

'No, never.'

'How long have you known John Simpson and Mandie Lane? They were both there again, helping you turn Peter, is that right?'

'I couldn't say really. Since I started shiftwork, I'm not great with timeframes. Just guessing, I would say that John has worked here for about ten years, and Mandie probably longer, maybe fifteen or twenty years.'

'Have you ever had any issues with either of them?'

'Oh no, not at all. They are both amazing, really helpful. They both follow instructions and always help us get each patient comfortable. Some of the orderlies are less patient because their phones are ringing constantly, but those two are both excellent. I've never had any problems with either of them.'

'You have never seen either of them adjust equipment?'

'No, they are not qualified. They just bring the infusion pumps in closer if the lines are stretched or help us to reattach the ventilator tubing if it disconnects and our hands are full. Occasionally, they might silence a monitor alarm for us when instructed, but they only do as we ask. I have never seen them touch anything without instructions. Both are really experienced in helping us do cardiac compressions, positioning patients for chest X-rays and maintaining patients in specific positions for dressings or procedures like lumbar punctures.'

Julie nods to Vivienne in silent communication. Vivienne leaves the tearoom and returns with an infusion pump, the same make and model as the one in use at Peter's bedside.

'So, Carol,' Vivienne puts one hand on the pump, 'I could technically move this dial with my thumb to change the zero to a three without anyone noticing as I wheel the stand, couldn't I? Like the PEEP dial, it does not make any clicking or beeping noise when adjustments are made, does it?'

'No ... I guess not, I've never really thought about it. The ventilator would not be moved, though. We keep the brakes locked on it. But you're right ... the dial is silent on both the infusion pump and the PEEP dial.'

'So, technically anyone could turn three notches with their thumb when moving the stand without anybody noticing, because it does not make a noise when adjustments are made.'

Carol's eyes widened. 'No, it doesn't make a noise ... yeah, I guess that's true.'

'How do you find Lauren? Is she easy to work with?'

'Yes, Lauren's brilliant, very experienced and skilled. Lauren always makes sure we get our meal breaks, if it's humanly possible. If we miss breaks on the twelve-hour shifts, it is usually because she's attending MET calls or we're having our own unpredictable emergencies in the ICU. Lauren is a good resource person, especially when you can get frustrated from alarms going off and you can't figure out the cause. Lauren is really supportive. She will help us methodically problem solve, or if the equipment is broken, grab another from the storeroom. I have a lot of respect for Lauren; she's a team player and a hard worker. Lauren does not leave for home when she is team leader unless everyone else is gone. If you are still finishing up, delayed by an unstable patient or emergency procedures, Lauren will always come over to help.'

'Sounds like you get on.'

'Yeah, Lauren can look cranky when she is in pain or has "underslept", but she is always professional. Lauren often takes risks when protecting junior nurses from the belittling supervisors. Lauren won't let the novices get demoralised. She kind of shields them, often to her own detriment.'

'Are there many crabby supervisors?'

Laughing, Carol says, 'There is definitely no shortage! It seems like you have to be a narcissist or sociopath to get promoted here. Gail and Ray are exceptions, though; they both try to defend us from the destructive upper echelons.'

Julie and Vivienne make eye contact before turning to face Carol. 'You make it sound like there is a great divide between the clinical staff and management.'

'Definitely,' Carol smiles. 'The clinicians possess the conscience and compassion which is sadly lacking in the leadership here.'

'Why's that?'

'Only egos and budgets matter to them. That would be their budget, of course, not ours. Their dysfunctional power games are endless. The managers will abuse you one minute, then ring you at home wanting you to do overtime for them the next. They aren't bothered about ringing every household, waking up children and babies all hours of the day and night, until they find someone.'

'So, you already work full time and they expect you to work overtime as well'?

'Not expect ... *demand! The line managers here are like nothing I have ever encountered before. They will cancel your holidays if there are too many on maternity leave or unexpected sick leave, even if you've paid for a cruise or airfares. They hang up when the ICU is functioning over capacity and you need overtime approved to organise staffing. That is why I avoid* team leader roles. I have no respect for bullies.'

'Hmm … well, here is my card. If there is anything you think of later, you'll let us know, yeah?'

'Sure.'

'Thanks for your time, Carol,' Vivienne and Julie say, leaving the tearoom.

Vivienne turns to remind her. 'We will need a written statement from you when you can.'

Both officers check their phones for messages while Carol returns to her patient.

'No one seems to have seen anything,' Julie says in frustration.

'And Peter's family were not in then, either.'

'I wonder when John and Mandie are rostered on duty again.'

'Looking at the rosters Human Resources provided, Mandie is on shift this evening and John is already scheduled on today from 7 am to 4 pm.'

'There are really only four staff members present at both incidences.'

'Yes, but Carol arrived after the alarms triggered at the PEEP incidence and was at the head of the bed during the noradrenaline event, so we can probably rule her out.'

'Hmm, unlikely, I agree. You would not think the orderlies would have the medical knowledge and skills to be adjusting PEEP and noradrenaline dials to potentially lethal values, though, would you?'

'I suppose you can search the internet for anything these days. All of the other three were moving freely around the bed areas. Yes, Lauren, John and Mandie would have to be the main suspects.'

'What about those staff in the green striped shirts that restock all the syringes and gear in each bed area?'

'Nah, they don't work at night and would not enter a busy bay with limited room, cluttered with staff, unless they were asked to get something, I'd imagine. We will check with Gail, though.'

'So, we can probably rule those Assistants in Nursing out then, hey?'

'Yeah. We will check with the unit manager, Gail, but I expect so.'

Chapter 10

Friday 14 February

Interview with John Simpson

'Hi, John. Did your supervisor let you know that he was taking you off line for a brief chat with us?' asks Vivenne.

John Simpson was about 180 centimetres tall with a trim build. His dark brown hair was styled in a short back and sides neat cut that drew attention to his friendly, chocolate coloured eyes and charismatic smile. He wore a navy blue shirt, with black trousers and a wide black belt weighed down with a bulky mobile phone.

'Yeah sure, I'm off line for fifteen minutes before I'm due home.'

'Did you hear there has been suspected tampering with equipment attached to Peter Robinson, the ventilated patient in bay six, in the ICU?'

'Yes. I did not really understand much of the medical talk, but I got the impression that settings were wrong on the breathing machine and fluid pumps.'

'Yeah, that's what the concern is. Did you see anyone doing anything suspicious?'

'No. I was just there helping move him off the hydraulic trolley onto the ICU bed Friday night when he was being admitted. Then we both got called in Wednesday to do a turn, our first day shift after we came back from days off.'

'Do you usually work with Mandie?'

'Often, yeah. Most of the orderlies doing the lifting and patient movements work in pairs. There are so many heavy stroke patients and disabled or weak critically ill patients that you usually need two people to reposition or lift them upright.'

'How long have you worked here, John?'

'Since 1996. We transferred here from Newcastle Hospital when the mother-in-law took ill.'

'Do you like working here?'

'The nurses and doctors are great, but the managers are not as friendly as I was used to.'

'Any bullying?'

John sighs and says, 'Daily. This is one of those places where you keep your head low and try to navigate the bullshit rather than step in it.'

'Oh, that bad, hey?'

'Yes, I am here purely to pay the bills, increase my superannuation and keep my family provided for. I don't get involved in any politics.'

'How would you compare this facility with Newcastle?'

'Well, Newcastle was a bigger hospital. We had a warmer atmosphere there and good humour. Here, the morale is dismal. Everyone is paranoid about avoiding any contact with their line managers. The orderlies here get pissed every time they get hideous directives, like the latest on "how to walk downstairs policies".'

Vivienne leans forward. 'What?'

'Yeah, exactly! A nurse tripped down the stairs at the end of a night shift, so the Human Resource response was to protect the entity by creating a ridiculous policy to shield them from liability. So, if you fall down the stairs, you have to say you had your hand on the rail before you tripped and lost your grip; otherwise, you will not be complying with the Bounty Hospital policy. Not that they pay for work injuries anyway!'

'What else don't you like?' Julie enquires, maintaining eye contract.

John's eyes crease in amusement. 'Honestly, you could write

a book about this place! We have heavy workloads, but the management stupidly expects us to keep going to an external building for basic equipment, like the low resistant HoverMatts that should be available in clinical areas where patients are being transferred from ward beds onto the ICU or bariatric beds. Unlike Newcastle, here they keep the clinical equipment in an external storeroom for the convenience of the maintenance team monitoring equipment, rather than in the clinical areas where it is actually needed. Everyone hurts themselves lifting because they don't use the lifting equipment that's inaccessible. We are too busy to keep leaving the clinical areas to get equipment that should be available. Most of the issues at Bounty Hospital are caused by ridiculous management directives, which drive the busy clinical staff nuts. Just think about it – why would you have HoverMatts to shift every patient over ninety-five kilograms in theatre from a narrow theatre table to narrow trolleys and back again, and not have them in an ICU doing wider ward bed to ICU bed transfers every admission and transfer out? It is sheer stupidity!'

John continues. 'If you document these hazards on the risk reporting computer system, they are downgraded with no action taken and without anyone discussing your concerns with you. We have been waiting eight years just to get fifty per cent differently coloured slide sheets for lifting, so that staff on either side of the bed can determine that they are all lifting with the same top sheet. When the two slide sheets are the same colour and staff are lifting but accidently not all holding the same top sheet, the patient can move unpredictably, hurting our backs or the patient's lines, catheters and tubes get dislodged. Yet, the business managers continue to buy slide sheets all the same colour because they are cheaper.'

'So, you're saying that very few staff members experience any job satisfaction?'

'How could you get job satisfaction when there's no respect, no voice, no support? It's more like a circus, not what you would expect from a health facility,' John replies, frowning.

'I am sorry to hear that, John. Well, thanks for your help. Here are my contact details in case you think of anything else you feel we need to know. We will also need to get a statement at the station from you when your line manager can cover your workload.'

'Thanks,' says John, putting the card in his pocket as he goes off.

Vivienne suggests, 'Why don't we go to security and see if they can pull up the surveillance of the ICU foyer and stairwells while we are waiting.'

Julie nods. 'Probably a long shot, but we can look.'

Vivienne checks her notes. 'There were three other minor crimes that night. Four wheels were stolen off an antique car belonging to a children's ward nurse parked near the helipad. Another nurse who was shifting house had a brick smashed into her back car window near the maternity ward after she left a box on the back seat. Later, a night nurse driving down to the back car park wound down her car window, offering assistance to a man who appeared lost near the mental health unit. She had to go to Emergency to get a hepatitis and human immunodeficiency virus screening when he spat in her face.'

'Night shifts are bad enough – wouldn't that be the dizzy limit!'

Chapter 11

Friday 14 February

Interview with Mandie Lane

Mandie Lane worked part-time as an orderly but had an unusual physical shape for one. About 157 centimetres tall, Mandie's scrubs pulled tight across her abdomen. If it wasn't for her sixty-two years of age, Mandy could have easily been mistaken for a woman in advanced pregnancy. Her arms and legs were thin and wasted, amplifying the weight centralised around her trunk. Mandie weighed about 80 kgs but she looked older than her age, with her short, light brown, straight hair and dry brittle skin.

'Hi, Mandie, I am Julie and this is Vivienne. We're officers from the local station, and we're hoping you might be free for a chat.'

'Yes, sure. I will just let my buddy know I am with you. How long will I tell him I will be unavailable?'

'Maybe twenty minutes?'

'Okay. In the central dining room?'

'Sure, we will wait there.'

Mandie arrives about two minutes later and checks for messages before placing her phone on the table.

'Do you want to grab a coffee?'

'No, I'm fine, thanks. How can I help?' asks Mandie, curiously.

'Mandie, we are interviewing everyone about the two suspicious events that occurred in the ICU on Friday night, the 7th of February, and on Wednesday the 12th, when you had returned to work on day shift.'

'Oh, I am not sure I can really tell you much about what happened. I am not medically trained. That Peter did look a bit crook, though.'

'Sure. We are just wondering if you saw anything unusual, anyone touching the ventilator and infusion pumps, before the emergency alarms began?'

'Er ... no ... not really. We don't do much with equipment other than transport it.'

'Hmm, and you are not aware of any conflicts in the ICU with Peter or amongst any of the staff?'

The rapid 'no' response is slightly louder than Mandie's other answers. Maybe anxiety? Mandie looks towards the door and begins fiddling with her phone, as though begging it to ring.

'So, you didn't hear or see anything suspicious?'

Her 'no' response is even slightly louder and more abrupt in pitch and tone. Mandie now looks anxious. When a silent pause does not elicit any further information, Vivenne changes to some more personal questions.

'Do you have a family, Mandie?'

'Yes, two daughters. I am widowed.'

'Do any of your daughters work here, Mandie?'

Another, louder 'No.'

'Do you like working here, Mandie?'

'No, no one likes bullies.'

'Bullies?'

'The line managers ... not the clinical staff.'

'Are the line managers abusive?' Julie questions, thinking, *This has become a regular theme!* 'Yes, they are ridiculous. They harass the staff over ridiculous things, such as a relative putting flowers in a five-dollar plastic water jug instead of a vase. They don't focus on real issues.'

'What real issues?'

'Safety issues, like not replacing orderlies when they call in sick, leaving only four orderlies for all the clinical areas in a hospital this size at night. When two orderlies are swapping every two minutes for cardiac compressions or attending emergencies, it only leaves two more for all the clinical areas. Then it just needs a drama in Emergency, or the helicopter to arrive, and the security need help as well.'

'And you have raised this issue with the operational manager?'

'Yeah,' scoffs Mandie. 'Nothing will change, because he gets a bloody bonus for coming in on budget. Us slaving our guts out, running from one end of the hospital to the other, understaffed, doesn't worry him.'

'So, that is why you don't work full-time here?'

'Honestly, I couldn't bear it.' Mandie's hand subconsciously gravitates to resting on her rotund abdomen.

'You haven't seen any suspicious or shady medical events?'

'Oh no. I'm not sure that I would recognise much. There was a kerfuffle those two shifts, though,' Mandie says, her eyes gravitating towards the door and the phone again.

'Have you ever met Peter before? We understand you also work a few shifts with Brumbie Football Club.'

'Oh, he's a footy player, is he?' Mandie's eyes open wider in surprise.

'Yes. You didn't recognise him?' Julie queries.

'Bit hard to tell when they're lying down with all that junk in their face.'

'So, you haven't seen him before?' persists Vivienne.

'You've got me curious now … I'll have to take another look, maybe when he's sitting up with his eyes open … or perhaps if I saw the family? I don't think I've run into them yet. I usually take the meals out for Chef, so I could recognise them.'

'Ok, well, you will probably see us around the hospital over the next few days. If anything else comes to mind, here is my contact details. Feel free to give me a ring.' Julie hands Mandy her card.

'Sure, I will, thanks.'

Mandie grabs her phone and walks rapidly from the room.

Vivienne raises an eyebrow. 'Was that odd or what? That departure reminded me of the expression, "if fear would lend me wings",' Vivienne whispers, her eyes following Mandie's hasty exit.

Julie contemplates, checking Mandie's side profile as she waits for the lifts. 'For a health worker, she looks quite ill, doesn't she?'

'Yes, she looks stressed and agitated too. She looked at her phone a lot. Do you think she was worrying about getting in trouble for not working?' Vivienne speculates. 'How can she have such scrawny limbs and be so distended in the trunk? She was nervous.'

'It's hard to tell around this hospital. They all seem apprehensive. Mandie did look off, though.'

'She was present at both events, near the equipment that was tampered with both times, My instincts are saying she's cagey.'

'Mandie and Lauren are looking like the best suspects so far, but Lauren would have more ICU knowledge for sabotage, don't you think?'

'Mandie's a funny shape. You reckon she's a drinker?'

'Maybe, but Lauren is the one with the major debts,' says Julie.

'If she was being paid for an attempt on a patient's life, she may not have got cashed up after two failures. But Lauren seems passionate about defending nurses and she just doesn't seem the type.'

Chapter 12

Julie Wright

organise to collect my car from Ray's on Saturday. He arrives to pick me up at 10 am after he's finished his hospital rounds. I bring an extra towel for the back of his car so I can take Rosie for another long walk along the beach. Ray grabs his surfboard and walks over to the beach with us, enjoying a few waves.

I spent the rest of the morning at Ray's house. Ray replaces a few of the butterfly bandaids that were lifting off my eyebrow. I sit mesmerised, gazing at those skillful, soft, warm hands, answering the questions Ray asks me about my parents, brothers and sister. I have bought Ray two chilled bottles of Tasmanian sparkling apple juice and a platter of dried fruit and nuts as a small thank you for looking after me, the car and Rosie. Ray heats up his barbecue, preparing Rosie and me a light lunch before I head home to drop Rosie off and do some shopping. Rosie and Ray are besties after he cuts a few sausages in half for her followed up with another game of catch.

We sit on his patio sun lounges while he teaches Rosie how to shake paws with his 'high five' command. Rosie laps up the attention. I am developing such intense feelings for Ray that I don't really want to leave. Ray's phone has rung about a new admission, so he is heading back to the hospital. He walks me out to my car. As I unlock my silver Toyota Camry to strap Rosie into her harness on the back seat, I noticed there is a cellophane-wrapped object with curly pink ribbons on the front passenger seat. I discover the most adorable pink teddy bear, wearing a pink tutu and butterfly bandaids on her left brow, in a basket of flowers. The card reads: 'Hey, when you're feeling a steady teddy again, would you like to come out for dinner?'

I cannot help myself. I give Ray a thank you hug, pressing the right side of my face to his chest, with my arms wrapping around to his back. He certainly knows how to brighten up my week.

'I would love to,' I reply, not keen to be disembarking from the warm, cozy hug. Ray is twirling my ponytail gently in his fingers, and like myself, appears reluctant to move.

'So, you're not dating anyone, then?' I clarify, almost as an afterthought.

'Well,' he strokes his bearded chin, placing one hand on my shoulders to look at me, 'there is this Sergeant Wright who is a hot contender – that is, when she's not walking like she's drunk and disorderly.'

He chuckles. Those gorgeous, captivating eyes light up in jest. I look up, smiling into his magnetic blue eyes and warm grin as he gently kisses the middle of my forehead. I am thrilled, and when the corners of his mouth quirk up in a smile, my heart flutters. I experience an intense longing in my chest that makes me want to remain in his firm, masculine hug. The message is clear – we are taking things slowly, which is just how I like a relationship to begin. I reluctantly let go of this embrace.

'How about you come over for some pan fried barramundi and salad after you finish at the hospital?' I suggest, wanting to make the most of the time we have off together.

'That would be lovely,' Ray agrees.

Ray is smiling, looking at me, with both hands now on my upper arms. Now, I really don't want to leave him, but I know he needs to return to Bounty Hospital. After another light hug into that strong, muscly chest, followed by another high five for Rosie, we part for a few hours. I dash home and prepare a shopping list, wanting tonight to be perfect.

Soon, I am home again, preparing the salads and tidying up the bathroom. I can't wait. Ray feels like the man I have waited all my life for, despite us meeting socially in such hideous circumstances. I cut up fruit salad, in case Ray is hungry before dinner. I am just returning the food back to the fridge as the doorbell rings.

Chapter 13

Ray Fischer

I t is alarming that two suspicious events have now occurred on the same patient, and within a few days, involving a team we both trust. It is inexplicable really. The frequency and the seriousness of both events are too much of a coincidence to be accidental.

Sitting in the HEAPS analysis a few days ago, I spotted the two female police officers again. Julie and Vivienne had already interviewed Gail and me about the PEEP and noradrenaline incidents. Before the HEAPS analysis began, I saw the taller one, Julie, looking at me. I was just checking my principal house officers and residents had arrived when Julie whispered something wicked to Vivienne. Vivienne, obviously entertained at the comment, had looked up at me immediately afterwards.

Then, the same afternoon, when I was feeling so relaxed from the great waves, I had just finished showering when a labrador come bolting into the spray too. The pup raced back towards the path, pawing at the ground, looking frantic. I looked down the rocky slope to find the focus of the pup's distress was the dishevelled sergeant sprawled out on the path! A shade pastier than her normal cute self, the sarg looked stunned, with blood dripping down her face and smeared on both hands. Rather than gently supporting her to stand up, I really would have preferred to carry her back to my man cave like a Neanderthal.

Out of uniform, the sarg looked pretty and sexy. Her loose, long, wavy, honey coloured hair was catching the sunlight. It was probably a good thing that she had one eye swollen; two of those sapphire blue eyes could have been overpowering. There were few things more attractive to me than the sight of this delicate beautiful female looking so vulnerable. Looking at her, I wondered how all those elegant feminine features were contained in a police uniform! In all the first aid manuals I have read, nowhere does it say the first act should be to check there is no wedding ring on her finger, so why was that my initial response?

During her interviews with me, the sarg had emitted 'career woman' vibes without the usual aggression. In her unguarded moments, she portrayed sensitivity, humour and, from what I saw in the HEAPS analysis, a touch of mischief. If I wasn't attracted to Julie before she had answered the door in her shortie pyjamas with her hair tussled from sleep, my interest was captured intensely now. It was quite endearing the way she instinctively hugged me when she read the teddy bear message I had left in her car with the flowers. I swear she almost melted into my frame. She was so cuddly, and dare I say for a cop, disarming. The first night of her head injury, I wanted to ask her straight out if she was dating but had to settle for subtle questions, like whether she lived alone.

While Julie only had a minor concussion, I instinctively needed to keep her with me safe. ... probably for selfish reasons of my own! I felt unbelievably attracted to her, wanting more of her company. Even that charismatic smile had the power to turn me into a shameless fool. That adorable puppy, Rosie, was just as enchanting. Her boundless energy and endless appetite for play made me feel instantly part of the family. Strangely, before I met the sarg, I had always known what I didn't want in a partner, but not what I did crave. My previous relationships had taught me that I should never date a health professional. Medicine as an occupation became too stressful if forced to engage in medical chatter 24/7. I physically needed to switch off and engage my mind pleasantly elsewhere. And my mind was definitely elsewhere while rescuing that cute damsel in distress. A female police officer was not even on my radar until my interest was piqued by her stimulating questions and charming intellect. There was also a subtle strategy about her interview technique that was an intricate combination of both direct and sensitive.

Over dinner, I ask, 'How's your investigation coming along?'

'Nowhere, to be quite blunt. No one saw anything,' Julie sighs in frustration. 'The common theme resonating from all the staff is how unsupportive and destructive the management is.'

'Yes, I hear you. When I started work there, the original contract negotiated was a one-in-four deal. I was required to work one weekend out of every four and one night a week, I was required to be on call. Then my friend, Charlie, another intensivist got severely depressed, his marriage broke down and he virtually drank himself to death.'

'Oh, how awful!' Julie gasps.

'Yes, he was a great mate. Everyone truly loved him, but he was too depressed to realise it. He was so funny, a brilliant doctor, excellent father. When he went into self-destruct mode, he had had a few days off sick. I rang to see if he was okay, but he didn't answer the phone. I didn't realise he and Joanne had separated, and she had moved out with the boys.'

'What a shame!' empathises Julie.

'Yes. Those boys seemed to be how Charlie measured his success as a father, doctor and husband. To Charlie's depressed mind, the marital separation meant he was an epic failure. Charlie had shown the boys how to work the washing machine if Joanne was working. When they did the washing, he told his sons it was a magic washing machine. Their mother asked the boys what was magic about it, and they said, "You put two socks in and only one comes out".'

'He sounds like the best dad. Humble, too, for an intensivist to be doing housework.'

'Yes, his boys would activate their robotic vacuum cleaner, then have fun hiding the docking station when the robot returned to recharge. The boys would put the vacuum's docking station in a cupboard or up on the step of a staircase. Charlie could make anything amusing. Charlie was a sport with the staff, too. He engaged the nurses in silly banter, and they would all joke around. Charlie was great for morale. On my first day in the department, Lauren came over with her hands on her hips saying to Charlie in a "mother, no nonsense" voice, "Doctor, come and have a look at what you have done!" Totally intrigued, we all went over there like sheep. We saw what had happened after Charlie had given neostigmine for a bowel obstruction. With the patient's head elevated on a pillow, there was diarrhoea from the patient's neck to their heels – it was like liquid mud.' I laughed at the memory. 'So, the negotiations began, with the nurses all deciding whether it was going to cost him a Black Forest cake or pavlova. Charlie, who was using the suction equipment to slurp up the brown liquid, said, "What about a mud cake?"'

I grin, cheerfully reminiscing.

'I am so sorry to hear you lost a lovely colleague like that. How devastating.'

'Charlie's death was such a tragic loss for the ICU. He was truly loved by everyone, except the executive. The first I knew Charlie was in trouble was when Lauren came and pulled me by the sleeve towards the isolation room. I was in charge of the floor for the day, so I knew we had no one in there. Lauren was coming from the utility room, where she was collecting blood tubes, a syringe and tourniquet, pathology bag and forms. She said to me urgently, "Come with me, Ray. This has to be stopped." Taken by surprise, I said, "What does?" Lauren whispered, "Charlie asked me to take his bloods, but he needs more than that. Charlie has fulminant liver failure.' She mouthed, "You must not let him go home. We need to get him to a tertiary centre." You can imagine my shock when I saw Charlie so severely jaundiced. It was so humiliating for the depressed Charlie, because we needed to admit him into the ICU and get him flown to Brisbane. Tragically, he died from a major haemorrhage.'

'What got him so depressed?'

'Budgets, and the executive trying to cherrypick their ICU patients. The managers wanted revenue from patients not requiring a lot of resources to recover, and the nursing directors were trying to force Charlie to send complex patients to Brisbane. Charlie resisted these transfers by patiently trying to persuade the nursing directors, not wanting to approve overtime, that sending critically ill ventilated patients to Brisbane put them at risk of equipment failures, like running out of oxygen. Aeromedical transfers also exposed vulnerable critically ill patients to the effects of turbulence and atmospheric pressure changes, for no treatment benefit. Every time Charlie refused to transfer a patient to Brisbane, the nursing directors would ring the executive director of medical services. The ICU would get swarmed with suits, conspiring to outnumber Charlie and prevent him doing any procedures or work. Charlie always held his ground, sincerely advocating what was best for his patient's wellbeing. However, Charlie chronically found himself in a nightmare of having the same circular arguments, with the same futile debates, happening over and over.'

'So, they drove him to drink'?

'Eventually, yes. Charlie got some funding arrangements changed though our ICU network to influence health policy to get improved funding for dieticians, pharmacists, physiotherapists, occupational therapists, social workers and speech therapists. Charlie was also trying to elevate the ICU's functional operation level to a higher category, to improve funding to appease the managers. A higher ICU category would also stop the separation of elderly and vulnerable patients from their social supports. However, the nursing directors changed strategies by trying to allocate excessive workloads to the clinical nurses. They would attempt to rationalise dangerous directions, like assigning two unstable patients to one nurse, by suggesting that this was acceptable if neither patient was ventilated'.

With Julie listening intently, I elaborate.

'Charlie and Gail would insist the ICU patients needed a one nurse to one patient ratio for safety, which is another ICU standard the accountants wanted to ignore. Again, the Nursing Director arrived with the Executive Director of Medical Services, challenging Charlie and Gail's clinical decision making. The nursing directors would insist the nurses should buddy up "simple patients", when any patient not requiring complex care was already being discharged rapidly to the wards, to alleviate the high bed demand. Gail and Charlie would be defending their clinical judgements, by saying this patient has been returned to theatre five times for complications, this one has required over twenty blood product transfusions, this patient is in septic shock. No one could do their job, for all the dysfunctional power dynamics and ridiculous politics happening daily'.

'Good God, it sounds like a diploma in head banging.'

'It truly was, and still is.'

"How do you find Lauren? She seems very skilled and knowledgeable.'

'Lauren is a pleasure to work with. She has amazing equipment expertise and extensive clinical knowledge and experience. Unfortunately, she is a bit of a martyr. If Lauren catches any of the young ones crying, she shields the novices at her own expense. Lauren encourages the new grads to develop the mindset that absolutely nothing at work is worth crying over. After Charlie's death, Lauren educated the novices about not letting destructive people into their headspace. Lauren puts her hands on her ears and says, "Between here and here is a sacred site they don't get to trespass". I pissed myself laughing when Lauren told a novice crying in the tearoom that in her head she needed to give the bullying line manager a "travel plan". The impressionable trainee looked up at Lauren confused, cautiously asking what kind of travel plan. Lauren whispered, "Tell them to fuck off." It was hilarious. Neither Gail nor I compromise on safety standards, but morale has plummeted with Charlie's death. ICU nursing and the impact of shiftwork is extremely exhausting without adding battle fatigue with unscrupulous bean counters'.

'Sounds like Lauren's a great mentor.'

'Yes, she is invaluable, and she's fun, too. One of the new nurses straight out of university was setting up to put in a urinary catheter to monitor kidney function. She set up her tray immaculately, with everything was organised and sterile. Then when Lauren pulled back the covers, the poor nurse couldn't find the gent's penis. Lauren said, "What did you do with it?" The poor little novice could not see Lauren laughing under her mask and was panicking about having to do all this paperwork, when she didn't actually know where the gent's penis had disappeared to. Lauren put some gloves on and helped her find it.

Then at Christmas time, the rookie got a secret Santa present, one of those water fountains with a tap and bucket, in case she needed "spare plumbing". Lauren's so funny, even in the most repulsive circumstances.'

Observing Julie's interest is captured, I continue.

'Another greenhorn nurse was allocated to care for a schizophrenic patient who had just arrived from Emergency, with a head so infested with nits that her hair was moving. The worst part of the predicament was that the patient had pneumonia and needed a CPAP mask and strap put over the hair for ventilation. The nurse was squealing when the black band of the CPAP mask instantly got covered in brown flecks that began moving all over the pillow. Lauren sprayed the sheets and pillowcase with lice killing spray so that any nits landing on the linen died. Lauren was laughing so much at the novice's horrified expressions that tears were tracking down her face. Fearing infestation herself,

Lauren wasn't game to wipe them away by bringing her hands near her face or hair. Being a sport, Lauren got out the hair wash tray and lice killer shampoo to wash the poor lady's head. The poor young nurse was shrieking just holding the CPAP mask on her patient's face. Lauren washed the lady's hair, and then proceeded using a nit comb to remove the eggs. Just as the nurse thought she was safe, Lauren told her to keep the lice spray on standby for new hatchlings.'

'So, you find Lauren a leader and a hard worker?'

'Yes, a genuine role model in the most practical sense of the word. The only ones who don't like Lauren are the executive. The after-hours line managers don't like Lauren not compromising on safety to satisfy their budgets. If they refuse overtime by making the nurses double up unsuitable patients or delegate heavy workloads, Lauren raises her voice, telling the managers that she has the phone on speaker and has several witnesses who have heard her refuse their unsafe requests that breach the Australian and New Zealand Intensive Care Society's care standards. In most hospitals, treating staff members with respect is an expectation, but at Bounty Hospital, respect is a privilege that very few experience. As a team leader, Lauren insists that staff be called in for unstable new admissions, if necessary.'

I grimace before adding, 'I'm afraid for Lauren, because the nursing hierarchy is either trying to mentally break her with their Public Service Act directed assaults, or physically trying to harm her by refusing her rehabilitation support. Without consultation, the managers removed the only cupboard in that office Lauren could reach and replaced it with a ladder. After spinal surgery, which affected her balance and after five faints from arrhythmias, the Bounty Hospital concept of safety was to add height to the falls. If Lauren breaks her neck, that could be criminal negligence or even manslaughter. When Lauren complained about the ladder, the nursing director held a "reading" where discussion was refused.

The nursing director read out a typed, dated, signed decision that the ladder was fine because it was within Lauren's ten-kilogram lifting restrictions. Have you ever heard of anything so stupid?'

'How can those managers be allowed to work in an accredited health facility?'

'Criminals Charlie called them, criminals with the luxury of always investigating themselves to avoid accountability. Yet, the legislation protects these perpetrators. That's why Lauren taught us all to document breaches, together with the safety standards not being complied with, on the risk reporting system. Lauren has got us all doing that now for our own protection, so that these administrators can't claim ignorance. Bounty Hospital is like a giant domino stack. The pressure is building, and when it falls, the accountants, executive and managers won't be found in the rubble. Bounty's legal team obstructs right to information requests and hides reports, even when the individual has a right to access information about themselves. When Lauren asked for a Work Health and Safety investigation, which is the right of an employee sustaining a serious permanent injury, the executive went to extreme efforts to get her injury dismissed as "personal". A physio was sent to adapt Lauren to the non-ergonomic ICU, injuring others. Yet, despite freedom of information laws, Lauren was not able to access that grossly inaccurate report for four years. When Lauren did access the physio report using lawyers, it showed that the physio had accepted an inaccurate opinion of a line manager at face value. The line manager had instructed the physio that Lauren could get a medical clearance, which was never possible, because the cervical 7 disc tear was beneath a cervical 4 central haemangioma. The Human Resource Department correspondence, which was generated by staff with no medical knowledge who never leave their office, also suggested that Lauren could get a medical clearance, which was also not possible. Why would you comply with the instructions of the spinal surgeon and neurologist treating her when you economically fabricate misinformation and false diagnoses to deflect all work injury costs to financially compromise workers?' I ask sarcastically.

'Are you worried about Lauren's safety and how far this nursing hierarchy will go to harm her?'

'Yes. So far, they have financially strained her and deliberately increased her pain and injuries by ignoring medical requests. We all worry what the next criminal action will be. It is hard to intervene because nurses are a separate professional division, independent from the medical stream. As lower income earners, nurses are much more exploitable, because they have fewer resources to challenge fraud. Sorry, I did not mean to get into a heavy conversation.'

Julie was looking down at the floor at the chicken neck that I had bought as a treat for Rosie.

'Talking about harm,' Julie looks up with a cheeky grin, 'I thought she'd dismembered you for a second.'

I looked down at the chicken neck and laugh. Julie's laughter is a delightful musical melody that you could listen to all day. She even blushed at the sexual connotation! She's a keeper. I want to spend every moment I am not at work with her. I find her so intriguing.

Chapter 14

Monday 17 February

Interview with Brad Robinson

Julie and Vivienne approach Brad with a friendly smile after watching him end the call he was on in the relative's waiting room. Brad looks exhausted and sleep deprived, sighing as he returns his phone to his trouser pocket.

'Hi, Brad. We were hoping to catch up with you again.'

'No worries. Is there a problem?'

'Honestly, we are not sure. In our first conversations, you emphatically stated that Peter did not use illicit drugs.'

'Yes, he doesn't do drugs at all!' Brad looks offended and angry. 'Peter just has a few rums with the footy guys now and then. He stays busy with his work, the farm and footy training. He usually has a few drinks at the club at Christmas and on weekends after the games, but that's about all. Peter and Craig often stay for a meal after the match with some of the team so they don't have to go home and cook. Peter's not one of those party boys that drinks regardless of whether they win or lose. Both my boys put their money into the farm to get ahead.'

'Did Dr Fischer mention that Peter's urinary drug tests were positive for narcotics?

'That's rubbish!' Brad says in a raised voice, both hands curling in tight fists.

Julie frowns, puzzled. 'Then, how do you explain Peter being found in the Brumbie Club car park, behind the wheel, unconscious and needing ventilation?'

'I don't know ... Maybe he hit his head during the match or something?'

'The doctors have ruled out a head trauma. Can you think of any reason why there might be foul play – any conflicts or fights over girls?'

'My boys don't do drugs. They're not criminals! Maybe he hurt himself on the field, and the sports doctor gave him something. He probably had a rum or two, and if he was already given some kind of pain pill, that could have made him sleepy. How would I know?'

'His GP covered the games on Sunday as the first aid support. He says he did not give Peter anything.'

'Well, I wasn't there. I can't help you. All I can tell you is Peter does not do drugs, Craig neither!' Brads looks annoyed and exasperated.

A smiling Carol appears through the ICU locked door, giving permission for Brad to visit Peter when he's free. 'The physio has just finished with Peter, so just pick up the phone and I will release the door for you when you're ready.'

Brad glances over at the police officers, hoping their questions are done.

'Go ahead, Brad. Thanks for your help again,' Julie says, dismissing him.

Julie notices by the clenched jaw and frowning that Brad is confused and furious at the implications surrounding their questions.

Chapter 15

Thursday 20 February

Carol Bryant

have just come on duty at 7 am and realised that I have not yet been allocated a patient. Steve Jacobsen, the team leader, smiles on his way over to me to explain.

'Hi, Carol, we are getting a new admission. Do you mind taking him?'

'No problem.'

'Can I get you to take the Emergency phone handover then? Paula will be ringing back shortly. She said they are about to leave for CT scanning on his way here. This admission is not ventilated; we just need two infusion pumps available, apparently. I'll put them over in bay one ready for you.'

'Thanks, Steve.'

As if on cue, I pick up the phone with the screen displaying the Emergency Department number. Paula Biggs begins telling me about a thirty-year-old male farmer presenting with an insecticide smell on his skin and lung changes on his X-ray, thought to be Paraquat poisoning. Paula identifies her patient as Craig Robinson.

'You're shitting me!' I exclaim. 'Is he the brother of Peter Robinson in bay six?'

'It's true, he's Peter Robinson's older brother. The police were notified and have requested all body secretions are to be sent for forensic analysis. The doctors have ordered the viral and bacterial screening tests for animal carers, just as a potential differential diagnosis. Craig's blood, urine and saliva samples have been sent.

He's just got a dry cough, so no sputum has been available to collect yet.'

'Both brothers needing ICU admission within a week, with histories that don't make sense, is a bit dodgy. Too many coincidences here,' I insist.

'Yeah, I totally agree. This situation is beyond suspicious. There have been discussions about sending an agricultural and veterinary services team to the farm. None of it would explain Peter's positive narcotic screen, though. The house would need to be searched for narcotics as well.'

'Did they use Paraquat on the property?' I enquire.

'Craig says not. He reckons he's never even heard of Paraquat as a herbicide before. Craig has been told how critical this situation is. We are getting a CT scan of his chest to send the results to a professor in Brisbane who specialises in Paraquat poisoning. Until he reviews everything, no oxygen is to be given, unless the oxygen saturations drop below ninety per cent. The professor at the Royal Brisbane says that if you give oxygen to someone with Paraquat poisoning, it can kill them quicker.'

Paula whispers, 'Another odd thing, considering we don't know the source, is that Craig has only given the police permission to check the chemicals in his shed but not to enter the house, for some reason. Without permission, the police can only check the house if Craig becomes a coroner's. With both brothers being admitted to ICU one after another, the police had tried to convince Craig of the need to investigate the house for foul play and the source of the narcotics. Craig's every response had been a firm no. Sandy and Brad have tried to persuade Craig as well, but he remains adamant. Craig insists that there are no narcotics or Paraquat in the house, and that the brothers do not want strangers in their home. Although Craig has been shown his X-ray and alerted to the potential seriousness of his suspected diagnosis, my impression is that he is still in disbelief. I suppose that would be natural, since for both these brothers, their hospital admissions have been serious and dramatic. Craig might need some time to come to terms with all this sudden information.'

I continue writing quickly rapid abbreviated notes while balancing the phone against my ear in my other hand.

'Apparently, Craig stores his pesticides, insecticides and chemicals in a locked cupboard in the shed closest to the house, so he removed only that shed key from his key ring for the police. Craig has told the police he has no idea why his chest X-ray is abnormal. Although potential viral and bacterial causes are yet to be ruled out, Craig said he has not had any recent coughs, temperature or flu-like symptoms. We are wearing gowns, gloves, a N95 respiratory mask and a face shield as a precaution for the moment. Craig insists that he has not taken chemicals or illicit drugs and that Peter did not, either. However, it is the chemical smell of his skin and breath that suggests the Paraquat poison. Craig maintains that he has not been spraying weeds; he has just been mending fences.'

'Both these brother's cases are odd and scary,' I say, puzzled at this continually unfolding odd scenario.

'The doctors and police asked Craig about his activities for the last week. Craig was not aware of any neighbours doing aerial spraying. Craig said he began feeling unwell early Tuesday morning. He drove himself to the hospital because he was feeling worse Wednesday and declined further today. Craig reckons he was fine Sunday when he had visited Peter in the ICU, played footy and had his usual evening counter meal at the Brumbie Footy Club. Craig said he left the footy club early just before 7 pm to feed a calf. The calf is fine.'

On admission, Craig is alert and orientated, but the CAT scan shows lung consolidation bilaterally. The toxicology manual states that a very small amount, as little as a teaspoon of Paraquat, can be lethal. It is absorbed rapidly when in a liquid concentrate, and if oxygen is administered, patients die faster, as oxygen accelerates the severity of the pulmonary fibrosis. Organ transplants don't work because the Paraquat can move out of other body organs into the transplanted organs. Craig is nauseated, complaining of gut pains and becoming increasingly short of breath. Craig's laboratory tests are consistent with the signs of renal and liver derangement, anticipated after twenty-four hours of Paraquat ingestion. I put on the protective garb to protect myself from any accidental absorption.

Craig's urine and plasma tests have confirmed Paraquat toxicity, with his predicted chances of survival being estimated at less than ten per cent. Unfortunately, Craig is likely to progress to irreversible fibrosis and multi-organ failure prior to his death. The delayed onset of symptoms, a common feature of Paraquat poisoning, makes it difficult to determine when this exposure or ingestion occurred. Although requiring analgesia for the abdominal pain, Craig remains fairly lucid. The police visit, organising another officer to remain at his bedside. The ICU team is hyper-alert, and not just for equipment alarms. With the two brothers on either side of the ICU requiring police protection, everyone is wondering what the hell is going on. With Craig unable to identify anyone wanting to harm him, the police begin interviewing his extremely limited social contacts.

Chapter 16

Sunday 11 January

Mandie Lane

I was exhausted from working three night shifts in a row, with three consecutive days of poor daytime sleep, constantly interrupted with phone calls, dogs barking and car horns. The night was an endless series of phone calls for assistance all over the hospital in a shift that seemed to drag on forever. That was until I got a phone call to come down to the bright lights of the Emergency Department to assist a young female at around 6 am. The traumatised lady had been found naked, cold and confused, wandering along the local beach, by early morning walkers exercising their dog.

With two males rostered to cover security in Emergency, I was asked to sit and comfort the shocked, dishevelled girl, suspected of having been the victim of a sexual assault. Dr Suzie Murtagh, a female doctor, was chosen to do the rape kit, which required the intimate collection of vaginal secretions, the combing and plucking public hair, anal swabs, fingernail cuttings and the extraction of a few scalp hairs.

Tahlia Bennett's face and left eye were so swollen that I did not recognise her until Suzie confirmed Tahlia's identity for the labelling of the forensic specimens she had collected. There were four, deep, circular abrasions on both wrists and ankles as though, the police suggested, Tahlia had been tied with some kind of thin nylon rope. Tahlia's nipples were bruised as though she had been tortured. Suzie gently warned Tahlia before the vaginal speculum was inserted that she might be uncomfortable due to her extensively lacerated labia. These abrasions were photographed as evidence. The traumatised Tahlia became intermittently confused, at times, defensively trying to fend off the speculum being inserted.

'No more turns,' she cried, weeping loudly, 'no more turns!'

When I tried to wipe the snot off Tahlia's face with a wet washer, I had to take it away because Tahlia panicked. I could not continue to clean her face in her stressed state without her feeling threatened and becoming defensively combative again.

As Tahlia gradually warmed up and became more orientated, she began to recognise me. For most of her primary school years, Tahlia had often stayed at our house, since she had gone to school with both my daughters, Melanie and Penelope. Tahlia had always fitted in like one of the family. When her mother was working long hours in their family accounting business, Tahlia had often stayed overnight or entire weekends. With my daughters born only two years apart, the trio played, shopped and planned most adventures together. Whether they were swimming at the pool, visiting the movies or meeting friends at the mall, their activities were always accompanied by the delightful sound of giggling. The girls would choose an activity each and the bubbly Tahlia, who was in Melanie's class at school, would always predictably pick visiting the zoo or helping at an animal refuge. Tahlia absolutely loved animals. It was always her passion to pursue a career in veterinary studies either as a vet nurse or surgeon, depending on the university offer.

Melanie loved fashion, so she was always taking the girls to look at makeup and dress shops, while Penelope engaged them in sporting activities like surfing. On birthdays and public holidays, the girls would often visit the movies as well. Tahlia was such a darling girl. When my husband, Jack, died, Tahlia was only twelve years old. Tahlia hugged us all through our tears, asking her mother, Beth, if she could stay over for the weekend. Beth had hesitated, to make sure Tahlia was not an added burden during our grief. However, Tahlia did all those little endearing things that were comforting, like answering the phone, checking if we were up to talking with callers, making toasted sandwiches, supporting the girls during the funeral arrangements, providing hugs at the funeral and even visiting Jack's grave with flowers.

How could anyone destroy this beautiful little gem? Maybe that was the problem. Tahlia was gorgeous inside and out. Tahlia was slim, with tanned olive skin and she wore a warm welcoming smile that made her light blue eyes shine. Tahlia's mousey brown, sun-streaked hair flowed down to her shoulder blades. Tahlia's natural love of animals was an extension of her gentle, kind soul. Loving animals was Tahlia's way of helping humanity, Beth always said. We had all laughed when she had applied for job training at the Toowoomba zoo. Tahlia was glowing from a day in the large animal enclosure, while we had retched when she got in the car, reeking from all the various forms of smelly zoo poos.

When she recognised me, Tahlia buried her face in my embrace. There were tears in my eyes. I gently rocked Tahlia and spoke reassuring words until her distraught mother arrived. Tahlia's dad had died suddenly from a heart attack during her senior year. Although Beth managed her finances and their accounting business effectively, with only one wage coming in, there were suddenly heavy workloads and major expenses, like building maintenance, to be covered. To fund her university studies, Tahlia was working about twenty hours at the local veterinary practice each week. During her university semester breaks, Tahlia did waitressing work with me at the Brumbie Football Club.

As I sat there looking at the rope burns, bruises and the terrified look on Tahlia's swollen face, my thoughts wandered to the Bounty rape, reported the night of Penelope's school prom. After Penelope had graduated, the local news had reported one of her classmates was sexually assaulted on their Prom night. It was about five years ago now. I remember many parents expressing disgust at the horrific event and concern for the distressed student victim. Most parents had also conveyed an undisguised relief that it was not their daughter harmed. Another female teenager had been assaulted at the Bounty showgrounds almost two years later. After Beth arrived and began hugging and comforting her now sedated daughter, I reminded the police about those assaults, worried that a serial offender had not been caught. Tahlia's drug urine screen was positive for benzodiazepines. The laboratory result suggested the date rape drug, Rohypnol, may have been added to Tahlia's drink at some stage as she slept on the beach.

Tahlia's memory was foggy. She could only recall suddenly waking up in a panic in the dark room, restrained and being assaulted. A wave of nausea swept over the blanching Tahlia as she recalled the smell of a garlic breath and salty perspiration spraying down on her. Later, when the groin pain began again, Tahlia awoke, panicking, to a husky male voice muttering vulgar words. The lighter silhouette had loomed above, issuing menacing threats that the drugged Tahlia could not remember as he violated her. Tahlia could only remember her abject fear and powerlessness. The terror inflicted from recalling this memory for the police rose within her again. Suzie prescribed sedation and analgesia to dampen Tahlia's profound grief and distress.

Chapter 17

Sunday 1 February

Mandie Lane

The football club dining room noises rose as the day's games finished and daylight faded. As the teams and spectators begin straggling in to order meals and drinks, the smell of sweat and beer invaded our nostrils. It was Tahlia's first Sunday back at the club since the assault three weeks ago. Tahlia remained fragile but showed a rigid determination to keep her life goals on track. Since Tahlia and I were both rostered on the kitchen and dining room from 2 pm to 11 pm, I had picked her up on my way. Extra kitchen staff members were rostered to cover the anticipated semi-finals crowd watching Gynter play Bounty. To limit Tahlia's interactions with the public, I took out the meals while Tahlia wiped down the tables and returned the dirty dishes and cutlery to the kitchen.

The bar attendant, Trudy O'Neill, was delivering several coffees on a tray when her foot caught on the handles of a sports bag protruding out into the aisle. Suddenly Trudy fell, spraying the Brumbie team table with hot coffees as saucers and cups flew from the tray, shattering as they hit the floor. Trudy landed heavily on her right elbow, which immediately swelled, causing shock. Tahlia, collecting dishes from the table nearby, returned the laden tray to the table and rushed over to help.

'Clumsy bitch,' an aggressive husky voice cursed. More bar staff and some of the players arrived to help the stunned Trudy into a chair. The drenched Robinson brothers were offered tea towels to dry their sopping shirts. Amid the chaos, Chef came, pulling me away from the ruckus towards the kitchen, a panic-stricken look on his face, just as the ambulance arrived to take Trudy to Bounty Hospital.

Tahlia was lying on the kitchen floor curled up in a foetal position, shaking violently in shock, uttering, 'Bitch ... bitch ... bitch ... no more turns ... no more turns.'

I rang Beth. She finally answered her phone just as the ambulance arrived around the back at the kitchen's external door. Before moving Tahlia, the paramedic, Ian, had inserted a cannula and administered midazolam. He diagnosed a panic attack caused by post-traumatic stress disorder. With Tahlia unable to walk or respond, Ian and the ambulance driver loaded her onto a stretcher. Ian explained that post-traumatic stress disorders occurs when a trigger or cue from a previous traumatic event causes extreme fear and alarm.

'Bitch, bitch, bitch, bitch, bitch,' mumbled the sedated Tahlia.

At 11 pm after finishing my shift, I drove to Bounty Hospital to reassure myself that both Trudy and Tahlia were okay. Trudy was resting with her arm elevated in a back slab. When her eyes opened, I lifted up Trudy's handbag to show her that I had brought it with me in case she was worried. When I offered to grab some toiletries and clothes for her and feed her pets, Trudy pointed with her good arm to where her keys were.

'What a shocker!' I said, looking at Trudy's arm.

'Yes. One minute I was delivering drinks, and then next thing, my breath was knocked out of me. I don't even know what happened.'

'Your foot got caught up in the handles of a sport bag that a Brumbie player had carelessly dropped between their chairs. The bag was jutting too far into the walkway,' I say.

'Well, if I hadn't been in so much pain, I'd a' bloody punched his flamin' face in!' exclaims an angry Trudy. 'Fancy calling me a "clumsy bitch" like that!'

'Who said that?'

'One of those Robinson brothers – the older one, Craig!'

'Bastard!'

'Yeah, he should have been apologising if it was his bag, not abusing me.'

'Well, I hope that bloody coffee was boiling hot!'

'Me too!'

'I'll bring you some gear up in the morning, love. Try 'n get some sleep,' I say, ready to depart the dimly lit room.

'Thanks, Mandie, you're a godsend.'

'Night, love.'

I left after giving Trudy a light kiss on her forehead. When I arrived in Tahlia's room, she was thrashing her head from side to side, with her arms and legs extended, splayed wide, as though she was still tied to the single bed.

'Bitch, bitch, bitch, no turns!' she suddenly screamed.

Beth's sodden face and swollen eyelids told me she had been reliving the rape along with Tahlia for hours.

'I can stay with Tahlia if you want to get some sleep,' I suggested. 'I've got days off tomorrow. She could be like this for days. You go home and get some sleep, love. I'll stay here till you get back. That way, you can be here for Tahlia tomorrow if she is awake.'

Beth looked at her watch; it was midnight. After loads of persuasion, Beth reluctantly went home. Although I tried to discourage her from setting an alarm, Beth wanted to be back by 6 am.

Minutes after Beth left, Tahlia sat bolt upright, let out a high-pitched shriek and touched her groin, as though in pain.

'Bitch, bitch, bitch, no turns!' she yelled.

The medical ward night nurse, Katie, entered the room, giving Tahlia another midazolam bolus into her cannula for sedation.

'I can't imagine her mother listening to this for hours,' I said to the nurse.

'Me neither. From what I can make of this, Mandie, Tahlia seems to be reliving being tied down and possibly raped by at least two or more perpetrators.'

'Oh God, no!' I gasp.

'When Tahlia becomes catatonic, her arms and legs assume postures like she is tied up. Then she starts thrashing her head like she is trying to stop an offender but is pinned down, unable to move. She also seems to be repeating words uttered by the assailants during the attack,' Katie says. 'It's almost like they were calling her a bitch and telling her they were going to take her in turns. I can't be sure, though.'

The more I listened the more I had to agree with Katie's interpretation. My mind drifted back to Trudy's fall and how she was pissed that Craig Robinson had called her a 'bitch'. In the kitchen, they were the words Tahlia had been mumbling. Clearing dishes from the nearby table, Tahlia had been within earshot. Instead of racing to help Trudy up, as Tahlia automatically had, both brothers had remained seated. Even though both Craig and Peter were closest, I could not recall either of them even moving. Most of the other Brumbie players had instantly erupted out of their seats to help us stand the shaken Trudy upright. I had always thought it was odd that neither of those brothers had ever dined in with any partners or family, especially when they leered at attractive girls like Tahlia and Trudy.

In fact, unlike most of the other Brumbie players, there was no jovial joking with the Robinson boys. When on my breaks, watching parts of the odd game and training sessions, I had noticed that both brothers played to win without any concern about hurting other players. While often the other team members might check if an opponent was all right after a tackle or fall during practice, I could not recall any occasion where either brother had even looked back. I had also noticed how Trudy and the other barmaids were naturally cautious around both those players. If a few of the younger kitchen and bar staff preened their hair while serving, or smiled exhibiting subtle flirty gestures, it was never to attract either of those brothers. Although, from a distance, the Robinson brothers appeared to fit the 'eye candy' appearance and lean physique model the young girls often jested about, neither brother had ever displayed any charm, compassion or manners. In fact, both brothers appeared to display an intense dislike of confident females or any competitors on the footy field showing weakness.

Chapter 18

Sunday 29 February

Craig Robinson

Craig Robinson lay in his single room dying, every breath slowly arriving, rattling and laborious. After being notified of his grim prognosis, as consecutive days of blood testing demonstrated progressive organ failure, Craig had remained puzzled about the cause of his demise. As Craig's deterioration advanced, he began engaging with the palliative care team to discuss his terminal care options to ensure he died in comfortable oblivion. Brad and Sandy had assumed responsibility for feeding and watering the cattle until Peter could be discharged.

As the kilograms shed, Craig's ribs were visible corrugations, his pelvic bones were prominent and no fat softened the hollows around his eyes. Craig's former good looks and buffed physique were replaced by wasted sinews of muscle and bone in loose, crinkly, malnourished skin. Craig's severe emaciation was the result of his increasing shortness of breath, forcing his body to prioritise ventilation over nutrition. Every breath became a struggle until the accumulating effects of the toxins in his brain and the morphine infusion synergised, dulling his ability to communicate. The palliative care team had begun a subcutaneous infusion that kept Craig pain free and relieved his awareness of nausea or breathlessness.

Occasionally, Craig opened his eyes, as the nurses and orderlies repositioned him from side to side on the humming pressure relieving mattress, which inflated and deflated to prevent bed sores. As his level of consciousness fluctuated, Craig opened his eyes to see a woman come into his room to wash her hands in the sink.

Noticing his eyes were open and that he was watching her, she moved close to his ear and whispered, 'Now it's an even playing field ... It's your turn now, bitch!'

She threw her paper towel in the bin after drying her hands and exited his room. Twelve hours later, Craig drew his last breath.

Chapter 19

Sunday 29 February

Interview with Lauren Poulsen

Vivienne and I met up with Lauren to review her evidence of Bounty Hospital's alleged criminal activities. Newspaper clippings supported Lauren's claims that extracts of her subpoenaed testimony had been published prior to her disc tear diagnosis. The payroll and MRI evidence substantiated that Lauren had indeed been left on twelve-hour shifts with a diagnosed disc tear and placed on a three-month waiting list for the staff spinal surgeon until, six weeks later, she was unable to walk.

It was quite disconcerting to be shown confronting evidence that Bounty Hospital had intentionally subjected a nurse to this kind of deliberate retaliation as a consequence of testifying without whistleblower protection. The medical receipts also validated that, as a result of Bounty Hospital's negligence, Lauren had required the complex management of seven consultants for the twenty-seven surgical procedures she had described.

Rather than any display of remorse, Bounty Hospital had escalated its adverse actions by weaponising the Public Service Act to direct two assaults upon Lauren, using non-independent, insurer-funded doctors from Brisbane. It appeared to be no coincidence that the Chief Executive Officer directing the Public Service Act assaults had, once again, chosen the same doctors who, in 2008, had dismissed the proven disc tear as a Morton's neuroma by ignoring MRI evidence.

A 2019 pay slip confirmed that the Australian Industrial

Relations Commission (AIRC) had granted approval for Lauren to receive a payout of her thirty years of long service leave. The AIRC's direction for the long service leave payout, to cover the $20,000 medical gap fees she incurred, appeared to have instigated the Public Service Act weaponised assaults. Bounty Hospital correspondence provided by Lauren validated that the CEO's instructions had indeed directed these two medical assaults, by alleging 'concern for safety', despite photographic evidence of this employer providing ladders to her to climb to shelves three metres from the floor while leaning over the wider table that had replaced her desk. It was alarming to view the supportive evidence of Lauren's assertions that, with her balance impaired by spinal surgery, the Bounty Hospital managers might have negligently caused manslaughter. Why else, after five episodes where Lauren had lost consciousness from arrhythmias caused by a congenital accessory electrical pathway in her heart, would a ladder be provided to facilitate falling and potentially breaking her neck?

This ongoing victimisation was alarming given that Bounty Hospital had refused seven medical requests for sedentary duties that avoided bending, twisting and lifting from their own pain consultant and spinal surgeon. Medical receipts also validated that Lauren had still been unable to afford the desperately needed botox instillation into her bladder after the Bounty Hospital had forced her to fund her family's travel and accommodation to Brisbane to attend the two CEO sanctioned assaults. The CEO had directed these two Public Service Act assaults, despite her being competently managed by seven consultants who, according to the correspondence, were all satisfied with her progress. Reliving this trauma, Lauren was tearful at the insensitivity of a CEO not even permitting a health professional autonomy over her own body.

Lauren's documentation revealed that under the Rehabilitation Standard, the Public Service Act should only be weaponised to direct assault for 'personal injuries'. Regardless of how the disc tear occurred, the disc tear injury had progressed due to the negligence of her employer prioritising the clinical indicators monitored by Work Safety over her health. Numerous statements supported Lauren's assertions that Bounty Hospital focused on reducing the clinical indicators like compensation claims, emergency waiting times and absent days, monitored by Work Safety rather than complying with the Work Health and Safety Act or Rehabilitation Standards.

Further correspondence from Bounty's CEO contained accusations of 'diminished performance' for 'not working a roster schedule that matched her contracted hours', despite Lauren having no intrinsic ability to speed up the spinal nerve regeneration rate of one millimetre per month, requiring a four- to five-year recovery. Lauren's evidence had supported the common theme recurring in many staff interviews where employees had individually alleged that the Bounty Hospital 'choose vulnerable targets'.

For Vivienne and me, the dilemma was that, since Lauren was the most ICU skilled and experienced person in the bed area when the two episodes of sabotage occurred, we still needed a statement from her. With Lauren waking hourly to void day and night and returning after spinal surgery to full eight-hour duties, Lauren was prioritising her physiotherapy to improve her leg strength. The leg weakness and Lauren's arrhythmias causing fainting episodes still prohibited Lauren by law from driving. Out of compassion, we decided to wait another week before booking in a time to get Lauren's statement, given that she was already physically, financially and psychologically stressed from the two Public Service Act assaults this week. With Lauren's consent, we had recorded her statement about the two ICU incidences on our phones in the interim, to draft a statement for signing.

Lauren's predicament of having to fund lawyers instead of crucial medical procedures had her arced up. Lauren was paying off a car with an electric adjustable driver's seat and reversing camera, gym gear and an electric bed. Lauren was required to fund the additional cost of an electric bed after she required multiple courses of antibiotics for chest infections, caused by aspirating saliva into her lungs when sleeping flat on her back. With no rehabilitation support forthcoming, Lauren even had to fund uniforms that fitted over her full body spinal brace. Despite working at Bounty Hospital, Lauren could not even get disability parking assistance for when she was permitted to resume driving.

Our interview with Carol Bryant had also raised our awareness of other reasons for Lauren's mounting debts, as two other family members had also been left paying for work injuries. Lauren's husband, Glyn, a qualified boilermaker, was also left funding a work injury, after a shoulder injury caused by operating faulty equipment in the manufacturing industry was not compensated. Like Lauren, Glyn had also been required to take 'annual leave offered as flexible working arrangements' while on painkillers for a month after his trauma. Glyn had paid privately for two years of physiotherapy for his frozen shoulder complication when his employer had refused to submit his compensation claim to their insurer. Recent Australian Government taxation reforms also meant that these expenses could no longer be claimed as a tax deduction.

After returning to the same unsafe workplace designs and equipment with no risk mitigation or rehabilitation support, Glyn's pain had become so severe from repetitive injuries that he was intermittently waking up if he turned onto his right shoulder in his sleep.

Glyn had no choice other than to resign when the frozen shoulder symptoms causing arm weakness began affecting his ability to operate power tools safely. After Glyn had applied for Job Seeker payments and assistance from the social security services provider as a disabled person, he was instructed to enter his data into their website himself. Glyn's six online applications were continually erased from the broken Social Services system, which erases applicants from their system every thirteen weeks with no income. Still financially strained due to funding ongoing health costs, he had received no Job Seeker assistance, disability assessments or job plans.

When Glyn rang his foreman to see if there had been any calls from his social security service provider validating his previous employment and skills, Glyn overheard a volatile conflict between the foreman and the company's business manager. The foreman was advocating for the rights of another worker who had accidently cut a finger with a Stanley knife, requiring stitches. The business manager was furious that the foreman had submitted the injured employee's compensation application online, costing the company a $300 expense and a future potential increase in premiums if the injured employee had surgery.

As Lauren's financial crisis deepened, her brother, Jeff, was diagnosed with prostate cancer, requiring surgery. While still totally overwhelmed by the cancer diagnosis and prognosis, Jeff's stress had plummeted into depression when his boss's response was 'just lucky you have plenty of annual leave'. As with Lauren, Glyn and Jeff, who worked for two separate companies, were each denied the use of their combined two thousand hours of sick leave.

As Lauren validated the information we had been given, she astutely pointed out that she would not have incurred $20,000 worth of medical gap fees or been paying off the car and bed had she received the rehabilitation entitlements she was eligible for when the disc tear was diagnosed. She would not have sustained the second disc tear, either, had she not been on an operating table as a consequence of her employer's negligence and fraud. Yet, even appeals to the Industrial Relations Regulator, and providing evidence of three consultants and MRIs validating the disc tear, had the regulator's powers limited to permitting the same insurer to investigate themselves with 'procedural fairness to both parties'. As Lauren had rightly pointed out, why would procedural fairness be expected after twenty-five years of fraud was permitted by insurers abusing the onus of proof laws, leaving seventy-four per cent of injured employees funding work injuries?

Incredibly, Lauren's folder had even provided email evidence that Bounty Hospital had actually got an Australian award for quality and safety, while nurses were shunting furniture from bay to bay to receive admissions. The floors remained so cluttered with equipment that they could not be cleaned. This danger was a recurring hazard, after the original ICU building plan had been modified and no longer accommodated the standard that required a third of their floor space to be dedicated to the storage of equipment. However, with creative spreadsheet illusions, the managers, failing in their duty of care to patients and staff, had a demonstrated an astounding ability to unethically navigate all legislation and standards to preserve their budget integrity – and win awards for doing so.

Another AIRC commissioner, confronted with photos of chronically obstructed fire doors in an ICU caring for immobile ventilated patients, notified Lauren that his powers were restricted to having the same ineffective occupational health and safety team re-audit Bounty Hospital again. Six weeks after Bounty had passed their own audit, by temporarily shunting furniture to an external building after being warned in advance, they were issued with an improvement notice when a safety inspector arrived unannounced. One year after the improvement notice was removed, the fire doors were blocked again, according to the dated photos Lauren provided.

Generally, most of the clinicians interviewed described the executive as 'maiming, shaming and blaming' their workforce or 'diluting and polluting' any attempts to enforce health standards to improve safety. Many doctors and nurses interviewed blatantly expressed a desire to migrate to the private system. One ICU nurse informed us that the staff spinal surgeon had resigned because Bounty had failed to respond to his concern about hammering in orthopaedic appliances on an unstable theatre table. Worried that the appliance might end up getting inadvertently hammered through, rather than along, the bone, the risk was documented on a risk register. However, after the irate surgeon received notification that no action would be taken until the next financial year, he became so afraid for patient safety that he instructed the theatre bookings clerk to cancel his operations list.

Lauren's plethora of evidence clearly demonstrated that highly paid executives were underperforming. Other staff interviewed had reported underhanded tactics like line managers not providing contracts for individuals' relieving higher duties. However, when the union was contacted about the payroll discrepancies of unpaid increased responsibilities, the managers and accountants falsely alleged that the roles delegated were an integral part of the employee's portfolio. While no one had anticipated that the hospital administrators, displaying the ethics of an alley cat, would suddenly develop a conscience, a distinct pattern of systemic failures and obscene corruption was emerging. After the shameful media publicity of several inquiries, Bounty Hospital was clearly still willing to sacrifice the health of its workers and vulnerable patients for profits. What was the point of maintaining risk systems aimed at protection if profits were prioritised rather than safety?

Unable to afford lawyers and never having been inside a courtroom, Lauren was so livid that she had presented irrefutable evidence of fraud, negligence and grievous bodily harm to an Industrial Relations Commissioner (with limited powers to intervene), only for the maltreatment to escalate to where she suspected manslaughter. With Lauren doggedly demanding accountability, a dangerous situation was spiralling out of control since the determined nurse was not backing down. Another persistent feature of Bounty's failure to comply with health standards and legislation was that, with so many clinicians risking their career opportunities by approaching government authorities to report systemic failures, this entity remained permitted to investigate themselves. Most government authorities alerted to unsafe operational functions were more focused on protecting themselves by hiding reports or obstructing right to information access than maintaining patient or staff safety.

Lauren had even provided evidence in the Industrial Relations Commission hearing that simple heart tracings had not been performed to standards for four years. This standard breach exposed patients with long QTc medication restrictions to an unacceptable risk of fatal arrhythmias, with no interventions forthcoming. Lauren entered the risk of lethal arrhythmias on the risk reporting system, as she was concerned that patients on anticoagulants to prevent clotting could fall from arrhythmias, sustaining fatal brain bleeds. Lauren was apprehensive that fatalities could be occurring with the cause remaining unidentified, since heart tracings were not being performed to standards, which required a patient's age and gender to be entered. Once again, these concerns were dismissed by administrators alleging that the doctors could calculate the QTc measurement on heart tracings, when the pharmacists and nurses checking and administering medications also had a professional responsibility not to administer medications that were contra-indicated.

Cautious not to be diverted by this Bounty Hospital misconduct, we again reminded Lauren of our need for a formal statement. Lauren's response portrayed no 'lizard brain' survival instinctive alarm. Like most of her conversation, Lauren's nature displayed more of a maternal instinct to protect young nursing novices, coming out of university with $30,000 Higher Education Scheme debts, needing a healthy spine to carry pregnancies. While Lauren admitted she was fed up with employees being bankrupted self-funding work injuries, while corrupt government departments designed laws to protect themselves, she emphatically denied causing any patient harm, in the two instances under investigation.

Chapter 20

Ray Fischer

On my way home from work, I pop into the dry cleaners to collect a suit I need pressed and cleaned for a Bounty Hospital executive meeting. I am just leaving the doorway when I spot Julie coming out of the doctor's surgery in the mall.

As Julie looks fine, the bruise and laceration having healed nicely, I wonder why she needed to see a doctor. I am worrying that something is wrong, so I follow her to say hello. Before I can catch up to her, Julie enters the pet store to get some treats for Rosie. Julie has her arms loaded up with bags, so I grab a trolley for her. I am about five metres behind her when Julie enters the lingerie shop. Aware that Julie is purchasing intimate apparels, I hang back prudently so as not to embarrass her. It is too early in our friendship for that kind of familiarity, so I grab a coffee for myself and a hot chocolate for Julie while I am waiting for her to finish her purchases. Finding myself loitering now with intent, I enter the newsagency and grab the *Courier Mail*, browsing through the pages while I am waiting. Seeing Julie walking in my direction, I approach her with a smile and a quick peck on the cheek.

'I saw you in the pet shop, so I grabbed you a hot chocolate.'

Julie's eyes light up in a welcoming grin. While I unload her purchases into the trolley with my dry cleaning, I experience an intense desire and reigniting sense of passion just being in Julie's company. The taste of her skin and memory of her embrace linger to taunt me.

'What have you been up to?' Julie asks.

'Just had to grab some laundry. What about you?'

'Mainly treats and toys for my gorgeous girl.' She smiles.

Recalling the doctor's surgery, I ask, 'How's your eye going?'

'You did a good job, doc,' the cheeky minx replies, raising her hand subconsciously to the wound.

'No headaches now?'

I am wondering whether Julie is being tight-lipped about her doctor's visit or whether it was trivial.

'No, as fit as a flea again, thank goodness,' she says, beaming.

'Are you off tonight?' I ask. 'Would you like to come out for dinner? There is a new Italian restaurant on Beach Road just opening, if you are interested. Or we can go somewhere else.'

Julie looks at her watch. 'How about you follow me home to my place? We can feed Rosie and I can take a quick shower and go with you.'

'Sounds terrific,' I say.

I head back to Julie's car with her, load her boot with her items and follow her home. I have a ball game with Rosie, reinforce a few 'high fives' and check out some of the framed photos in her lounge room. Julie's unit, though small, is tidy and clean. Rosie has a few toys scattered on the floor, with the rubber chook being her favourite after the ball.

My breath is taken away when Julie returns in an elegant blue and grey wispy dress in a tiny floral design that flatters her trim figure. The thin shoulder straps of her dress and discreet neckline highlight her defined neck and arm muscles. Julie's stylish dress is a sharp contrast to the bulky masculine uniform I am used to seeing her wear. Julie's face is freshly made up with blue eyeshadow and a pink-toned lipstick. Julie smells so much like a floral bouquet that my hormones are raging at the smell and sight of her. I am deliriously besotted by this warm, charming sarg. I move in for another embrace. I could honestly hold the cuddly sarg all night.

'You look amazing,' I tell her, as she lifts her heels encased in glittering silver sandals.

After a final pat for Rosie, Julie grabs her matching handbag and we depart, leaving the light and television on for Rosie. Small, silver, diamond-studded loop earrings catch the light and shine out from under Julie's wavy curls. Oh boy, I am batting above my weight, I think – this girl is refined and polished. I open the car door for Julie and shut it after she scoops up her dress.

'I'm so glad we caught up this arvo,' I assure Julie. 'I was going to text you, but I had a few events at work, waylaying me. In the end, I dashed out to get my suit for tomorrow night's meeting before the dry cleaners closed. You are the perfect end to my turbulent day.'

I lean over to give Julie another gentle kiss, with my hand tenderly caressing her unblemished jawline and neck.

At my place, Julie surveys my lounge and kitchen, taking in all the photos and novelty items that she did not get to see on her first overnight stay. I turn on the television to entertain her while I shower and dress hastily in a light blue shirt with coal coloured trousers and black loafers. I take Julie's hand as we return to the car. I feel so attracted to her beauty, her smile, her wit, that she has me enthralled. At the restaurant, I hold Julie's hands across the table, suddenly feeling lost at what to say. We have ordered our drinks and entrees. I really want to get to know all there is to know about the sarg. I am gently stroking Julie's hands with my thumbs when I look up and see her watching me with keen interest. I take a deep breath for courage and tenderly make eye contact with her.

'Julie, I was glad you came out with me tonight. I was hoping that you might like to spend a lot more time with me.' To my relief, Julie smiles, as though she feels the same. 'I am hoping we might be compatible enough for a long-term relationship,' I blurt out.

'I trust that you are meaning a mutually exclusive relationship,' Julie's eyes search mine, subtly outlining her boundaries.

'Yes, definitely. What would your ideal relationship look like?' I ask, clasping both her hands, squeezing them tenderly.

'Well, to be honest, Ray, I have not been in a relationship for about eight years. I do feel an attraction to you, but I know myself well enough to recognise that I need love from a partner, rather than just lust. I am sure we will need to compare our schedules a lot to make this work for both of us. What would your expectations be?'

'Honestly, I would like to spend as much time with you as I can, Julie. I find you fascinating. I hope our feelings for each other can develop and grow, at a pace that is comfortable for you. Realistically, we both understand there will be some evenings and weekends when I'm on call or you're on shiftwork. When we are not, though, it would be great to go out and enjoy ourselves together and do anything you want.'

In my head, I am wondering how one separates love and lust when Julie is so beautiful and alluring.

'I really like that you are fond of Rosie, Ray. She is important to me. I appreciate that dogs are pack animals, so when I am not at work, I don't want to be leaving her alone a lot.'

'Rosie is welcome at my house – you both are. If you're having an evening off, you should feel welcome to just drop in or call me. I am really enjoying your company,' I say, kissing her hand in sincerity.

'Slow would be good,' Julie says, shyly.

My heart skips a beat. That was a yes to a relationship. I am delighted!

'Do you have family in town here?'

'Yes, my mum and my brother. They live over south side. Would you like to meet them?' I ask.

'Yes, sometime. Do you like nature walks? Trips to the zoo? What are your pleasures?' Julie enquires.

'Mm, surfing. I like country drives, good movies, great books, music, jigsaw puzzles, most things. I am tempted at some stage to try stand up paddleboarding – that's on my 'to do list' – but I don't have the gear yet.'

'Are you on call this weekend? I am rostered off. I'm keen to take Rosie to a puppy school sometime before she gets too big. Ten am Saturday, there is a puppy class.'

'That would be fun,' I smile, imagining how hard the boisterous Rosie will find it to obey the 'sit' command. 'What time is it on? I should be free most of this weekend. I thought I probably should catch up with Mum. Would you like to come with me on Sunday?'

'I'd love to meet your family.'

Julie looks so serene I want to kiss her. I move my chair so that I'm not on the other side of the table. After we finish our meal, I take Julie back home, and we laugh as the excited Rosie greets us with her ball. Julie gets us both a sparkling apple juice as we sit and 'high five' Rosie on the lounge. I hold Julie's hand, not looking forward to having to leave her. It's 10 pm.

I have finished my drink and stand up, reluctantly preparing to leave. I give Julie a warm hug and kiss, enjoying the chemistry between us. I should be migrating towards the door, but Julie's body is pressed closely to mine, so comfortably that I am unsure. Julie's soft lips have me buzzing in a hormonal chemical bliss.

'I don't want sex just yet,' the sarg tentatively offers, defining her terms of engagement, 'but you could sleep here the night if you wanted.'

Julie breaks away from our embrace, heading for her laundry. She returns with my laundered T-shirt and drawstring board shorts, offering them back for me to wear in her bed.

'I would love to spend more time cuddling you,' I confirm, not wanting Julie to feel any pressure to advance our relationship to a more intimate level.

I lie on my back with Julie nestled inside my right arm, with her head resting on my shoulder. I can feel her breath on my chest. I run my fingers along her outer arms as she strokes my chest.

'Do you mind if I ask you something personal?' I enquire.

'Like what?' comes Julie's guarded response, as she looks up at me abruptly.

'When I came out of the dry cleaner's today, I saw you at the doctor's surgery. Is everything okay?'

Julie's head drops suddenly in awkwardness. I freeze, then backpedal, suggesting that she does not need to answer. Julie is silent for a few seconds before confessing candidly.'I had to get a close encounter.'

'A what?'

I look at Julie, surprised at a foreign medical term I did not recognise.

'That is what Vivienne calls a PAP smear. She reckons it's as close as she ever gets to a bonk these days. I was enjoying your company and worried that I was feeling attracted to you,' Julie explains anxiously. 'So, I made an appointment with my GP to get a prescription for the pill. But she said I needed to get a close encounter first.'

Julie squirms. I laugh impulsively.

'Well, just be glad you don't have a prostate,' I announce. 'You get a finger up your butt, then they grab your nuts and asked to cough for a hernia check! That would be an alien encounter, although by Vivienne's standards, it is certainly up close and personal.'

Julie smiles up at me, looking at me intently, before climbing astride me in her shorty, pale pink pyjamas for a full body hug. I tighten our hug, tenderly rubbing Julie's back and I feel her softness against my chest. I rub my fingers gently up the outsides of her smooth legs.

Distributing her weight on her elbows, Julie clarifies. 'I hoped we might see more of each other, after your teddy bear note. So, I wanted to get my contraception sorted. My GP said that it is routine to wait to get the PAP smear results back before they give me a script, to make sure there are no cancers.'

I raise my hands to Julie's face, tucking her hair behind her ears so I can see her clearly.

Reflecting on our dinner conversation, I say sincerely, 'I am honestly unsure how much I can distinguish lust from love in my feelings for you, Julie. All I can say is that my attraction is beyond physical. I love your clever humour, your intellect and so many unique things about you. Rest assured, though, that in our relationship, we will only go at your pace, my lovely.'

I hug her again. I spend the night with Julie, holding her and pashing her until her heavy sighing breaths signal she is asleep. I watch the sarg, admiring her relaxed, unguarded posture. Her hair is spread all over her pillow as she rolls, sinking down to cuddle more into the blankets. Rosie has climbed onto her hammock in the corner.

I am too excited to sleep. I am bathing in the contentment of such a wonderful evening and Julie's confession that she feels the chemistry between us, too. I am longing to spend more time with her. Ideally, I'd like every night and every weekend to be with her, but I don't want to crowd her or push things too fast. She is like an addiction that I cannot get my fill of. I wake up with the sarg's fingers discreetly wandering under my T-shirt combing the coarse hair of my sternum, with her fingers splayed. I don't move a muscle. Her warm hand rises and falls with my breathing like a chemical defibrillator, sparking purges of hormones and electricity.

'Are you trespassing my person, Sarg?' I joke.

'No, doc, you're in my bed. That implies consent,' comes her smug reply. 'Also, there are no signs of a struggle.'

'Mm, definitely not. I am besotted with you, Sarg.'

Chapter 21

Julie and Vivienne

After such a romantic evening, Julie is requiring more effort to focus on the Bounty Hospital case.

'I'm beginning to think that if we got shot, our first words should be "I've got private cover",' jokes Julie. 'This is so wrong. The only truly independent party enforcing accountability, integrity and transparency appears to be the media.'

'That is why the nurses and orderlies report that Bounty Hospital has generated a Human Resource policy to prevent them from commenting on social media platforms. There seems to be no laws that Bounty Hospital cannot strategically navigate or manipulate,' Vivienne acknowledges.

'I'm gobsmacked that you can run a health facility and not even acknowledge the human right of an injured employee to visit an Emergency Department. It beggars belief that Bounty can put clinical indicators and profits even before the law. I had always presumed it would be a basic right of an injured worker to access their sick leave, but when you see pay slips where sick leave hours accumulated are increasing after twenty-seven surgical procedures and witness a disabled nurse with mobility issues and medical exemptions for cardiac compressions, responsible for attending ward emergencies, it robs you of any faith in humanity.'

Julie looks miffed.

Vivienne says, 'We are in a tricky situation. With Lauren being the only health professional possessing the most intensive care skills and knowledge of PEEP devices and potent inotrope drugs like noradrenaline, we will need a statement from her sooner rather than later. Otherwise, it will appear as though we are not doing our jobs.'

'Let's see if Gail Tontine has any suggestions.'

'It seems callous that we must force a statement from someone who is sleep-deprived, in pain, not sleeping from bladder spasms, struggling to work eight-hour duties and still having to perform a rigorous physio regime at the end of the day,' Vivienne says.

'We can't ignore that two highly suspicious events have occurred, either,' Julie asserts, 'even though I don't believe any of them were orchestrated by Lauren.'

'How about we see if Gail would be able to organise someone to relieve Lauren's duties? We could ask Gail if she would allow us to use her computer to get the signed statement, or alternatively, since she can't drive, we could come and collect her,' suggests Vivienne.'That is probably how we need to play this,' Julie sighs in frustration. 'Someone with the courage to front up at an Industrial Relations Commission hearing without a lawyer, having never been in a court before, to expose dangerous practices, would be less likely to perpetrate them, you'd expect ... unless another part of this puzzle is missing.'

'Yes, I agree, we need to err on the side of caution. Honestly, you have to admit Lauren's behaviour and mannerisms give off more of a victim being hunted than of being cruel, don't you think?' Vivienne responds, looking just as bewildered about who is the perpetrator behind these medical dramas.

'Mm, Lauren's actions suggest that she will break before she bends. Lauren's mentality is that safety should not be compromised. There will be no flexibility in her ferocious determination to stop Bounty Hospital's exploitation. Lauren's behaviour is almost at the extreme of self-sacrificing, like she is willing to jeopardise her own safety and take actions to her own detriment, albeit from a precarious position of powerlessness.'

'God, this would be disturbing for her family to watch! It would be like watching a mouse limping on a wheel with unscrupulous players lubricating every step to prevent traction,' Vivienne angrily replies, appearing frustrated at our lack of progress after so many interviews.

'Even though we feel sympathy, the bottom line is that we must do our jobs, and sensitively try to get a statement,' Julie contends.

Chapter 22

Interview with Gail Tontine

Vivienne and Julie knock on Gail Tontine's door, interrupting a binge-eating episode. With both cheeks bulging, Gail cannot greet us in her usual friendly manner. We wait patiently until Gail is finally able to swallow the food she had been rapidly shovelling into her mouth. Witnessing this personal crisis, you could almost feel the tension and stress caused by Gail's disobliging line managers, as though they were literally fuelling her destruction. Gail looks so guilty and ashamed that she instantly tosses all the remaining sugary foods into her rubbish bin.

'What has happened?' we ask, taking in Gail's miserable expression.

'I've just had in-service training on how to add sticky notes onto contracts from a total tosser in the tearoom,' Gail responds, anger etched on her face. 'Marcus Maitland loves an audience when he's intent on humiliation. Would you believe, he then bloody left without even signing the flaming urgent contract!' Gail explodes.

'You're kidding?' Julie shakes her head disapprovingly.

'No, you never need to manufacture drama in this place. One of the other nurse unit managers just rang me to say that Marcus was boasting of his antics in the lift,' Gail reports, looking defeated.

'We have heard so many complaints this week we wondered how anyone works here,' commiserates Vivienne.

'It's due to poverty, not choice,' assures Gail. 'My colleague just rang to tell me that Marcus just bragged to a lift full of staff that if he sees me coming, he walks faster, pretending to be running late for a meeting. Not to be outdone, another nursing director blatantly admitted to hanging up on her subordinates trying to organise staffing when their units or wards are functioning over capacity if they ring asking for overtime. It is not like we can control who comes through the bloody door. They are just pathetic, the whole bloody lot of them!' Gail declares, pointing towards the executive domain. 'The only legitimate use society could find for that lot would be as organ donors, and then you'd no doubt think twice.'

'We feel for all of you, we truly do,' Vivienne says, shaking her head in revulsion.

'While those accountants and managers are watching their bottom lines, my nurses are getting titanium implanted in theirs,' growls a furious Gail.

'It is amazing that, after the whole inquiry and media exposure, they do not even seem bothered sufficiently to change their tactics,' Julie replies.

'The clinicians would rather soak their heads in bile than have meetings with any of these criminals,' reports Gail. 'The whole nursing career structure is futile because no one wants higher duties. The nurses call this a "stealth service", because it is not a credible "fit for purpose" health service. I have to literally beg the experienced nurses to be team leaders because no pay incentive is worth exposure to administrators focused on disempowering nurses. The nurses ask me how they can make responsible adult decisions in an atmosphere where this dysfunctional leadership engages them in parent–child conflicts. The leadership amplifies minor issues, like people parking cars on the grass, but takes no interest in the quality of care delivered or patient safety. After the ICU was evacuated twice for mould, which is a hazard for ventilated patients, no solutions were found other than for the executive to direct the nurses to function like lumberjacks, moving furniture from bay to bay according to whether the admission needed the dialysis, isolation or paediatric bays.'

With Gail having saved a few kilograms from venting rather than bingeing, we depart her office for teacher interviews at Bounty Public High School.

Chapter 23

Wednesday 3 March

Bounty Senior Public School

With the summer vacation over, excited children have returned to school. Most classrooms are loud hives of activity as enthusiastic children and teachers begin settling into their new routines following their long summer break. Trevor Jones, the principal, needing relief from anxious parents ringing constantly with trivial questions, looks out the window at the school oval's manicured lawn, inhaling deeply. Trevor finds his attention drawn to the blue and white cruiser that has just arrived in the car park. Two female police officers are strolling down the path towards the administration building. Shortly afterwards, his desk phone rings and his secretary ushers them in.

'Thank you for seeing us, Trevor. We appreciate you are very busy at the moment. We are hoping you might be able to give us some background on two of your former students, Craig and Peter Robinson.'

'Oh, I remember them all right. They left here over fifteen years ago now. I was their maths teacher then. I taught both brothers and their sister in grades ten to twelve.'

'They had a sister?' Julie suddenly looks up, her surprise evident.

'Yes, Charlotte. She left to live with her aunty mid-term in year ten, if I remember correctly.'

'We knew nothing about them having a sister,' Vivienne confirms.

'Charlotte was Brad and Sandy Robinson's biological daughter, whereas Craig and Peter were adopted as Brad had always wanted sons. Charlotte was always a happy, bubbly girl, but that seemed to change rapidly after the brothers arrived. Charlotte began falling asleep in class, was anxious not to go home and was suddenly getting into trouble a lot. I remember Charlotte, because Family Services became involved in her custody. Charlotte went to live with her aunty, her mother's sister, in Brisbane. I understood that this was initially intended to be a temporary arrangement, but I can't say that I ever saw Charlotte again after that. Charlotte accused the brothers of setting her cat on fire. She was absolutely terrified of those boys. According to Charlotte, the brothers taunted her, broke her personal property and ripped up her homework. Things came to a head one afternoon when the brothers tried to walk her home. Charlotte would not go. She ran and locked herself inside a classroom.'

'So that was not the Charlotte you were used to?'

'No, not at all. We had to ring Family Services. Charlotte always had a very close relationship with her parents until the boys arrived. Brad and Sandy seemed to be misunderstanding Charlotte's fear. Charlotte was awake all night and sleeping at school. She went from being a straight A student to being either sleepy or hyper-alert. Charlotte stayed with another family that night until her aunty arrived to take her to Brisbane. I can't remember the aunt's name, but Charlotte told her music teacher that if they took her home again, she would run away. The teacher tried to calm the situation down by reassuring Charlotte that both her parents loved her, but she dug her heels in. Charlotte said that her parents no longer believed her, but she remained adamant about wanting to live with the aunt in Brisbane. When the teacher hinted that Brisbane was a long way from her parents, Charlotte was extremely clear about needing to be well away from those brothers.'

'So, this was really unusual behaviour?'

'Yes. Charlotte had been at this school since grade seven. She loved her music and playing tennis. She was popular with her classmates and teachers. Charlotte was a high achiever academically, but she was beyond terrified of those boys.'

'How did you find Craig and Peter?'

'Both boys were mentally and physically traumatised from living with their abusive, alcoholic father, who had been beating them up all the time. The boys arrived here with bruises all over from his assaults. When we asked Family Services about the scars and festering sores on their arms, we were told that their father awoke them by burning them with cigarettes when they were asleep. Craig and Peter were only enrolled here after their father had died. I can't remember ... there may have been some story about him dying in a house fire? The older brother, Craig, had a smaller stature compared to Peter and was very thin, as though he had not got regular meals during his early childhood.'

'How did the brothers adapt to their new home and school?'

'Sandy and Brad had doted on the boys, so both brothers were well looked after. Craig and Peter were always well fed, clean and tidy, but both had a natural distrust of others. I suppose if you could not trust your parents, the primary carers supposed to be protecting you, it would be difficult to bond with others. Peter and Craig only tended to socialise with each other, at lunchtimes and at their after-school sports training. They did not really make friends with other students. Even though Brad and Sandy spent a lot of time and money taking them out to sporting and social events, there was no natural warmth or friendliness about either of those boys.'

'Craig and Peter were loners?'

'Yes, exactly. Peter and Craig were well cared for, but they were too broken to integrate with their peers. The boys displayed no ability to return any of the love and affection they received. At the same time, both the brothers were highly reactive and became a formidable force if picked on or criticised. Any student who took on one brother took on both. It did not matter what size the other student was, there were two of them. We heard rumours of a few male students being ambushed in the toilets, but we could not act because no one was willing to formally report anything. The best we could do, when parents complained, was to have our security teams patrol the toilets and the sporting sheds, but they were never caught.'

'Did the brothers see a school counsellor?'

'I don't know that six months of counselling would have an impact on the cruelty of living for years with an abusive father who was physically torturing them. But they went for the standard six months of government-funded free service.'

'Counselling didn't really make a difference?'

'Not really. Those boys were intelligent and street smart. Craig and Peter were happy staying with Brad and Sandy, so that was what happened. It tore at Brad and Sandy's hearts that Charlotte would not come back home to integrate with the family unit they were trying to establish.'

'Do you know where we could contact Charlotte?'

'Sorry, I can't help you there. We destroy the school records five years after the students graduate. You would probably have to search for her license or ask Sandy for her sister's address.'

'I wonder if Charlotte is still in contact with her parents.'

'I'm really not sure.'

Chapter 24

Saturday 20 March

Peter Robinson

Peter Robinson was finally receiving oxygen via a mask after the breathing tube that was inserted for ventilation was removed. After the aspiration of vomit into his lungs in his unconscious state, Peter had taken quite some time to recover from the septic shock and pneumonia complication that developed. Following his critical illness and prolonged immobilisation, Peter was now battling severe muscle weakness, which affected his ability to coordinate muscles to swallow, speak and walk. The speech therapists and physiotherapists continued their daily exercises to strengthen his muscles in preparation for his ward transfer. Peter was continuing renal dialysis through a large bore catheter to remove the toxins which would normally be eliminated by his kidneys. Peter's kidneys were damaged by the prolonged low blood pressure, a feature of his septic shock.

Security camera footage, played retrospectively, found that at 10.48 pm, a person wearing a theatre cap and an isolation gown ran down the dark fire stairs at the back of the medical ward. The individual placed a thick black object, possibly a sock, in the door jamb to prevent the one-way door from shutting completely. At 11.36 pm, the same person entered the hospital grounds wearing a black shirt, trousers, hoodie and sandshoes. The offender was barely discernible, walking stealthily in the shadows to avoid detection. The shadow entered the unlit stairway, climbing cautiously to the second-floor exit beside Peter's single room.

The figure of the person was briefly outlined in the hallway light as the second-floor door opened, before continuing to ease their way stealthily into Peter's room. Peter would have been snoring softly, exhausted from his daily therapies. From the footage, it appears they used a double-gloved hand to remove his large bore dialysis catheter, allowing blood to pour from the wound. The scant trail of blood found at the scene suggested they may have folded their gloves over each other to remove the tube and prevent spills. The gloves and catheter appear to have been placed into the plastic locker bag, discovered missing from Peter's bedside table. Since no fingerprints were found on the blanket thrown haphazardly over Peter, the individual may have used a second pair of gloves that were taken with them when they exited.

The assailant, with their face mostly concealed by the hoodie, appeared to be briefly checking the corridor was clear before descending rapidly down the pitch-black stairwell. Both doors appeared to be closed gently behind them to reduce the risk of discovery.

Peter's concealed hemorrhage flowed rapidly in expanding pools, initially absorbed into the bed linen before spilling over to drip onto the floor as he slowly exsanguinated. It was thirty minutes before the medical nurse shone her torch on him during her ward rounds.

The MET team arrived too late to be of assistance. Even the rapid plasma expanding solutions, that were commenced while blood was being retrieved from the blood bank, could not be delivered in time to replace the severely diminished circulation which had persisted too long.

Chapter 25

Sunday 21 March

Mandie Lane

On 3rd February, Mandie's bloated abdomen, weight loss and chronic fatigue had been diagnosed as stage 5 ovarian cancer. According to her doctor, the cancer was too advanced in its spread to other organs for any treatment options to be of benefit. The only treatment deemed suitable for Mandie consisted of only pain management. Therefore, Mandie's final days on the planet were going to be spent ensuring her three girls were safe. Protecting her daughters from the predators who had raped several Bounty girls, Mandie believed, was a mother's obligation. Mandie may have had no choice about the cancer invading her body, but she felt a moral duty to keep the girls protected.

Tahlia was not the same bright bubbly girl she had been months ago. Tahlia was fearful and paranoid of strangers, following the assault. The rape had not just traumatised her body. Those brothers had defeated her spirit, compromised her sense of safety and crushed her optimistic ability to see the good in others. Notably missing was Tahlia's constant effervescent smile and naivety. Both were replaced with hypervigilance, as Tahlia began endlessly checking her surroundings for threats and strangers.

While Mandie may not have given birth to Tahlia, the only difference in her love for the three girls was that her love for Tahlia grew from within her heart, not beneath it, like the daughters carried in her womb. Now that their safety was assured, Mandie could resign from Bounty Hospital and the Brumbie Footy Club to go to her grave in peace. Tonight would be heavy, though. Mandie needed to share her alarming diagnosis and dismal prognosis with all three girls at dinner. Mandie wanted to give them a little time to prepare for the changes that lay ahead, in a life without her.

Mandie had used her remaining time constructively to finalise her will and funeral arrangements so that her girls would celebrate their life journey with her rather than grieve her absence.

Chapter 26

Thursday 4 March

Interview with Sandy Robinson

'Hi, Sandy, how are you?'

'Fine, thanks,' responds Sandy, slightly deterred by our sudden appearance.

'We were just hoping that you could provide us with the contact details of your daughter, Charlotte, please,' asks Vivienne Hale.

Shaken by the request, Sandy queries, 'What's Charlotte got to do with any of this?'

'We are just finalising our enquiries,' says Vivienne apologetically.

'Lotta good that did my boys,' sobs Sandy, searching for a tissue in her handbag.

'I am so sorry, Sandy, truly I am. That is why we would like to talk to Charlotte. We are hoping we might have some answers for you and Brad soon,' says Julie in a soothing tone.

'Nothing will change two bloody funerals, will it? Those boys had such terrible childhoods. Their lives were finally just getting on track. No one deserves to have their lives taken away like that,' sobs Sandy.

'No, they don't.' Vivienne's soft voice displays compassion for Sandy, whose actions for over twenty years had demonstrated that she had cared deeply for her adopted sons.

Sandy fossicks around in her handbag and retrieves a small address book. Under 'L' is a phone number with no name above it.

Surprised that her daughter's name is not written above the

number, Vivienne validates that the number offered is in fact Charlotte's number.

'Yes, yes, it's hers. I put it under L for Lotte. Charlotte was so paranoid that the boys would find her.'

'Why was that?'

'Honestly, I don't know. Charlotte would not talk about it. Said we sided with the boys, which wasn't true. We were just trying to give them extra attention to make up for the miserable lives they'd had. When they first arrived, the brothers kept stealing biscuits. There was stolen food stashed in their bedroom, in pockets, in shoes, under mattresses, inside pillowcases, everywhere. We did not growl at them. We just reassured them both that they were welcome to help themselves to any food in the pantry they liked. The only condition stipulated was that they needed to remind me if our stocks were running low so that I could get more from the shops. When they were settling in, Charlotte and I took Peter and Craig shopping for groceries with us so they could pick the snacks and foods they liked.'

'So, they both got on well with Charlotte then?'

'No, no, not at all! Initially, Charlotte came shopping with us to get the boys set up in the spare room and for school. We wanted the boys to pick things they preferred, like sheets, doonas and cartoon pyjamas, and to make sure their clothes and school uniforms fitted. Charlotte was welcoming and her usual friendly self. Then overnight, instead of playing with the younger brothers, Charlotte started acting up. Charlotte was demanding they stay out of her room, which we supported, because a girl should have her privacy. Then Charlotte's orange kitten, Pumpkin, disappeared, and she accused the boys of setting her kitten alight.'

'You did not see any bad behaviour from the boys?'

'No. We encouraged the three of them to get along together, but that made Charlotte worse. Charlotte kept insisting that we did not believe her, that we were siding with the boys. We could not reason with her. Charlotte's maths teacher rang to say that Charlotte had not done her homework and was sleeping in school, worried that she was sick. Next a music teacher rang and said that Charlotte had locked herself in a classroom. She said Charlotte would not walk home with the boys and wanted to go to my sister Heidi's house in Brisbane to live. Charlotte would not even come home that night. She insisted on staying at her friend's home until Heidi flew here.'

'Could something have happened on the way to school, do you think?'

'I don't know. Charlotte would not talk to me about it. Before I left for work that morning, I had offered them all a lift. The boys wanted to walk, so Charlotte walked the three blocks with them.'

'Has Charlotte come home since then for visits?'

'No. When Craig and Peter got their mortgage for the farm, we flew to Brisbane to spend time with her, but she has never been home again. Charlotte insisted that Brad and I could only ring her when we were on our meal breaks at work, not from home.'

'That sounds like she was terrified of the boys,' Julie says, expressing her mounting concerns.

'Yes. I am not sure what happened. Charlotte's friend, Amie, did not like Craig, or Peter either. Charlotte and Amie were in year ten, Craig was in year nine and Peter was in year seven at that stage.'

'So, you are saying that from when she went to live with your sister, Charlotte's communication with you was on your daughter's terms, and that Charlotte did not return home after she left?'

'Yes. I tried to get Heidi to talk to me, but she was evasive. Heidi said she was happy to have Charlotte living there with her, and Charlotte was keen to stay.'

'So, Charlotte never came home, even after Craig and Peter moved onto the property?'

'No. We would mail gifts for her birthday and Christmas. We would webcam and talk a lot on the phone, but we never contacted her from home.'

'Is there a good time to ring Charlotte?' Vivienne asks, her spiral notebook still open.

'With the traffic congestion, she's usually home after 5 pm.'

'Okay, thanks for your help.'

Vivienne turns to leave before asking, 'Did Charlotte come home for either of the funerals?'

'No. She is coming home for a month at Christmas, though. She has holidays then. Charlotte wants to catch up with her friend, Amie, then too.'

'Okay. Well, I will probably call you next week then, yeah?' ask Julie.

'Next week?'

'Yes, we are still following up on a few leads. I will give you a ring to arrange a convenient time for you and Brad.'

Sandy walks us to the door, her face flushed and her eyelids swollen with tears. She looks exhausted.

Chapter 27

Friday 5 March

Interview with Charlotte Robinson

Vivienne and I decide to teleconference with Charlotte who is at the Brisbane metropolitan police station. The technicians there can ensure privacy without interruptions, acquire quality images and support communication should problems arise.

Due to the sensitive nature of the issues we are hoping to discuss, we want get a close-up view of Charlotte's facial expressions to determine if she is becoming distressed. A female psychologist will be on hand during the interview, in case emotional support is necessary.

'Hi, Charlotte. I am Sergeant Julie Wright from the Bounty Police Station, here with Constable Vivienne Hales. We just would like to ask you a few background questions on Peter and Craig. Is that okay?'

'Yes, that is fine.'

'Firstly, we would like to ask you a few questions about why you relocated to Brisbane suddenly, in the middle of grade ten. In particular, about specific incidences, playing out between you, Craig and Peter when your parents were not around and what behaviours caused you to panic.'

'While the boys were settling in and my parents were organising their room, school uniforms, food preferences and clothes, everything was initially all right. As you say, it was when Mum and Dad were not there that the trouble began. Probably the first thing I noticed was my homework going missing. I had tried to encourage the boys to have their afternoon tea when we got home and then to do their schoolwork. Peter and Craig did not like being told what to do, particularly by a girl. As you know, they outnumbered me.'

Charlotte is sounding factual and emotionally mature.

'They were like sheep, meek and mild when Mum and Dad got home. I tried to be patient, but they were becoming menacing.'

'In what way?'

'Teasing me in an aggressive way, calling me a princess in a derogatory fashion, taking things out of my school bag, going into my room after I had asked them respectfully not to. Even when Mum and Dad told them they were not to enter other bedrooms, the defiance escalated when I was by myself with them.'

'Were you frightened?'

'Yes. It was like they were getting worse every day. They started breaking the heads and limbs off my dolls that I had treasured growing up and throwing them at each other, laughing when I cried, telling me if I dobbed on them, I would regret it. They pulled my kitten's tail and were rough with her until she shrieked. On my last night in the house, they came into my room. They told Mum and Dad they were looking for my sticky tape, but it was a lie. They were both right beside my bed, taking the covers off me and lifting my nightie.'

'Both of them?'

'Yes. They bolted, leaving the door open, when I screamed. Dad said he would put a lock put on my room, but the locks would have needed to be on every door. They pretended to "accidently" come in when I was in the toilet and in the shower. I would sit on the toilet with my leg or arms out to stop the door opening, in case they tried to come in. I couldn't relax. I did not feel safe being alone with them. It was not like a fun game they were playing; they were actually ganging up on me, so I was scared. Peter and Craig were calling the shots with Mum and Dad too. I was frightened because my parents would not listen to me. I did not want to walk to and from school with the boys. I wanted to stay in the library after school, not be alone with them. The last morning, when we were supposed to be walking to school together, I went to look for them. I found both the boys with the barbecue lighter setting my kitten alight. I called Pumpkin but she took off, still on fire. She was loudly howling, squealing in pain and would not come. I couldn't find her. Peter and Craig were laughing, saying they did that to teach me a lesson.'

'Was there any attempt to sexually assault you?' Julie hesitantly asks.

'I believed that was their intention. I was in a deep sleep that last night when they came to my room. They were pulling my knickers down when I screamed. I warned Amie, my friend, about them.'

'Did you ask them for an explanation?'

'When we were alone, Peter lied and said he was going to tickle me. Craig knew I wasn't fooled. He said something like if I hadn't screamed, we could have had fun, like the brothers could have had turns cuddling and kissing me. It was said in a strange way, as though neither had considered that I would not be interested. I really don't believe they planned to give me a choice. My scream took them by surprise.'

Charlotte's shoulders tighten. The psychologist eyes also divert, recognising Charlotte's body armouring posture.

'Did you tell your teachers?'

'Yes, I told them that Peter and Craig were bullies. I warned the teachers on that last day about their constant lies.'

Charlotte's eyes looking upwards to her right, like she is trying to recall more memories from that night.

'So, they did not actually sexually assault you, but you were afraid they were escalating.'

'Yes, escalating on every level. Invading my space, breaking my things, nuisance things like playing with my hair, making threats, calling me a bitch, lying about everything.'

'How did your mum and dad respond?'

'I suspect I might have complained so much that they thought I was being hysterical. I don't think they believed me. Both Craig and Peter pretended to smile like they were playing, when they were making it clear to me that there would be payback.'

'Did you ever get any apologies or signs of remorse after they hurt your kitten?'

'Definitely not. They said menacing things, like Pumpkin was theirs to play with, too. Only they were not playing – they were hurting her. I would try to rescue Pumpkin and she would try to run away from them. Both boys found pleasure in hurting and taunting us both after they invaded our home. The hair playing became pulling, and their threats began to include my friends. Later on, Mum and Dad wanted to get the brothers interested in farming so they could work for themselves. Neither Craig nor Peter socialised well as they grew older. They had no respect for others. They just pretended to be charming to go along with ideas that suited them. It was becoming evident as they grew older that they both needed to be kept away from people. Craig and Peter were constantly lying and could never be trusted to own up to anything they did wrong. They felt entitled to having my parents do everything for them, and Mum and Dad didn't stop.'

'As they got older, did they have any girlfriends, do you know?'

'I am not sure. They both had an emotional coldness about them, no empathy for others. They only appeared friendly when they wanted something. I don't think they could ever have a real relationship or connect to anyone. That was why my parents put a deposit on the farm for them, to try to give them a goal.'

'How do you think that was working out?'

'From what I heard from my parents, they were still helping Peter and Craig out financially. I know it sounds terrible, but I cannot relate to them as brothers – they acted more like predators.'

Charlotte's shoulders elevate towards her ears.

'You didn't return home while they were alive?'

'No. I love my parents, but I did not feel safe anywhere near Craig or Peter. Both had the same mindset, I am afraid. Living at home felt like I was being stalked all the time.'

Charlotte's shoulders remain raised and taut.

'Well, thanks for your assistance, Charlotte. You have been very helpful. Can I give you a phone number to call if you think of anything else?'

'Okay.'

When we end the call, Vivienne and I compare a photo of Charlotte to images of the other Bounty rape victims. Bounty Police Station has received an anonymous tip from a caller that has been traced back to a public phone. The female caller suggested that several rapes at the high school and showgrounds should be attributed to the brothers. The caller's concerns appeared to be valid when five female victims from as far back as 2008 fit Charlotte's tanned, blonde, blue-eyed, petite physical attributes. According to forensic psychologists, most psychopaths select victims with preferred attributes and hunt them in familiar territories. The abuse experienced by Peter and Craig as children was also suggestive of the backgrounds, documented retrospectively, for many psychopaths.

'Let's look at the rape victims' statements to see if there is any information that could remotely identify Peter or Craig as the offenders.'

'The school Prom assault would have been in the year Craig finished. We'll start there.'

Chapter 28

Saturday 6 March

Interview with Josephine Flynn

Reading through the files, Josephine Flynn had drunk two glasses of wine at the night club where the students had met up after the school formal. They had all arrived around 9.30 pm, had a few drinks, chatted and danced. Josephine went outside for a quick smoke by herself before driving home.

Josephine recalled someone violently grabbing her before she was thrown into the back seat of her car. In the tussle, her car keys slipped from her lap. The car park was poorly lit, so Josephine could not identify her attackers before a beanie was pulled down over her eyes and her hands were tied. Josephine could recall being in the back seat of her own car when the motor started and the car began driving away. Fearing for her life, she had kicked out at the assailant in the back seat.

Josephine was found concussed and semi-naked in a park by a bicycle riding group the next morning. The left side of her face was badly bruised, her lip was split and her dress was ripped. Josephine's shoes, handbag, phone and silver Subaru XV were missing.

'Two offenders,' says Vivienne.

'Yes. Let's take a trip to her home address. It will be better for us to talk in private at her home rather than draw unwarranted attention at her workplace,' confirms Julie.

Josephine's mother, Lillian, answers the door. She invites us into a bright, open-plan dining room for coffee. The room is lit by panelled windows framed in light coloured timber, with polished, uncluttered floors. We take our seats as Lillian heats the kettle.

Looking around at the family photos, our attention is drawn to a beautiful adolescent girl with wavy shoulder-length hair, playing volleyball in a beach photo. There are a lot of similarities between Charlotte Robinson and this girl. Both are petite, attractive and possess stunningly beautiful smiles.

'Yes, that is my daughter, Josephine,' says Lillian proudly, as she enters the room with a tray.

'Is she home by any chance, Lillian?' Vivienne enquires. A frown creases Lillian's brow as she looks down at her watch.

'She should be about ten minutes away. She finishes work at 4 pm. I can't imagine she would be in any trouble,' Lillian says, looking at us before setting the tray down on the polished timber table.

'No, not at all,' Vivienne says softly. 'We've had an anonymous phone call that we are hoping to talk to Josephine about. Someone has given us a potential lead into her assault case. We would like to ask her a few questions to see if she can provide any further information about the offenders.'

Lillian's facial expression is grim. 'I hope you catch them. It took Josey quite a while to get over that night, but it was not just the physical and psychological trauma. Josey's left cheek bone was fractured, and the concussion left her dizzy for ages. Josey would lose her balance if she turned around too suddenly. She also had ear trouble, hearing a noise like cellophane crackling in her left ear intermittently.'

'Was Josie's car ever found?'

'Yes, it was driven into a creek with the windows opened. Her keys and belongings were still inside. All her money had been taken from her purse.'

'How is Josey now?'

'Well, she has never dated since and still won't go out at night. Josey has no boyfriends or intention of dating, I'm afraid. Josey had been all set to go to Brisbane for university before the assault. Josie and two other girls from her class had planned to share accommodation. After her rape, Josie worried that her flatmates could bring home strangers. She worried about being assaulted on the university campus, something she would never have thought of before. Eventually, Josie decided it was best to stay home and do her business studies by correspondence. Josey is much quieter now. Josie gets anxious about going out alone or even going to public toilets alone.'

A car door closes. Josephine enters, greeting her mother with a warm hug and kiss. Josephine stops suddenly when she sees us. We have parked in front of the neighbours, mindful of compounding Josephine's stress.

We let Lillian do the talking. After explaining the reason for our visit, Lillian asks her daughter whether she would prefer her to stay or give her privacy. Without hesitation, Josephine reaches for the comfort of her mother's hand as both sit side by side. Josie's other hand trembles visibly as we introduce ourselves.

'Josie, as your mum has said, we received an anonymous phone call at the station, but we are still validating the timeframes and other information. We will definitely provide feedback to you when we know more, if you like.'

'What would you like to know?' Josie asks, her tightened biceps revealing she is physically bracing for impact.

'Did you have many offers to partner you for the Prom night?' Vivian enquires.

'Yes. I went with my best friend, Jamie Livingstone. We had been friends since Kindy, and he was also the first one to ask me. Cody Sommers asked me too, and since I already had a partner, I suggested he ask my friend, Amie, so we could hang out together. They went to the Prom together and are still dating. Craig Robinson asked me after that, so I had to apologise as I had already accepted another offer.'

'Was either of them angry or feeling rejected at all?'

'I don't think so. Cody was very happy to go with Amie. Craig and I were not really friends.'

'Did Craig go to the formal?'

'Not that I recall. Craig hung out mostly with his younger brother. He didn't really integrate with our class. I was really quite surprised that he had asked me to go with him to the Prom. It did not seem like the kind of thing he would go to.'

'Usually at formal occasions like Proms, most couples would go in their male partner's car. Was there any reason that you drove your own car?'

'That was the original plan. Jamie worked part-time at the Burger Shop till 10 pm. The night before the Prom, he had returned to his car to find all his tyres had been slashed. Jamie had been cutting and polishing his car so it would shine for the Prom photos, so he was really angry and disappointed. Jamie and his boss went to see the owner of the pub next door to see if they had seen anything, but there were no witnesses and no cameras in that area of the car park. It was going to cost Jamie two weeks' wages to replace the tyres, so Jamie's boss gave him extra shifts so he could afford more tyres and pay his parents back. Jamie and I had initially arranged with Amie and Cody that we would meet them at the night club. However, with Jamie needing to work the next morning, I had no dance partner, and he could not come out partying with us, so I only stayed until around 11 pm.'

Lillian leaned forward, looking curious. 'The police thought it was an opportunistic attack, since Josey was alone in the car park that night.'

'We are unsure ... After the anonymous phone call, we need to check ... Josey, had you had any conflicts prior to that assault?'

'No, we all got along well at school.'

After exchanging details, Julie and Vivienne drive to Tahlia Bennett's address.

Chapter 29

Saturday 6 March

Interview with Tahlia Bennett

Tahlia Bennett, almost another clone of Josie and Charlotte, answers the door after peeping through the viewer. After we introduce ourselves, Tahlia invites us to sit on her mission brown fabric lounge, scrambling to make space by stacking her study books on the coffee table. Accepting Tahlia's preference to discuss her rape in private, we continue our gentle probing questions, acutely aware from her tear-rimmed eyes how stressful recalling the memory of her assault is. Dressed in a baggy pink tracksuit, Tahlia sits on the edge of the sofa, nibbling at her fingernails.

'Thank you for talking to us, Tahlia. We hope you won't mind if we ask you a few questions. We are following up on some information received from an anonymous caller who contacted the station, reporting information about several Bounty assaults.'

Tahlia swallows before saying, 'I really don't remember much … just waking up in a quiet, dark room with a large heavy man's weight on me. When I tried to get loose, I discovered I was tied down. I was punched in the face when I screamed. When I woke up again, another, lighter man with a smaller silhouette, a husky voice and a filthy mouth was raping me.'

'That would have been very stressful,' Vivienne's soft voice emphasises. 'Prior to this, were you dating anyone, or had you rejected anyone who had asked you out?'

Tahlia shakes her head. 'No, I wasn't dating. I was trying to finish my degree in veterinary science by the end of the year. I was studying the last three subjects for the final semester and getting paid shifts at the veterinary surgery. I worked at the Brumbie Football Club in the semester break to reduce my university fees as well, so I was very busy juggling work and study.'

'None of the university students or footballers had ever asked you out?'

Tahlia contemplates before responding. 'Occasionally, a guy would ask, but when I explained that I was pressured, they seem to understand. An occasional uni student would ask me out for drinks or dinner. A farmer asked me out for a meal once, too. I was working on his property with Dr Bond, helping him turn the calf of a bellowing cow in obstructed labour. I remembered thinking it was such odd timing. I was covered in so much blood, shit and amniotic fluid that I could not even use my grubby arm to wipe my face.'

'Do you know any of their names?'

'There was a vet student, Elijah Drummond; he was in most of my vet science classes. He graduated just six months before me. Elijah said he would ask me out for a meal again when we finished our degrees. Dr Bond called the farmer Craig, I think. Craig had seemed familiar, like I might have seen him around at school, but I am not sure. He might have been in a different grade to me. He seemed familiar for some reason, before we met again on his Gynter cattle property. I don't really know his last name. I don't really do the billing or see the paperwork. I am still just working with Dr Bond to observe and learn his skills.'

'Were Elijah or the farmer upset or bothered at all when you declined their invitations?'

'No, I really don't think that either was really bothered. I simply explained that I was busy trying to finish up all my assignments and pracs for the last semester to qualify. They both seemed to understand. Dr Bond joked with the farmer that next time I helped on his property, I'd be a doctor. I remember that day because it was as cold as a mother-in-law's kiss. The breeze on the mountain was blowing right through me and my clothes had gotten pretty drenched in amniotic fluid … The farmer was really odd, actually. Although Craig had asked me out, he did not offer me a coat or towel when I was soaked and shivering.'

'So, no one got hostile from rejection or anything like that?' Julie clarifies

'No, I just gently declined, trying not to offend them. I did not really have the time nor the money. My car is getting old, costing me heaps too, so my finances aren't great.'

'Well, thanks, Tahlia. We better leave you to your books. We really appreciate your time.'

As she turns to leave, Vivienne reflectively says, 'If you're still studying, have you ended up having to delay your last semester?'

'Yes, I've had to get counselling. Dr Dalton advised me to postpone the final semester. He said I have post-traumatic stress disorder and has recommended at least six months of counselling to mentally process the rape. Dr Dalton said that after any assault, there is a mental wound, as well as my physical injuries, that need time to heal.'

'That's right. Okay, thanks again for your help. If there are any developments, we will let you know. And good luck with your final exams,' Vivienne says as Tahlia diligently relocks her door.

As Julie and Vivienne stroll back to their vehicle, both comment on Craig's rejection as a precipitant to both assaults. With all roads leading to the Robinson brothers, it is time to look inside their house. With little progress on solving the mystery surrounding Peter and Craig's deaths, Sandy and Brad Robinson have provided keys to their Gynter house without a warrant. Still reeling from the grief of two funerals one after the other, they have fed and watered the cattle, but no changes have been made inside the house.

Inside, the kitchen and living areas are sparse and relatively clean and tidy. No Paraquat or narcotics are found. Both Craig and Peter's rooms have king-sized beds, with only one bedside table in either room appearing to be used. Isolated from the main living areas and closed off at the end of the verandah, a small windowless room is found. The dark room contains a single bed with four thin nylon ropes tied to each corner. The forensic team has identified several strands of long blonde hair that DNA analysis confirms belonged to Tahlia Bennett.

The only common link between the Robinson brothers and Tahlia Bennett appears to be the Brumbie Football Club.

Chapter 30

Ray Fischer

Since our first dinner date, I have been staying at Julie's unit overnight mainly during the week, and the sarg and Rosie are spending most weekends at my house. When we have an afternoon off together, I often catch a few waves while Sarg walks or jogs with Rosie. Now attending puppy classes, the exuberant Rosie is learning to sit, albeit rotating vigorously on the spot as she changes direction to keep watching us.

Today, we've arranged to meet at Julie's unit. I arrive to find the door slightly ajar before I insert my key. Pink, white and red rose petals are sprinkled on the floor in a trail leading to the bathroom. Sarg is sitting in a two-thirds-filled bubble bath in a tiny red bikini, with frosted wine glasses filled with bubbling apple juice at each end. I lock the front door and return to the bathroom, where I strip off down to my smalls to join her. Rosie, after greeting me enthusiastically as soon as I opened the door, has settled with her rubber chook on one of the apricot bathmats. An Australian mix of country music is playing on a CD player in the lounge.

'How was your day?' I ask, leaning over to give Julie a peck on the cheek.

'Sad, really sad. Vivienne and I were interviewing sexual assault victims after we got an anonymous phone call at the station.'

'That would be confronting.'

I watch Julie intensely, recalling her dinner date comment about wanting love, not lust, from a relationship. It must be difficult with the sarg's sensitive nature for her not to be affected by the level of brutality she encounters daily.

'Sometimes, like in your job, we don't see the best kinds of people. I decided I needed to wash the day off me. I am glad you could join me.'

Julie comes over for a hug, sitting cautiously astride me in the tub which now has a much higher water level after my entry. Julie lays her head on my chest, wrapping her arms around my neck for a short while, before she turns around to settle her body between my legs, with her back lounging against my chest.

'How was your day?' Julie asks.

'Very pleasant, really. No administrators barging in, telling me how to do my job. No emergencies. We discharged two patients to the wards, so I had time to do two hours of staff training and intern assessments.'

'That does sound like a good day. What would you like to do this evening? I just finished making a seafood pizza, so I was hoping you might be up for dinner and a movie.'

'Mm, definitely.'

I gather Julie's long silky hair and place it over her collarbone, then grab the washer to soap up Julie's back. I feel the tension releasing from her muscles as I massage her shoulders in a circular motion. I clasp Julie's hands, wrapping my arms around her. Silently, I comfort her, recognising this is one of those moments when the tough persona of the cop struggles with the fragile feminine side of her. It is obvious to me that Julie sometimes battles with her inability to control the evil in the world she exists in. I even worry frequently about her capability of defending herself with those tiny fists she possesses.

'What are we going to watch?' I ask, intent on diverting her mind to more pleasant distractions.

'Do you like *Last Christmas with Emilia Clarke and Henry Golding?*'

'I don't know that I have seen it.'

'It's a rom com. Will that worry you?'

'Sounds perfect.'

We snuggled on the lounge, feeling so comfortable together that we end up both falling asleep. After a two-hour nap, we heat up the pizza and sort out our clothes, ready for tomorrow's shifts. I am accumulating so many clothes at Julie's unit that she has given me some closet and drawer space. I particularly need to be mindful of my shoes, unless I want to salvage them designed with a unique Rosie dental impression. Rosie picks them up and energetically kills my shoes as though they are imaginary prey, trapped in her death grip jaws. It only takes seconds before one shoe disappears. Rosie, keen to get a game happening, usually has me searching the yard or bartering to get its mate back from her.

Julie and I are still taking our relationship at a slow, steady pace. Julie has only just started taking contraceptives. We are growing progressively closer as we become familiar with each other's likes and build trust. We learn more about each other every day. I am relieved that Julie has never baulked about us spending every night together. We both feel our attraction building and experience a deep longing for each other when we are apart. We have been functioning as a team, sharing the domestic chores, shopping and cooking. Spending time together has taught us that we share many mutual goals. One of Julie's best traits seems to be her flexibility and her realistic outlook.

Julie often holds my hands, as we walk along, with her thumbs on top on mine, three fingers tucked between my thumb and pointer finger, and the little finger separately tucked into the other side of my pointer finger. We coordinate our busy lives using a paper diary of our rosters, left open for the current day, on the dining table. Our transition into being a couple has so far been free of conflicts. Maybe it is a sign of maturity, or the result of previous unsuccessful trysts, that we are both slowing evolving our deepening connection.

After the movie and pizza, I return from the bathroom to find Julie already in bed, with the covers over her and the light out. I climb into my side of the bed, rolling over to hug her when my hand lands on her naked back. Delightfully surprised, my hand migrates up and down in disbelief. My beautiful sarg is totally nude and ready to advance our relationship.

Looking up at me coyly, Julie says, 'Seems you're overdressed, doc!'

151

Chapter 31

Lauren Poulsen

We catch up with Lauren Poulsen at her home, after the Human Resource Department inform us that she has been forcibly medically retired, as she had predicted. We reluctantly advise Lauren that unless she wishes to file criminal charges against her employer for fraud, negligence and grievous bodily harm, we are not able to assist her in her plight for justice. The problems the Bounty Hospital staff are reporting result from the tendency of government authorities to pervert justice by generating laws that permit these entities to always investigate and protect themselves.

A small, short-haired beige chihuahua called Munchkin circles us, barking frantically in excitement. As Lauren pats her exuberant pet, she describes how her appeal for reinstatement through the Industrial Relations Tribunal has had to be rescinded when Bounty Hospital's lawyers used the gutter tactics of slandering Lauren as a 'vexatious litigant' to file an interlocutory application.

'How can I be a vexatious litigant, when all four permanent injuries were validated on four MRIs?' insists Lauren.

Therefore, after depleting all her superannuation for legal fees in her attempt to be reinstated, Lauren finds herself unable to even get an Industrial Relations hearing. Rather than Bounty Hospital having to defend their negligence of leaving Lauren on twelve-hour shifts with an MRI-diagnosed disc tear and on the staff spinal surgeon's three-month waiting list until she could no longer walk due to the disc herniating, Bounty Hospital have successfully exploited yet another legal loophole. Both the AIRC Commissioner and her barrister have informed Lauren that interlocutory applications are impossible to fight in a legal system that misuses the medical term 'degenerative'.

Lauren explains that while insurers exploit the term 'degenerative' to imply work injuries are the result of age-related wear and tear, medically this term covers the post-traumatic facet joint arthritis that she sustained in a previous work-related hyperextension injury twenty years prior. Legally, with the disc tear occurring in the same location (since post-traumatic arthritis alters the mechanical loading of joints), the injury should have been compensated as an exacerbation of a pre-existing injury.

Yet, since the interlocutory application skewed in an unfair and unwinnable manner how Lauren's case could be presented, rather than Bounty Hospital having to defend their negligence of leaving Lauren on the twelve-hour shifts with the disc tear, Lauren will end up bankrupt if she tries to defend her injuries as being not degenerative. Proceeding against this unsurmountable power gradient would leave Lauren homeless when liable for her own legal fees in addition to her opponents. Legally, Bounty Hospital would be able to acquire her home, as well as Lauren and Glyn's minimal superannuation funds, as compensation for their legal expenses, despite there being nothing degenerative about her employer's negligence.Lauren, who has worked most of her life on $20 to $50 per hour, cannot challenge these draconian laws, in a legal system where lawyers cost $690 an hour, without access to legal aid. Lauren, who has now applied for a disability pension, fears that the untouchables at Bounty Hospital will continue to maim her former colleagues. Lauren feels powerless to challenge this exploitation of predominantly female nurses, many of whom had left university with $30,000 of higher education debts and needed intact spines to carry pregnancies. Lauren can no longer afford the botox injections that reduce her face, neck and shoulder spasms or the rhizotomies to cut her pain nerves. It is ironic that the health service she has dedicated more than half her life to has discarded her as disposable.

'Bounty Hospital might have won the battle, but they will lose the war,' declares a defiant Lauren. 'If Bounty Hospital wishes to slander me as a "vexatious litigant", I am willing to oblige them by earning their label. God knows, I have earned the right. The one Australian law that works in my favour is that entities cannot sue – only individuals can.'

'What do you plan to do now?' Julie asks.

'Well,' continues Lauren, 'would you believe that even when the Crime and Corruption Commission investigated and validated at least two incidences of corrupt conduct, Bounty Hospital were still permitted to investigate themselves – *again*! The CEO's economic reply was "matters are now closed". When my family and I submitted protests to the CCC about these criminals being permitted to investigate themselves, a second CCC Commissioner identified even more corruption issues. That Commissioner instructed both the Bounty Hospital and their insurer to again investigate their actions. Recognising that the state government has incorporated laws that make public hospitals and their insurers virtually immune from scrutiny, neither party even bothered to respond to the second directive.

'Every injured worker ends up financially strained attempting to stop these protected entities avoiding accountability. Bounty Hospital and their insurers have all the resources that the financially strained workers funding their work injuries don't possess. The managers can use their legal services to obstruct any unfavourable right to information requests, like scathing Work Safety reports. The new National Australian Corruption Commission being formed won't remove draconian laws or provide whistleblower protection for any nurses testifying against their employer either, because they insist these criminal activities are state, not federal, issues. Therefore, state governments can successfully legislate to protect themselves without ever be held accountable.'

Lauren declares, 'Some exploited nurses are exposing Bounty Hospital's propaganda on social media, because they have to be stopped. All those impacted by the Bounty Hospital fraud and negligence are using the "365 rule", telling new people (one a day for a year) about all the unethical and criminal behaviours occurring. Truthfully reporting Bounty's activities to every tradesman, postman and neighbour and responding to posts on social media is placing the leadership and hospital board under immense pressure. Hopefully, we will soon get the overpaid, unresponsive politicians failing to act removed from office. Even if it takes another twenty years, we outnumber them and will eventually get an even playing field.'

Lauren smiles. 'Bounty Hospital left me with spinal rods, screws and a chronic pain in the butt. I am happy to reciprocate by giving them a chronic pain in the butt and screwing them over.'

'We are sorry to hear that this health provider and its insurer can manipulate the system this way, Lauren. I hope you all eventually get fair compensation and justice. With the kind of irrefutable evidence that you have, this should not be happening.'Both Julie and Vivienne empathise with Lauren's predicament.

'I will miss my crazy colleagues, though – and their bleeding teeth stories,' says Lauren, smiling.

'Teeth stories?' Vivienne queries.

'Yes, Carol and Cindy have some hilarious ones. One lady, admitted with chest pain into the ICU, had a large horseshoe-shaped injury cut deep into her back. When they asked how the injury was sustained, she admitted her husband had fallen asleep spooning her. After he'd fallen asleep, his front teeth had migrated out of his mouth, and the poor wife rolled onto them.'

'That would have looked funny!'

'Another lady Cindy looked after was admitted with an

anaphylactic reaction from an anaesthetic she required for a dislocated shoulder. When Cindy went to clean her teeth for her, they were excessively loose. The patient told Cindy that was how her shoulder had dislocated. The poor lady had gone shopping with her teenager. When she sneezed, her teeth torpedoed down the aisle like a missile. The lady was trying to get them out from under a bottom shelf in the supermarket, but her arms were too short. The lady said her "beyond embarrassed" teenager was nowhere to be found!

'Another male patient demanded food immediately after surgery, even after being warned about the anaesthetic side effects of nausea. The man was getting so upset about already having had to fast before the surgery that he was given the sandwiches he demanded. Naturally, he vomited the sandwiches back not long after he finished them. About twenty minutes later, as he woke up more from the anaesthetic, he realised he had vomited up his expensive partial dental plate, which had long been discarded irretrievably into the sluice with his vomit.'

'It sounds like the ICU team really enjoys their teeth humour,' laughs Julie.

'Oh, you have no idea how funny those silly buggers are. One gent had a cardiac arrest. Steve started the cardiac compressions just as Carol went to put the shock pads on. As Steve compressed down, the patient's teeth were airborne and nearly bit the nose off Carol's face.'

'But he survived?' Vivienne gasped.

'Yeah, but they had to find his teeth after the kerfuffle,' laughs Lauren. 'I don't miss the shiftwork, but I will sure miss the humour of those comedians. On another occasion, a lady was cleaning her teeth when one of the Aboriginal nurses made her laugh. The female patient said, "Stop making me laugh or you will end up with toothpaste all over you". "Then I will look like a lamington," the nurse replied.'

'It sounds like you have lots of funny memories.'

'Yes, the ICU team used humour as a coping mechanism, so there was plenty of intellectual witty plays on words and hilarious pranks. Carol and Cindy were always competing to outdo one another. One time, Carol arrived back from an aeromedical retrieval at 2 am. Cindy had filled her pop-up umbrella with rice bubbles and retied the external strap. Cindy opened up the pop-up umbrella right next to one of the executive's offices. The rice bubbles sprayed everywhere. There is no form of mischief that would not be entertained with that lot. At the Christmas barbecue, Cindy stretched a rubber urinary catheter over a wine cask tap and went around filling up everyone's glasses through the hole at the end of the catheter. The wine was the right colour, too,' laughs Lauren. 'Carol, not to be out done, injected a watermelon with vodka, so we had to be careful no one drove home. One of the guests, a police officer, had his legal notebook grabbed and thrown up on the nurses' quarter's roof by one of the young nurses. When the young recruit told the nurses that the police legal pads are used for their testimonies in court, it was sidesplitting watching them steal a ladder from the maintenance department to get the notebook down again.'

On our way to the car, Vivienne comments, 'It was good to leave Lauren grinning rather than teary.'

Chapter 32

Mandie Lane

We return to the hospital's Human Resources Department to find out when Mandie Lane is on shift, only to discover she has resigned.

There have been a few subtle signs implicating Mandie in the deaths of both brothers. Mandie was present during the two ICU incidences. Since Mandie would most likely have been involved in transferring Peter to the medical ward, she would have known where he was located. Peter, who had no external injuries on admission, had weakly shaken his head, unable to explain the narcotics in his system but denying any recall of foul play. When Peter awoke, Mandie would also have been aware that the police officer stationed at his bedside had been removed.

When Peter's dialysis catheter was removed, causing exsanguination, according to the satellite location of her mobile phone, Mandie had left that device at home before coming to work to make her movements untraceable. The night Peter Robinson was killed, Mandie's car was seen exiting the Bounty Hospital riverside car park at 11.10 pm when she finished her evening shift. Divers searching the waters beneath the fishing ramp, at the Stanley Bridge walkway at the rear of Bounty Hospital, discovered a bottle of narcotic pholcodine syrup, to be the likely source of Peter's narcotic overdose. Mandy's husband's name was on the label. An empty bottle of Paraquat solution with the lid firmly secured was also found nearby. Several metres further along the riverbed, police divers found a plastic bag containing the dialysis catheter filled with water to ensure the device sank out of sight. Another 200 metres along, swept by the current, were black, mud-silted men's trousers, a black shirt and black hoodie. In addition, both the staff member in the theatre gown and cap and the image in the stairway appeared to be wearing spectacle frames in a similar design worn by Mandie.

We ring the doorbell at Mandie's house and get a surprise – the door is opened by Tahlia Bennett. After greeting us with a warm smile, Tahlia's eyes widen when we ask to speak to Mandie. Tahlia hesitates in the doorway before stepping aside.

'It's probably not a good time,' Tahlia suggests. 'This is Mandie's last day at home in her own bed before she's admitted to Bounty Private tomorrow for terminal care. Dr Dalton wants to put her on a pain infusion to reduce her discomfort and anxiety. She is experiencing an abdominal, bloating kind of pressure pain that radiates through to her back. She was diagnosed in February with ovarian cancer.'

'Oh, that's terrible. I'm shocked' Julie replies, stunned. 'I am very sad to hear that. We had hoped Mandie could talk to us for a few minutes about our investigation.'

Julie pauses, uncertain. 'Would you mind just checking if Mandie's up to talking for just a few minutes? We won't stay long and tire her out.'

When we enter her bedroom, Mandie appears to be orientated and calm. Mandie rests a hand on her distended abdomen, absentmindedly rubbing in circles. Tahlia leaves us alone.

'How are you feeling, Mandie?' Julie says, as she approaches the bedside.

'Sad, truly sad,' sighs Mandie. 'My journey will be over soon enough, but I will hate to leave my three lovely girls.'

'We were surprised to see Tahlia here. How do you know her?' Vivienne asks.

'Melanie, Penelope and Tahlia have hung out together since pre-school,' says Mandie with a slight grunt, shuffling in her bed to relieve her discomfort. 'Tahlia is just like one of our family.'

Cutting to the chase, Julie impulsively asks, 'Is that why you did it, Mandie ... to keep them safe?'

'I'm not admitting to anything,' grunts Mandie warily. 'We'll just say there's an even playing field now.'

Mandie winks before becoming too exhausted to provide any further information.

Chapter 33

Julie Wright

Without mentioning any names, Sandy and Brad Robinson were notified that the most likely suspect implicated in both their sons' murders was deceased. The file was closed with no action taken due to Mandie's terminal condition. Mandie was considered to have had access to both the narcotics and Paraquat, as her deceased husband had been prescribed pholcodine, a liquid narcotic to reduce his persistent coughing immediately prior to his death from lung cancer. Mandie would also have had access to poisons like Paraquat, as her husband had been employed for most of his career as an agricultural chemist. The absence of Mandie's missing laptop remained a mystery to Penelope, Melanie and Tahlia, who had not noticed it was missing until it was requested by the police.

Sandy and Brad were shattered to learn the motives behind their sons' murders, which had been validated at least in Tahlia's assault by forensic science. Both parents were notified that each sexual assault appeared to have been preceded by the victims declining to date Craig.

Charlotte Robinson was finally able to visit Bounty regularly and resumed her loving relationship with her parents in safety. While Tahlia, Josephine and the other victims of the sexual assaults would always remain hyper-alert, all were informed by the police that both offenders were believed to be deceased. Tragically following their assaults, none of the rape victims had dated again, and all were living reclusive lives, socialising only in the security of family members.

Other than fulfilling work commitments, Ray and I have spent most of our time together since we met. Rosie and I are moving to the beach house to live with Ray full-time, after our instant physical attraction and chemistry was heightened by Ray's consistently kind and caring manner.

We both have such full work lives and study commitments that it was easier to move in together to make the most of our days off than to be cleaning and maintaining two properties. Ray has met my parents, my two brothers and sister and their families at my parent's cane farm, where we all gathered for a barbecue for my birthday. Rosie, who is now a hefty forty kilograms, has learned to roll over, play dead and walk more safely on leads.

For my birthday, Ray presented me with another gorgeous teddy bear floral bouquet. One teddy bear was wearing a red bikini and the other was dressed in board shorts. Behind the teddy bears was a surfboard, and at their feet was a toy labrador. The female teddy bear carried a tiny red heart-shaped pillow, while the teddy bear with the board shorts carried a box containing a Ceylon sapphire engagement ring.

So, we are now officially engaged. Ray tells our friends he is my Mr Wright.

EARS PAINTED ON

Imogen Pershouse

Chapter 1

31 July 2017

Suzi Saunderson

At eight months pregnant, I saunter in to have a shower. I am grumpy and fed up with Jamie Johnson, my partner of three years, who has been arguing with me all morning. I'm feeling grossly fat and uncomfortable. Thank God this is a winter pregnancy. I feel like I'm about to burst open. Sleep is difficult when you can only toss from side to side, with a massive girth occupied by a kicking tenant. My clothes don't fit after my pregnancy weight gain of twelve kilograms. I cannot go for a drive to get away from the tosser because I no longer fit behind the steering wheel. At 155 cm tall, and now a frightening 69 kg, if I pull the driver's seat out further, my short legs won't reach to operate the pedals.

All morning, I've tried to convince Jamie that we need to start getting nappies, singlets, cots and prams ready for the baby. Jamie is so immature that he insists I use the 'baby bonus' for those purchases after our neonate is born. Although Jamie maintains that his money will only stretch as far as rent, food and petrol, his recent purchase of a subwoofer car stereo and flashy car seats suggests our baby is not a priority. I suspect I may have hooked up with Jamie as a grief reaction to Mum and Dad's sudden death in a car-versus-train collision. Why do I seem to have this overwhelming need to belong to somebody, when no one else can possibly replace the profound void my parent's deaths have left in my life?

However, that need for belonging changed instantly when I found out I was pregnant. Finally, I felt needed. I am welcoming this new responsibility gratefully. This will be my most important demanding role ever – being a mum. Before my pregnancy, after a morning of arguments like this, I would normally be going to the shops, hanging out with mates or driving to reduce my agitation. Instead, I am constantly reflecting upon how many friendships I have sacrificed for this dysfunctional relationship. Many of my university and old school friends have stopped calling after establishing that they had little in common with Jamie. I should have recognised their 'you have to tolerate him; we don't' vibes.

I must now take the therapeutic option of removing myself from his provocation. I just have to walk away. I decide to take a shower and then write myself a list of what I am going to need before and when our baby arrives. Then I am going to ponder over baby names to interrupt my destructive thoughts with more pleasant diversions. This is what my Aunty Beth has always encouraged me to do rather than allowing my brain to manufacture grim thoughts.

I have just walked into the bathroom and stripped off, ready to go under the shower, when the bathroom door locks from the outside. Shit! What is that mad bastard up to now, I wonder, alarmed that I am trapped? Outside, in the lounge, it sounds as though he is moving his stereo. With a towel wrapped around me, I glance out the window down at the driveway to discover Jamie frantically packing his belongings into his blue ute.

Shit! Who thinks to take their phone into the bathroom with them? I shout out the bathroom window, 'Let me out, you wanker!'

I watch him down there, walking to and fro, loading up his car, before hearing him back inside again, rattling around in the bedroom. He's frantically opening and shutting draws and cupboard doors. Instead of being perturbed after the morning we have had, Jamie's actions are a case of 'thank God'. Well, life will be simpler with only one 'baby' in the house.

I have a quick shower, shampoo my sandy, shoulder-length hair and get dressed, concerned that I am going to have to call out to the neighbours to get the police. A sudden slide and clicking noise tells me that Jamie has finally unlocked the bathroom latch before bolting down the stairs to escape out the front door. Jamie's loaded vehicle squeals and skids, losing traction as it exits the gravel driveway. All I needed was this bloody waste of space pissing off, leaving me with debts. What a prick! What a pregnancy, for that matter.

I go down to bolt the front door, then grab my phone to call my older sister, Jenny. Jenny will know what to do. Jenny has always had the natural ability to think logically and calmly in a crisis. My sister comes straight over, while I put on some makeup over the sprinkle of freckles that cover my nose and fair skin. I look in the mirror, astonished to realise that this turn of events is actually so welcome that I am not even shedding a tear.

Together, Jenny and I make a plan. First, we call a locksmith to change all the external locks of my rental with a copy of the spare keys for Jenny. After she helps me clean out the cupboards, we go around to a few shops to select and put deposits down on a stroller and a bassinet. Finally, I can confidently reassure my unborn child that I am making progress towards my goals. My Aunty Beth will be so pleased that the 'dead wood' Jamie is out of my life. Aunty Beth always says you have to remove the things that are not working from your life before peace and harmony can prevail.

I am not really grieving the loss of Jamie the loser. I am focused on steering my life in the direction of a happy future. 'One door closes, a better one opens,' Aunty Beth optimistically says. I take courage from repeating her mantras to prevent my brain from generating negative thoughts. If I'm being honest with myself, I have to say that I am a bit freaked right now at my abrupt single status and the daunting prospect of raising a baby on my own. However, I must focus on using the positive self-dialogue I have been taught to rally all the courage I can muster.

Chapter 2

20 August 2017

Suzi Saunderson

With a sudden gush, the fluid running down my legs alerts me that my waters have broken. Jenny comes around to pick me up and take me to the hospital. She rings in for family leave, supporting me throughout the whole chaotic delivery. I heard that you leave your inhibitions at the door when in labour, and it is absolutely true. Never before have I experienced so many strangers staring at the same intimate part of my anatomy. If I wasn't drowning in so much fear and pain right now, I would be mouthing off, objecting to this total loss of dignity. As the contractions begin coming fast and strong, my panic rises, as suddenly everything seems beyond my control.

After the anaesthetist arrives to give me an epidural, a urinary catheter is inserted to prevent my bladder from over-distending and rupturing. When the epidural interferes with my ability to feel the contractions to push, I end up needing a Wrigley's forceps lift-out of my baby's head. I'm left with heavy legs and a lot of stitches down yonder between both exits. However, nothing elevates my spirits more than hearing the magical little human I made crying for the first time. She has pink, flushed skin, a beautiful splash of sticky dark hair, slate grey eyes and every toe and finger is present – I know, I've counted! Her skin is soft and covered in a cheesy layer of protective vernix caseosa. Her elegant, plump fingers instinctively clasp around my pointer finger, initiating our first bonding connection.

I am delighted with my greatest achievement ever! I want to proudly show the whole world my beautiful baby girl – Poppy. I am determined to give my precious daughter the best life, even though I know the single mother lifestyle won't be easy. I will need to be strong and independent to fill both parental roles now. Although I am fatigued from this lengthy childbirth, I am immensely proud to finally meet the adorable, tiny girl I grew. I will keep her safe. There will be no shirking of my responsibilities. I am capable! I am going to do this right, with one hundred per cent commitment and no excuses!

The first hiccup arrives eleven days after I get home with Poppy. While I am still trying to establish a feeding and sleeping routine, Poppy is readmitted to the maternity hospital with projectile vomiting. I may be young, but this is my baby! I don't know if I am hormonal, post-natal or just overreacting, but I am feeling ill-tempered and fed up. My patience is maxed from being ignored by the hospital doctors and nurses using their medical jargon to talk over me and exclude me from their conversations about my baby.

Chapter 3

5 December 2017

Suzi Saunderson

As the months go by, irritable Poppy does not settle into any established routine. She sleeps less, rejects breastfeeding often, then bottles, and cries in a high-pitched tone more and more. I try to persuade the doctors that something is wrong with Poppy, only to be persistently ignored for requesting urgent tests to identify the problem. I can feel my anger ramping when I hear the nurses and doctors discussing me with social workers and organising community midwifery support without even consulting me.

'This is not a child at risk,' I loudly assert from the consulting room doorway.

I sit in the post-natal clinic, fatigued and fuming. I'm absolutely arced up. I hear them all judging me as incompetent and referring to me as 'acopic'. The social worker, Wilma, comes to the room, timidly knocking and apologising for interrupting me. She reassures me that midwives take standard precautions to act in the best interest of mothers and infants, in case I have post-natal depression.

'I'm not depressed! And I'm not whacked with the dumb stick either.' I angrily plead before bursting into tears, 'I am trying to get help for my sick baby.'

Now I am even more frustrated that Wilma is silently observing me as though ticking off invisible boxes for post-natal depression. Wilma is 's p e a k i n g v e r y s l o w l y' in reassuring tones. I try again, mimicking her slow speech.

'Wilma', I say through gritted teeth. 'I have a business degree. I am not an idiot nor a neglectful mother. Something is wrong with my daughter!'

'You don't want your baby to have unnecessary blood tests, do you, Suzi?' Wilma says with a steely smile. 'Babies sometimes get a bit of colic. It sometimes takes their little bodies a while after birth to adjust to digesting breast milk.'

'I am not after counselling, Wilma,' I patiently persist, doggedly determined to get Poppy the assistance she needs. 'I need someone to find out what is hurting Poppy. This is supposed to be a hospital. What does it take to get *medical* help around here?'

'Perhaps we could admit you overnight. We could leave Poppy in the nursery so that you can get a decent uninterrupted sleep,' Wilma offers.

I lean down, eyeballing Wilma to get her full attention. I want no distractions to make it perfectly clear what my needs are.

'What I need is a doctor whose ears aren't painted on. What I need are actual professionals who are not getting their exercise by running me down or jumping to conclusions.'

Wilma nods to convey she is being attentive. We both know that she is not a doctor and that she is treating me as though I am the patient. But I am not after platitudes! I am after physical assistance, in the form of an investigation to find out what is distressing my infant daughter. In utter frustration, I silently pick up my mother's bag and wheel the pram out the door. If I don't leave, there will be two of us screaming. Better to cry than violently express the rage building inside me, I suppose.

No one is listening to me telling them that it is Poppy who needs the assistance. I overhear them discussing me with each other, labelling me 'acopic' again, as I wheel the pram past the nurses' station.

Chapter 4

June–August 2018

Suzi Saunderson

As six months go by, nothing changes, except that I am spending more and more time convincing myself that I am *not* acopic. I am exhausted from being awake with Poppy all night, every night until, utterly exhausted, she eventually cries herself to sleep. Poppy begins screaming every time I stop rocking her. Her blue eyes are red-rimmed and her cheeks are flushed and sodden. I tell the doctors and nurses over and over, but their ears are painted on. I have no tolerance for anyone wanting to do what is convenient for them and not useful for me. If I hear one more time the rationalisation that crying exercises a baby's lungs, I will be rocking in the corner. I am convinced my daughter is in pain. I know something is wrong.

Yet, when the midwife and child health nurses see Poppy, she is usually sleeping from exhaustion after being unsettled all night.

Poppy won't even sleep in the bed beside me. I tried packing pillows all around her, but we ended up sleeping on two doonas with Poppy lying on the cot mattress on the dark blue, carpeted lounge room floor. We are sleeping on the floor because I am terrified that when we finally fall asleep, Poppy could fall off the bed.

*

Poppy's first birthday is no cause for celebration. At one year, Poppy sleeps for about two hours at a time before the high-pitched screaming begins again. Paracetamol and ibuprofen are not working. Poppy screams every time I try to secure her nappy as though I'm triggering pain from touching her belly. The health professionals are still telling me the large lump under Poppy's left ribs is just constipation. However, with all their laxatives and stool softening treatments, the lump never goes away – it is growing bigger. I try to explain that Poppy does not seem to be able to push down to poo or pee without spasms of pain. Rather than testing to legitimise my astute observations, I am diplomatically disregarded as an inexperienced mother lacking a medical degree.

Health professionals should know that screaming is how babies communicate pain. I emphatically declare to anyone who approaches me that to relieve Poppy's pain, I need tests ordered. Instead, all the prescribed medications for constipation and antibiotics for urinary infections are not changing anything. I persist, to no avail.

I am so sleep deprived that I am starting to find my 'blame the parent if you dare' mode. I find myself confronting my accusers with the same disrespect they deflect to me. Our general practitioner, Dr Richard Stone, has prescribed three courses of antibiotics for Poppy now, insisting on treating her for urinary infections with antibiotics that have made no difference. Although the doctors and nurses insist that germs from Poppy's nappy are ascending into her bladder, I am not that dim.

'Wouldn't there be a temperature and germs showing up on the urine cultures if Poppy had an infection in the bladder?' I question.

I remain awake most nights rocking Poppy to sleep. At fourteen months, Poppy is getting even harder to settle and more frequently refuses her bottle or attempts to introduce solid food. The lump beneath her left ribs is larger, but no one will listen. I just need someone to acknowledge simple facts rather than generate conclusions that have no place in reality.

Despite my best efforts, I am failing my child. The house is a disgraceful mess. Jenny comes around to help me on her days off. Jenny has offered Poppy and me to stay at her place, but I decline, knowing that with Jenny frequently rostered on night shift, she needs her daytime sleep. Another deterrent is that such a move would only fuel the 'acopic' allegations. If I cannot sleep with Poppy screaming day and night, how could Jenny accomplish such a feat on her night rotations? Eventually Jenny convinces me to move in, insisting that two sets of hands are better than one, but the reality is that no one sleeps.

When I take Poppy to the hospital again with projectile vomiting, we are both admitted to the children's isolation ward. I am furious to be ignored again when I notify the health professionals of the huge lump in the upper left corner of Poppy's belly. After more laxatives are prescribed to stimulate Poppy's bowels, no one will acknowledge that the lump remains unchanged.

Rapid hospital discharge policies emphasise that budgets are the focus, rather than care. I return to my unit after we are discharged, beyond exasperated.

Chapter 5

21 October 2018

Jenny Saunderson

t's 9.45 am. I have been asleep for two hours, after surviving four twelve-hour night shifts in a row at the Bloomesville Gardens nursing home, when I hear someone practically bashing down my front door. I look through the curtains to see my little sister's silver Subaru XV out front. My sassy sister is taking the door down. Something is truly rattling Suzi's cage.

Paying no attention to my long, matted bed hair that must look like a birch broom in a fit, I wander down the steps. 'I'm coming,' I holler out to Suzi, but the forceful bashing continues. I suspect that Suzi is making such a racket that she does not hear me. Suzi has become more emotional and less tolerant lately from her accumulative sleep deprivation. Night duties are dismal but at least I get fifteen hours of silence between shifts and days off, unlike Suzi, who has the never-ending nightmare of attempting to pacify Poppy every night.

Suzi has shown a remarkable resilience in adapting to the demands of pregnancy and childbirth. From the moment of learning about her pregnancy, Suzi's strong maternal instincts motivated her to protect her little 'cargo'. During the pregnancy and childbirth, the delighted Suzi willingly put in her best physical and emotional effort. She was totally besotted by her dark-haired, chubby baby girl when she arrived. But now, Suzi, with her reddened sky-blue eyes and flushed face and wavy, sandy hair tied back in a ponytail, seems to be getting thinner with each visit.

Already fine boned, Suzi now looks about fifty-five kilograms.

Suzi was always a battler who seemed to sustain more hard knocks from life than most. Unfortunately, when Suzi's dependent personality encounters dramas, she tends to lean on the immature partners she attracts, only to be devastated when they behave in a predictably irresponsible manner. Even in her darkest depressive moods, Suzi had always asked for help rather than resort to alcohol or drugs. Poppy's birth has been pivotal in giving Suzi the courage she needs to become stronger and more resilient. Like today, there have been many times when Suzi has been totally challenged by her tiny twenty-two-month-old daughter, who has remained impossibly difficult to feed, settle or placate.

I climb down the stairs, in my old threadbare, faded, floral nightie, trying to clear my head. I open the door to immediately receive a screaming toddler thrust into my arms.

'I can't do it anymore, Sis, honest, I can't!' cries Suzi, weeping.

'Come in, come in,' I say, opening the door wider.

I hold the screaming Poppy in one hand and hold the door wider, trying to encourage Suzi inside with the other.

'I've been up all night, Sis. Poppy won't stop crying. She won't feed … she won't take water … she just screams! I've tried sleeping on the bed with her, but every time I stop rocking her, she resumes that high-pitched cry that's like nails on a chalkboard. I've tried putting her in the bath, taking her for drives, wheeling her in the pram. Every time I stop the movement, she shrieks.'

'You go up and lie down for a while,' I calmly suggest. 'I have days off now, so we can get you both some rest.'

'Noooooo! I'm leaving her here. I need some sleep. I can't cope!' Suzi cries in despair. 'I need a break. I am sorry that I'm such a failure. I desperately need sleep or I'll go mad!'

I have never seen my feisty sister this distraught. Alarm bells ring in my head. Suzi is desperate, as though she is tinkering on the brink of insanity.

'You go to your room and grab a nap,' I encourage, gently rocking Poppy, hoping to keep her quiet. Poppy, however, takes the opportunity to emit another loud bellow. 'We will try some paracetamol and ibuprofen.'

'Poppy's had two lots overnight. The last dose was just an hour ago. She won't shut up!' Suzi exclaims, putting both hands over her ears.

Next thing I know, Suzi is out the door and driving off before I can stop her. Although I worry about Suzi, I intuitively know that my sleep-deprived self cannot tackle both a raging Poppy and an upset sister.

Feeling quite agitated, I start with the basics, like checking to see if Poppy's nappy is dry and offering her a bottle. Nothing takes. I ring our GP but no appointments are available for two days.

'Bloomesville Emergency Department it is then, missy,' I say to Poppy as I dress, grabbing Suzi's baby bag and heading out the door with the keys.

My instincts tell me that Poppy is in pain, but as usual, after a half an hour screaming in the waiting room, she is asleep when we finally get called in to see the doctor. The young resident doctor is more distracted by his pager going off every five minutes than a sleeping Poppy with normal vital signs. We head home with me feeling like nothing has been achieved other than another episode of humiliation. Like Suzi, who is feeling ignored by her general practitioners, hospital doctors and child health nurses, I am irate at being dismissed.

Since birth, Poppy has been hospitalised twice for projectile vomiting. After Suzi and I have asked for help repeatedly for this screaming infant, seven general practitioner visits have been just as futile. With every doctor and nurse explaining away Poppy's signs and symptoms as constipation or urinary tract infections, Suzi is getting nowhere.

'If there are no germs growing on the urinary cultures, this can't be an infection,' I challenge the busy doctor. 'The multiple courses of antibiotics prescribed have never worked.'

Suzi had noted Poppy's enlarged lymph nodes under her jaw, which the child health nurse explained away as 'teething related'. One GP rudely dismissed Suzi's concerns, telling her, 'Babies get sick. Deal with it'. Not expecting that reaction and confused about the message being delivered, after being awake comforting Poppy all night and diligently notifying the doctor that she had already tried simple analgesics, Suzi asked the doctor to elaborate. The gruff, condescending response was, 'Bring the baby back in a week, if she's no better. Don't rush to the clinic every sniffle.'

Suzi was so livid and animated about the doctor being 'neither use nor ornament' that my attempts to diplomatically hush her had her loudly proclaiming in the full waiting room that she did not give a rat's crack who heard her opinion. Since she was no longer opening the door to the community midwives, Suzi was suspicious that they may have contacted her GP's surgery. I could not blame Suzi for being so angry that she did not even want to pay for that ridiculous opinion. Suzi was so livid about the doctor's 'wait a week' advice that she strenuously objected to paying for what was neither a 'professional consult' nor satisfactory service. At one stage, I wondered who was throwing the biggest tantrum – Suzi or Poppy – since both were extremely sleep deprived.

I actually paid for that appointment to reduce Suzi's vulnerability. I was worried that refusing to pay a debt could destroy Suzi's future chances of getting appointments, with so many doctors' surgeries having long waiting lists for new patients. I was also alarmed at his lack of concern about the abdominal mass which appeared to be getting bigger, as I also believed it to be the most likely source of Poppy's pain.

'A baby not eating and drinking cannot be left a week without medical attention.' reported the infuriated Suzi. 'It's been over a bloody *year*, and I still cannot get Poppy's pain relieved!'

The huge lump in Poppy's abdomen under her left ribs, almost the size of her head, has been dismissed by every doctor and nurse as constipation. I again unsuccessfully request an ultrasound only to receive a pitiful look.

'Simple things occur commonly,' replies the doctor, giving me the bum's rush.

Do your job, dickhead, I want to shout! Do your bloody job!

When anything touches Poppy's abdomen, like us securing her nappy, she screams a high-pitched squeal as though in pain, I report. Yet, all the medical professionals we appeal to for help only conveniently want to prescribe antibiotics for non-existent urinary infections. Each doctor justifies their unsubstantiated diagnosis, as 'female babies anatomically have short urethras'.

After listening to this dialogue again, with these professionals reiterating the ability of the athletic bowel germs in the nappy to get into a female infant bladder, I know the only way to get effective help will be to embark on a four-hour drive to Sydney. Poppy's relentless screaming warns me that it is better to drink something caffeinated and drive four hours to a tertiary hospital now rather than attempt to sleep first and encounter the scarcer hospital resources available after hours.

Chapter 6

21 October 2018

Jenny Saunderson

ring Aunty Beth to ask if we can stay for a while before packing some clothes for us both. I let the phone ring for a while to give my seventy-one-year-old aunty time to answer. Aunty Beth, my mother's sister, sounds delighted to be getting company. In an upbeat tone, Aunty Beth mentions she is looking forward to finally meeting Poppy. I sincerely hope Aunty Beth holds that thought after she discovers how difficult Poppy is to feed and settle.

Even after experiencing the immeasurable grief after the loss of her life-time partner, my uncle Bob, following his sudden heart attack, my widowed aunty has always been inspiring. Aunty Beth keeps herself motivated by perpetually listing her daily tasks, like the meticulous cleaning of her house. Aunty Beth is always dressed immaculately, with her pristine appearance always complementing her flexible, cheerful nature. Aunty Beth's positive and inspiring demeanour is exactly what I need in this overwhelming dilemma. Despite her advanced years, Aunty Beth lives independently and is still able to drive during daylight. Aunty Beth's greatest asset, though, has always been her calm, practical logic, which prevents me wasting excessive energy on emotional turmoil.

Even before our parents died, our cheeky Aunty Beth always seemed more of a friend than a relative. When we were attempting to shut out the world following our parents' deaths, Aunty Beth spontaneously arrived on our doorstep unannounced. Aunty

Beth was there for Suzi and me, helping to organise the funeral arrangements and legal matters. After we selected clothes and caskets and made decisions about their wedding rings, the next day we arranged a funeral date suitable for all extended family members who were intending to travel to attend. Then we were choosing the headstone ... The list grew. If it were not for Aunty Beth having us choose one item on her never-ending lists to tackle each day, we would not have kept soldiering on. While Suzi and I would have preferred ignoring every phone call and doorbell, Aunty Beth taught us resilience. When the shit hits the fan, you organise a list, then take baby steps, each day, she instructed. And it worked.Aunty Beth kept us moving forward during our grief until life's challenges became manageable again. Eventually, the delicate decision making was behind us. Aunty Beth had known that she would be always unconditionally welcomed into our home despite our heartache. Aunty Beth cooked, cleaned, answered the doorbell and our mobiles, all while providing the unlimited comfort she had exuded for our entire lives.

*

As Poppy started to walk, even her gait was an unusual stagger. Like Suzi, I was becoming more and more convinced that nothing was normal about Poppy. She did not even possess a normal hunger cry. The high-pitched, relentless scream appeared to be Poppy maximising her limited mechanisms to express pain that simple analgesics were not touching.

Thinking about how long this circus had gone on, I am determined that if I cannot get an ultrasound at the Sydney Hospital's Emergency Department, I will boldly activate the new Ryan's Rule that I have just become aware of rather than leave. I grab a coffee in a thermal mug for the trip. I am determined to get Poppy a pediatric assessment at a tertiary hospital. The more I think about it, the more my instinct tells me that something more than 'common things occur commonly' is happening here.

With Poppy currently emitting her ear-piercing howls again, I detour into a service station. I change Poppy's nappy, with her wailing loudly again in protest at my mild compression of her belly, as I secure her nappy. With Poppy still refusing her bottle, her urine is now a dark amber colour.

Concerned that Poppy is becoming dehydrated, I head straight for the Sydney Hospital Emergency Department rather than Aunty Beth's. After fighting the paranoia that I am going to be belittled again, I am relieved when the diligent resident, Toby Greene, gets a paediatric opinion. With Poppy awake and screaming loudly from the moment he touches her abdomen, the efficient doctor is responsive to my concerns. Dr Toby diligently checks both the statewide laboratory program and private laboratory network before validating that none of Poppy's urine samples have ever grown any microorganisms. Yet, tragically fictitious, unsubstantiated misdiagnoses like urinary infections, constipation and an 'acopic' parent is all Poppy has ever been diagnosed with.

Chapter 7

21 October 2018

Jenny Saunderson

After Poppy screams her way through a painful ultrasound, the test has revealed the large mass present under her ribs on the left is indeed suspicious. A paediatric anaesthetist is requested to sedate Poppy for CAT scanning. I remain with Poppy until she is asleep under the anaesthetic. Looking at Poppy so chemically relaxed, I am suddenly stunned to realise that I can never recall her sleeping that peacefully in her entire life! A wave of remorse and guilt washes over me. I instantly regret that, despite all our protests where we were advocating for Poppy with health professionals, we had not done enough.

I cannot imagine how much excruciating pain Poppy has been in, given the size of that lump and its location. No wonder the devoted Suzi was so exhausted and frustrated. Suzi was consistently attentive and diligently comforting Poppy during all that pain without ever getting the support she had persistently requested. Suzi had hung in there for as long as she could. With every professional minimising Suzi's concerns, she had begun to lose her confidence, self-esteem and eventually her tenacity.

The medical imaging tests performed confirm the presence of cancer, an aggressive stage 4 intra-abdominal neuroblastoma. For the MIBG nuclear scan staging of the cancer, radioactive isotopes are injected intravenously to confirm and locate the neuroblastoma metastases. The radiologists then provide a Curie prognostic indicator score by assessing ten areas and providing a score out of thirty, according to how many sites the cancer has spread. At each of the ten sites, images are graded from one to three, according to whether there is no involvement, involvement at one site, invasions at more than one site or diffuse involvement. Poppy's score of ten out of thirty, I am advised, gives her a fifty to seventy per cent chance of survival.

On the medical imaging, the entire left-hand corner of Poppy's abdomen contains a gigantic mass surrounding and compressing her kidney. Worse still, this aggressive cancer has already infiltrated Poppy's pelvic bones, confirming Dr Toby's suspicion of the bony spread of the cancer being responsible for her awkward gait. Poppy's diagnosis has swung from her being the victim of an acopic single parent for twenty-two months to needing a medical marathon of interventions after which she may or may not survive.

The diagnosis is a breathtaking slam in the gut. My fear for Poppy and Suzi is toxic.

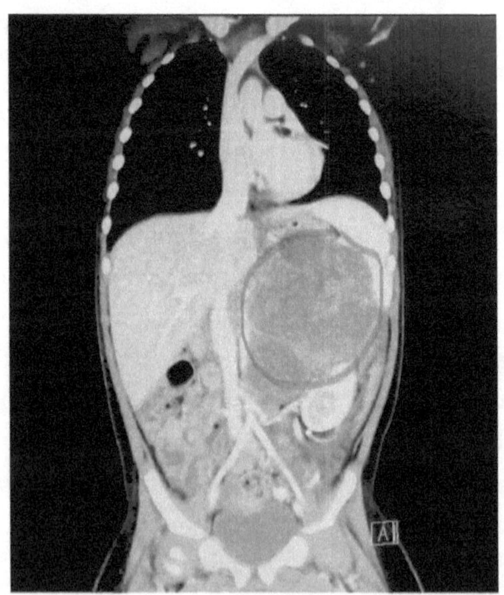

Poppy's neuroblastoma

Chapter 8

21 October 2018

Jenny Saunderson

After Suzi's maternal instincts have left her battle-fatigued from conflicts, I worry now about her future ability to engage with the professionals she has less confidence in. Fortunately, I can certainly assure Suzi that this Sydney team has comprehensively examined Poppy thoroughly. According to Dr Toby, Poppy will need to be subjected to a marathon of months of induction chemotherapy cycles, higher dose chemotherapy, major surgery, a stem cell harvest, a bone marrow transplant requiring six to eight weeks of isolation, therapeutic radiation, immune modulation therapies and hopefully, if accessible in Australia, cancer relapse prevention therapies.

I persistently shake my head in disbelief. Kind Dr Toby tries to rationally explain the fact that a toddler with a visible, palpable intra-abdominal mass the size of her head was not able to access a simple non-invasive ultrasound for twenty-two months – an ultrasound test that he performed within one hour of our arrival. While I understand Dr Toby's defence of his less cognisant colleagues, there is no excuse. Other infants in such dire circumstances need to be able to get appropriate access to paediatricians and tests sooner.

'Doctor, that mass did not grow the size of Poppy's head overnight,' I maintain.

After the shock of Poppy's diagnosis, my tolerance diminishes to a stage where I must consciously endeavour to remain respectful. My response is not just a reaction of profound grief to this life-altering diagnosis. The delayed diagnosis that has put Poppy's life in jeopardy is irrefutable evidence of a failing, budget-orientated health system. With as much respect as I can muster, I reiterate that a visible, palpable, persistently enlarging mass should have warranted an earlier ultrasound, albeit the odds of a neuroblastoma being a one in a hundred thousand chance.

While Poppy was under the anaesthetic, I had searched the internet, I informed Dr Toby. I found that, statistically, fifty per cent of children's cancers are diagnosed before four years of age. That statistic does not even include the congenital abnormalities commonly detected in children, such as being born with abnormalities like one kidney. As a non-invasive procedure, ordering a simple ultrasound is nowhere near as harmful as leaving aggressive paediatric cancers to proliferate unchecked.

'Keep in mind, Doctor Toby, that my request for an ultrasound in another Emergency Department was less than six hours ago,' I inform him, struggling to keep my irritability in check. 'While I have no energy to waste on anger, I cannot entertain idle stupidity. The impact of this negligence has been excessively traumatic for Poppy, who has been left in severe pain, most likely intensifying, for months as the tumour invaded more structures. Both Poppy and Suzi were left sleep deprived and driven to their mental edges. Even with Poppy expressing her grief more loudly than Suzi, I cannot imagine the devastating physical and psychological toll the last twenty-two months has had on both of them.'

I recall with extreme sadness how every visible sign and symptom Suzi had perceptively reported was minimised or discarded. Poppy's chronic screaming when her belly was touched, her refusal of feeds, the enlarged lymph nodes, the huge, constantly visible abdominal mass and her staggering gait had been consistently reported by Suzi. Yet all these pleas for assistance were futile when the only health response mounted was to slander her as an acopic mother to mobilise social workers for counselling.

Dr Toby explains that a neuroblastoma tumour forms from immature nerve cells in the sympathetic nervous system, which mature into cancer cells instead of nerve cells. The cancer cells form solid aggressive tumours by replicating and spreading quickly. According to Neuroblastoma Australia's figures, he cites forty children are diagnosed in Australia per year, with most being less than five years of age. Although this cancer can mimic other harmless childhood signs and symptoms, unfortunately, many doctors never see a neuroblastoma during their working life.

I am honestly not at all satisfied to be told by anyone that neuroblastomas are commonly misdiagnosed as urinary infections and constipation, because this was twenty-two months of unacceptable pain inflicted on an infant.

The neuroblastoma severity can vary from benign tumours that resolve spontaneously to aggressive tumours affording a survival rate of only fifty per cent. Therefore, high-risk tumours like Poppy's need strategic management based on research and drug efficacy. Early paediatric referral systems need to be in place, as more lives are lost in children under five years old with neuroblastoma than any other cancer, because these aggressive tumours have often proliferated extensively unchecked before diagnosis.

As in Poppy's case, a neuroblastoma often forms in the adrenal glands on the top of the kidneys, causing pain when it occupies space and compresses other tissues. When these abnormal cancer cells rapidly divided, grew and spread to infiltrate nearby structures, Poppy had exhibited the classic abdominal and back pain, leg weakness, weight loss, food refusal and bone pain signs of a neuroblastoma. As Suzi had suggested, this pain had no doubt prevented Poppy from tightening her abdominal muscles to pee or poo.

Poppy's survival is now pivotal on the coordinated efforts

of paediatric oncologists, haematologists, surgeons, radiation oncologists and transplant teams. Poppy's diagnosis of a stage 4 neuroblastoma indicates that the aggressive cancer had spread from the adrenal glands to the lymph nodes, bones, bone marrow, liver, skin and other organs. Therefore, the initial investigations and treatment plans initially focus on identifying, or 'staging', how far the cancer has spread.

Various sites on my internet search report that a major problem with paediatric cancers is that less than eight per cent of cancer funding is allocated to paediatric cancers, the remaining ninety-two per cent delegated to funding adult cancers. Consequentially, in the last thirty years, this lack of crucial resources has meant that only six new drugs have been approved, despite all those medications having serious side effects. Although these chemotherapy drugs are mostly effective, after surviving these lengthy treatment schedules, many survivors experience delayed developmental growth, hearing loss, abnormal spinal curvature, thyroid and neurological dysfunction, secondary cancers like leukaemia, psychological trauma and, later, fertility issues. Dr Toby therefore emphasises the need for constant and lifelong surveillance during and after these extensive therapies.

Since Suzi has left no stone unturned in her fight to save Poppy's life, my turbulent emotions fluctuate from livid to heart-broken. I want to ring my sister to reassure her that she has done such a brilliant job, despite the resistance she encountered. However, my reality is that, despite feeling emotionally overwrought, I cannot even update Suzi on Poppy's diagnosis as she is not responding to my texts. I delay further attempts at ringing Suzi, sincerely hoping she is getting well-earned rest. I can honestly tell Suzi that I have faith in this Sydney medical and nursing team, who have conscientiously validated our concerns in a supportive, open, professional manner.

I think if I had the power to write the procedure for the medical notes to be recorded by every doctor on the planet, the records would begin with a heading of 'Parental Concerns'. Those with a lower socioeconomic status simply do not have the funds to afford petrol and the cost of multiple medical visits, while health professionals ignore these children's vital advocates. From Suzi's perspective, little was accomplished at most of those appointments other than the 'normalising' of aberrant signs and symptoms. Health professionals should not be minimising and disregarding the concerns reported by parents supporting a child they care for for twenty-four hours a day, seven days a week. While parents may not possess the scientific knowledge of nurses who spend about seventy-five per cent of their time at a patient's bedside as full-time carers, many parents intuitively observe, recognise and report deviances from normal developmental milestones that warrant investigation.

Although none of this was Suzi's fault, I'm not sure that Suzi will be relieved that her instincts were accurate when confronted by this devastating, now established diagnosis. I check my watch and decide that it is too early to ring Suzi back. With horrendous news like this, it is best that Suzi has slept first. Once I contact Suzi, I plan to leave Poppy in Sydney with Aunty Beth to drive home to collect her, so I can deliver this heart-wrenching news in person.

*

We arrive in the children's ward, where Poppy is being admitted. I was feeling a bit guilty up until that point about taking Poppy out of town without Suzi's permission. Now I am thinking that since this neuroblastoma is at stage 4 already, any further delays in her treatment could have been catastrophically fatal. I ring my boss, requesting immediate leave for what I describe as a family emergency. Not wishing to invade my sister's privacy, I tell my line manager, Joanne Hosking, that I am not sure how much time I will need off or when I will be back. Sensing my panic, Joanne completes a sick leave application form for me so I can be paid during what is obviously going to be extended leave. It's 6 pm and I still cannot raise Suzi on her phone. I ring Aunty Beth to notify her that Poppy has been admitted to the hospital in a critical condition.

The nursing staff has recorded me as Poppy's next of kin. With the same surname, they are making assumptions that I fail to correct. With Suzi misjudged as acopic, there has been enough turmoil without adding Family Service conflicts into the unfolding drama. Ironically, it is never an even playing field. There are never apologies for responsible mothers whose reputations have been slandered by health institutions, possessing a profound ability to always investigate themselves.

Tragically, the parents and children bear the full brunt of any misdiagnosis or treatment delays, when their lives are jeopardised by a system that forces them to pay, whether they accessed a correct opinion or not. In contrast, the budget-orientated health systems, failing to provide safe supervision for the junior practitioners destroying the lifetime opportunities of vulnerable patients, are rarely scrutinised. I look at Poppy's little chubby, bubby fingers, cuddled around Hopper, her fluffy, lemon coloured rabbit, contemplating the terrifying maze ahead.

Poppy's face is so blissfully peaceful, sleeping off the anaesthetic, that I am still astounded by the contrast between her usual grimacing appearance and what a normal, relaxed toddler sleeping soundly should look like. This dreamy placid little face is not the Poppy I recognise. This is not the irritable, clingy child we have battled to pacify for twenty-two months. I take the opportunity for a brief nap before Poppy wakes up. I have requested the lovely paediatric nurse, Sarah, to wake me if the doctor does rounds to ensure that Poppy is provided adequate analgesia to avoid another night of screaming.

Chapter 9

22 October 2018

Jenny Saunderson

Poppy wakes up, once again distressed from pain and inconsolable, prior to analgesia being administered.

After so many months of inaction, Poppy has had such a busy day. A nasogastric tube was inserted into her nose, with the line continuing down to her stomach, to deliver adequate nutrition and prevent weight loss. The paediatric oncology team has visited, explaining the need for a central line to be inserted into a large vein at the top of Poppy's heart to administer potent chemotherapy drugs, monitor blood counts and check electrolyte levels. After a bit of difficulty and multiple chest X-rays attempting to feed Poppy's central line into an ideal position, a final X-ray confirmed the pediatrician's success. A Blugard central line was inserted, as these devices are designed with an antibacterial coating to prevent bacteria colonisation.

The paediatric oncologist, Dr Seth McKenzie, describes chemotherapy as feeding the cancer a poison, that will be taken up in greater quantities by the fastest growing cancer cells, to kill the tumour and produce remission. Dr Seth warns that since hair grows at a centimetre a month, Poppy's hair is likely to fall out as a side effect of the chemotherapy.

The other side effects Poppy will be monitored for range from mouth sores, nausea, vomiting, constipation, lethargy and tingling or numbness in her hands and feet. Since the neuroblastoma chemotherapy also lowers the numbers of white blood cells available to fight infections, Poppy will need to be kept away from others to reduce her susceptibility. Dr Seth states that another aim of chemotherapy is to prevent the tumour forming new blood vessels to keep growing and expanding. The numerous chemotherapy cycles aim to kill and shrink the tumour ready for its surgical removal.

Dr Seth provides me with a detailed schedule, listing predicted dates for the next planned cycles of induction chemotherapy, radiological reviews, surgery to remove the primary tumour, high dose chemotherapy, stem cell harvest, bone marrow transplant and the radiation therapies. Dr Seth also mentions that at the end of these gruelling treatments, he and his colleagues are hopeful that Poppy may be able to access the cancer prevention relapse therapies the Rare Cancer and Neuroblastoma associations are attempting to get approved for use in Australia at an affordable cost.

While I am keen for the chemotherapies to begin killing these cancer cells, I am stunned to learn that the debris released from the dying cancer cells entering Poppy's circulation poses even more dangers. Dr Seth informs me that since stage 4 neuroblastomas are solid tumours, when large numbers of neoplastic cells die rapidly from successful chemotherapy, they release their cell contents of nucleic acid, phosphate, calcium and potassium into the circulation. Therefore, one of the problems created by effective chemotherapy is that the vast amounts of these dead cell waste products can exceed the kidney's ability to eliminate them. Unless well hydrated, with intravenous fluids before the chemotherapy begins, the acids released from the huge numbers of dying cancer cells can create an acidity that will exceed the body's buffering capability to neutralise them. Intravenous infusions are therefore administered to provide the hydration necessary to lower the risk of the renal tubules becoming blocked by calcium and phosphate deposits or uric acid crystals.

Another unusual feature of malignant cells is that they contain around four times the phosphate present in normal cells. When the calcium binds with this excess phosphate released from the dead cancer cells, the calcium levels in the blood can become dramatically low. Particularly in the presence of dehydration or low levels of vitamin D3, the calcium and phosphate bonds can form crystals, lowering calcium levels and increasing the potential for an acute kidney injury. Compounding the nauseating side effects of the chemotherapy drugs, low levels of calcium can reduce Poppy's appetite, increase vomiting and cause potential bleeding, muscle cramps or seizures. These calcium phosphate deposits can even disrupt sleep, inflame parts of the eye and joints or cause severe itching and severe skin problems. My mind implodes with all these never-ending hazards to be navigated that I had not even imagined.

Dr Seth informs me that these signs and symptoms can begin within twelve hours but are more common within forty-eight to seventy-two hours of successful chemotherapy. The doctors begin ordering blood collections to monitor Poppy's blood for dangers like rising potassium levels, one of the first signs of cancer cell death. Unless checked at least every eight hours, untreated high potassium levels can widen the heart's electrical complexes on the cardiac monitor, slow Poppy's heart rate or cause progressive muscle weakness and paralysis. Although doctors say they don't like taking too many blood tests, for ill children at risk of anaemia, they emphasise that close observation is essential to prevent further complications during this interval.

The elevated uric acid levels excreted from dying cancer cells can also produce electrolyte imbalances. High blood urea nitrogen levels can inflame the heart lining, causing a metallic taste that compounds nausea and adversely impairs the function of the platelets in the blood that prevent bleeding. Naturally, with the risk of increased kidney impairment, Poppy's urine output is monitored to prevent excessive body water accumulating in her lungs, affecting breathing. The nurses weigh Poppy regularly and place cottonwool balls in her nappy to measure and test for abnormal urine components like blood.

Dr Seth, who will be coordinating the chemotherapy cycles, informs me that Poppy will have five days of chemotherapy followed by two days of rest. This seven-day routine aims to maintain sufficient drugs levels in Poppy's blood to kill the cancer.

A few weeks after the chemotherapy begins, as anticipated, Poppy's hair begins breaking off and falling out, with clumps visible on her pillow and in the bath. Even after simply removing any shirts or dresses over her head, more hair clumps disappear from Poppy's head. The rate of hair loss is so dramatic that I hesitate to use her soft brush to tidy it. Each time Poppy's bed linen is changed, I become more conscious of the tufts of hair coming out as her chemotherapy cycles continue.

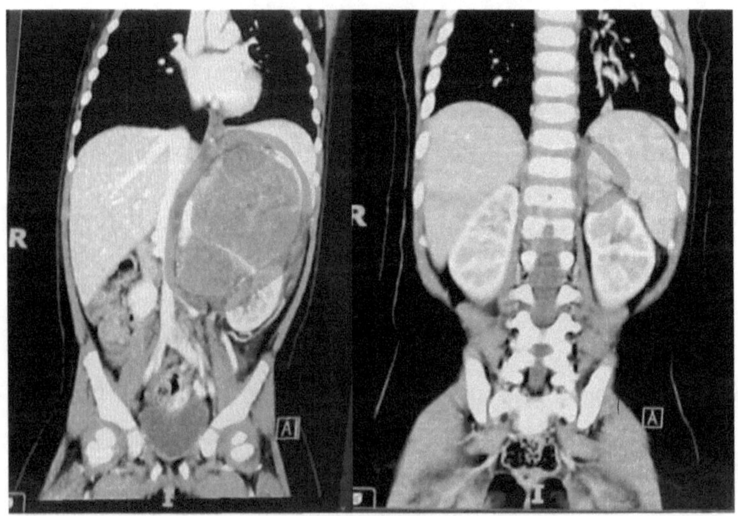

Before and after of successful chemo treatment

In contrast to the beautiful, thick, dark hair present about two months ago, Poppy's head is littered with sparse, short, brown fuss and broken-off hair follicle shafts. Mentally, I reprogram my thinking to process this hair loss as a sign that the chemotherapy is working. The fastest growing cells are dying, I tell myself, the tumour is shrinking. As Aunty Beth would say, opportunity is often disguised as loss. Hair loss is a small sacrifice to pay for the opportunity to live. Since neither Suzi nor I colour our hair, we will most likely donate our ponytails to Variety Australia in the future for wigs to help Poppy and older children undergoing chemotherapy.

Poppy's nausea and vomiting make her irritable and clingy again. Often when Poppy does eventually settle after exhaustive efforts, alarms from infusion pumps or monitoring equipment will break the silence, disturbing her again. Poppy's lethargy makes it increasingly difficult to distract her attention away from infusions and the strangers approaching her bedside to play on her butterfly-shaped toddler tablet.

Chapter 10

October–November 2018

Jenny Saunderson

The dietician has mathematically calculated the calories, vitamins and minerals Poppy needs to titrate the volume of her nasogastric feeds to prevent excessive weight loss. Poppy seems to be craving salt, as she is currently only interested in eating plain potato chips. Perhaps with all her nausea and vomiting, salty potato crisps may be all that Poppy feels she can retain. I watch, infatuated, at how Poppy's smooth, plump, tiny fingers grasp the small chips and take them to her mouth, transporting them as though the chips are the size of a large sandwich.

As the weeks go by, Poppy is allowed intermittently out of hospital for brief periods before returning for the cancer staging radiological tests, which assess the effectiveness of the chemotherapy cycles. Even though I desperately need to go home to talk to Suzi, it feels as though even the briefest escape from the sterile hospital environment is interrupted with infections requiring intravenous antibiotics or readmissions for blood product transfusions of platelets and red cells. Poppy has also been commenced on granulocyte colony stimulating factor injections (G-CSF) to stimulate her body's production of white cells after her count plummeted, reducing her ability to fight infections. While Poppy is relatively oblivious of the blood samples collected from the central line in her chest, her intolerance of the weekly changes of the central line dressing is countered by the delightful toys donated by various children's charities.

When Aunty Beth arrives to relieve me, I take the opportunity while Poppy is sleeping to attempt further contact with Suzi, who is still not answering her phone. I have not been able to contact her since she left my house, intending to go for a sleep. If Suzi does drive to my home, she'll find I forgot to leave a note in my haste to leave and because I was intending to return. Suzi is likely to get upset when she does not know where Poppy and I are.

In desperation, I report Suzi as a missing person to the police. However, since I forgot to bring my phone charger to the hospital, my battery fades before I can finish the conversation. I rationalise that not leaving my personal details is not a bad thing. What I worry excessively about is the need to avoid Poppy becoming swept up in what could become a Family Services custody debacle. I am so stressed and exhausted from comforting Poppy that the last thing I need at the moment is a guardianship battle in the middle of these back-to-back intensive therapies.

With a day off from hospital treatments, Poppy is wearing her little pink and white checked hat, sunglasses, pink shorts, white T-shirt, socks and sandals. She is zooming around in her little pink toy car on Aunty Beth's tinted glass-enclosed patio. After a short break for morning tea, Poppy colours in scribbly pictures in her drawing books with her grossly uncontrolled toddler movements while I catch up on washing and repacking the hospital bag with clothes and snacks. After lunch, supervised by Aunty Beth, Poppy is playing with a new book of stickers, obtained as bribery for the last central line dressing.

I hear an urgent 'Jesus, please us!' from Aunty Beth. Since that expression is as close as Aunty Beth ever comes to swearing, I know something is wrong. I dash onto the patio. When Aunty Beth had gone to answer the ringing phone, Poppy had managed to get her feeding and central line tubes caught up in the clothes she was attempting to remove. Fortunately, due to the amazing skills of the nursing staff, the tapes and dressings securing the central line and feeding tube have both held firm.

Blissfully unaware of Aunty Beth's heightened stress levels, Poppy begins blowing bubbles and excitedly clapping her hands as the rainbows reflecting on the soapy surface of each bubble drift upwards. Poppy, contented at mastering her new skills on this soapy, manual bubble maker, giggles and blows the bubbles she cannot catch towards us.

It has been great to spend a full day away from the hospital. While we can take Poppy alone outside for short intervals to see birds, trees and sunlight, we must limit her exposure to non-immunised people in shops. If Aunty Beth and I are together, usually to buy groceries, one of us remains in the car with Poppy. We also need to restrict Poppy's socialising with other children and playing in sand to reduce her risk of recurrent infections.

Poppy has chosen another pink, button-up pyjama shirt to wear, in preparation for her return to the hospital. Poppy's Bella, a light-brown teddy bear with a candy pink tutu, is packed. Bella's pretend central line, complete with a dressing and a nasogastric tube, appears to provide Poppy with immeasurable comfort. I administer Poppy's paracetamol before her trip to the hospital, as her bone pain from the neuroblastoma spread appears to be increased by her sedentary positioning in the toddler car seat. We pack Poppy's favourite patchwork quilt blanket before strapping her into her toddler car seat.

As Dr Seth does his rounds again, he reminds me that Poppy will need another hearing assessment soon to monitor the chemotherapy and antibiotic side effects of deafness. Poppy's hearing had remained unchanged until she acquired a blood infection from a crack in her central line that required mending, then eventually replacing. Unfortunately, the intravenous antibiotic used to prevent the sepsis from blood-borne infections was also detrimental to Poppy's eighth cranial hearing nerve. Poppy's hearing has therefore deteriorated slightly from the baseline level, recorded at the end of the previous cycle of chemotherapy.

With Aunty Beth inside the ward with Poppy, I take a small walk around the hospital to get some fresh air. As I return to the waiting room, two of the other mothers I had waved to through the glass petitions, when their children were getting admitted, look gloomy. Both mothers seem frightened, as though subconsciously shielding each other from adversity. I approach them both hesitantly, wondering if I should be getting one of the oncology staff to help.

'Are you both okay?' I ask, concerned.

'We've just both received devastating news,' Daisy replies, shaking her head with a defeated sigh.

I recognise Daisy with her olive complexion after seeing her with a little four-year-old boy wearing bright red Spiderman pajamas.

'My son, Ian, just had his MIBG score results come back at twenty-four out of thirty. He is riddled with cancer,' Daisy reveals, weeping. 'I am so shocked. We kept taking him to doctors for his pain. I just can't believe he was being treated for urinary infections all this time.'

I grab the tissues from the coffee table and sit down, reaching my arm around Daisy's shoulders to hug her. Daisy's head drops and her shoulders shake, releasing another crying jag as sorrow and powerlessness overwhelm her.

'I am so sorry to hear that,' I commiserate, rubbing Daisy's upper arm to comfort her. 'Our Poppy had a similar experience. I remember feeling like we were on an emotional roller-coaster. Our predicament shifted from having our worries dismissed as benign to be confronted with a life-threatening cancer diagnosis.'

'I asked the doctor how accurate the MIBG score is,' sobs Daisy, 'hoping it isn't real. He said it's about eighty-five per cent precise.'

'Today has been such a shocker,' the other sad mother, Rachel, says, wiping her sodden face and tear-filled, sad brown eyes. 'We were both down in medical imaging, one after the other. My Emma's cancer has returned, despite all that chemotherapy, surgery and radiation.'

'Oh no, how dreadful!'

My hands reactively reach up to cover my face instantly, as hearing any more demoralising news is unbearable. I walk around to hug Rachel as well, sensing her overwhelming misery.

'After I got that news, all I heard about were side effects and complications. The one thing you never get here are any guarantees,' Daisy says, commiserating with Rachel.

'At least the oncology team never gives up, I suppose,' Rachel adds. 'Dr Seth was just as distressed as we both were. I just wish they would put more funding into helping these little ones.'

Rachel's head shakes in frustration. 'At Emma's treatment stage, I was more worried about the fundraising for those expensive cancer relapse prevention drugs than this news. Emma going out of remission was not even on my radar.' Rachel sobs helplessly. 'I just don't know how I am going to tell my husband, Michael.'

'I know,' says Daisy. 'I haven't told Graeme yet either. After we got the horrendous diagnosis, Graeme was so relieved to learn that there were treatment options available for Ian that I don't believe he was really processing all the side effects and complications or how long these high-risk challenging treatments will continue.'

'Yes, it's so overpowering ... all these invasive tumours, side effects, tests ... All you can do is pray for survival. There seems to be no energy left to worry about the outcome. You just try to cope with the challenges each day presents. When they tell you about risks, it's not like you have a choice. It is like a gamble you have to take, like grasping for that small glimmer of hope,' Rachel says.

'We thought Emma was almost through the end of this Russian roulette nightmare. Now we begin again – only this time, we'll be probably even more desperate for any positive news'.

Rachel's frustration is palpable. As the veteran amongst us, Rachel had endured over twelve months of this cancer battle. Now she appears absolutely defeated, as though what she had been interpreting as progress was just an obscene hideous illusion. With Emma's cancer reappearing, Rachel feels as though everyone's colossal effort has been futile.

I empathise with Daisy and Rachel, shaking my head in despair.

'So far, with Poppy's therapies, we have only experienced about half the hurdles that your brave Emma has navigated. I pray there are effective medical solutions for both your children. I try to keep soldiering on with the hope that new technology, more scientific research and medical advances will help all these children to survive'.

My body shakes with the realisation that although I said 'hope', we are all living in abject fear.

Chapter 11

3 December 2018

Jenny Saunderson

After five cycles of chemotherapy, Poppy is admitted for a stem cell harvest and the removal of the 'metabolically inactive' abdominal mass, which has now shrunken considerably. Poppy is sleeping while we are waiting for this surgical review. Suddenly, an almighty squeal shatters the silence as Poppy is woken by a huge machine entering the doorway.

'Monster!' cries a terrified Poppy, pointing. 'Monster!' she squeals, looking alarmed and backing up the bed towards us.

The stem cell harvest machine, with fluid and plasma bags primed and hanging from the hooks above, is wheeled in through the door, arriving with a new, cuddly puppy toy, to add to Poppy's growing collection. As the professionals distract Poppy using play, giving her time to adapt to the machine, her panic subsides dramatically.

We are informed that the stem cells can be harvested from bone marrow in the hip bone or the peripheral blood when cancers are in remission following chemotherapy. With Poppy's MIBG score of zero out of thirty, healthy stem cells are collected from Poppy and filtered through the specialised machine before being frozen and preserved. Although the transplant team has warned us of their concerns about not getting adequate samples, enough stem cells are acquired to facilitate ten future bone marrow transplants, since the specimens can be stored for twenty years.Our next consultation is with the paediatric surgeon, Dr Branson, who advises us that Poppy's left kidney will need to be removed along with the tumour to improve her chances of survival, as the tumour tissue has calcified around the renal structures. With Poppy having fasted, the anaesthetist, Dr Greyson, briefly examines her before methodically listing off the usual general anaesthetic risks prior to my signing the consent form. Aunty Beth arrives just as Poppy returns to the surgical ward after hours of surgery in theatre. Dr Branson informs us that he believes he was able to excise about ninety-five per cent of the neuroblastoma, with the remaining calcified mass being too closely adhered to vital structures like the aorta.

Poppy's first post-operative night was dreadful. Several different narcotics were prescribed, with each analgesic triggering bouts of vomiting, exacerbating Poppy's pain at the surgical site. Since waking, pale Poppy has worn a perpetual frown as she is unable to have any psychologically comforting milk drinks until she passes wind or her bowels move, following the surgery. Although Poppy is grumpy, we are reluctant to handle her too much for cuddles, as her major surgery has left a large horizontal scar extending from above her umbilicus around to her left side. Once again, I attempt to contact Suzi, without success.

Poppy grimaces intensely as Aunty Beth and I try to distract her using her pink butterfly-winged toddler tablet to play her favourite Bluey cartoons or hug her cuddly toys. Gradually, as the days go by, Poppy needs less pain relief and mobilises more, allowing more infusions and tubes to be removed. Finally, ten days later, Poppy has once again rallied enough to return to Aunty Beth's home. With a short interval before her bone marrow transplant, Aunty Beth and I again contemplate making the four-hour trip back home. We hesitate for the first few days, worrying about whether the car's multidirectional forward, side-to-side and up and down movements, along with the prolonged immobilisation in a toddler capsule, will increase Poppy's pain and nausea.

Another concern is the dilemma of being out of town if

post-surgery complications, like bleeding or infections, occur due to Poppy's chronically low immune status and platelet count. In the end, we both decide to wait a few days, since Poppy has a few weeks to recover from her surgery, before the bone marrow transplant is planned.

Just as I am again considering the four-hour drive home, Poppy is readmitted for more red cell and platelet transfusions. It seems we are no sooner back at Aunty Beth's when Poppy has to be readmitted for another cycle of chemotherapy and the bone marrow transplant.

I am still exasperated about not being unable to contact Suzi.

Chapter 12

21 January 2019

The bone marrow transplant is to be immediately followed by six to eight weeks of hospitalisation in a dedicated isolation ward, with all visitors wearing disposable masks, long-sleeved gowns and powderless non-sterile gloves to reduce the risk of Poppy getting infections, as the transplant and medications lower her immunity further.

As we enter, we discover that the isolation ward has been made very enticing with rainbow coloured fairy light bulbs reflecting a glittering array of mermaid stickers, fish, bubbles and cartoon characters welcoming Poppy on the walls. On the cream coloured wall directly in front of her bed are large sparkling letters spelling Poppy's name, and the large television mounted on the wall above is playing children's programs with songs.

Sadly, the only windows installed offer a view of the medical and nursing station rather than the outside world, which would help orientate Poppy to day and night. Aunty Beth and I soon become both exhausted from keeping Poppy distracted and entertained when she is awake. Although Suzi has still not returned my calls, I make a note that I now have to remember to ensure that Suzi is immunised with influenza shots, like Aunty Beth and me, before she can visit Poppy. Poppy's head is now virtually bald, with wisps of fine, dark brown hair of irregular length less than three centimetres long.

Poppy's first major complication of her chemotherapy and high dose chemotherapy is mucositis. The mucositis appear as painful ulcers in Poppy's mouth that extend throughout her gastrointestinal tract. Just as the chemotherapy affected the fast-growing hair follicles, the rapidly dividing cells lining the gut are also impacted. Synergistically, these chemotherapy symptoms will most likely be worsened by the medications required following the bone marrow transplant as well. Although Poppy was given ice chips before and during her chemotherapy, to reduce this common side effect, the mucositis appears as a dry mouth before progressing rapidly to painful bleeding and inflamed gums that cause difficulty swallowing and talking. White pus-like patches appear on Poppy's tongue overnight, causing an offensive breath. Poppy's oral hygiene is boosted by us using a soft toothbrush, saline and sodium bicarbonate mouth washes to reduce the microbes present.

Antibiotic covering is implemented to prevent the loss of the integrity of the cells lining Poppy's gut from permitting bowel bacteria to enter her circulation, causing systemic infections. Combinations of artificial saliva, topical pain relief and numbing agents, anti-inflammatory solutions and mucous cell repairing agents are used to protect and repair the cells lining Poppy's mouth and gastrointestinal tract. Poppy sleeps poorly and becomes increasingly irritable and clingy as the protective antibiotics amplify the nauseating effects of her chemotherapy and the preventative transplant rejection drugs.

To further minimise Poppy's gut bacterial colonisation, she is intravenously fed with total parenteral nutrition containing glucose, fats, vitamins, minerals and insulin through the central line. The calories and volumes of the intravenous feeds required for Poppy's nutrition are calculated by the dietician using formulas that consider her weight, liver and kidney function and metabolic rate. These solutions arrive from the pharmacy covered in large black bags to protect the vitamin and lipid compounds from instability caused by light exposure. With the mucositis preventing Poppy's gastrointestinal tract from containing microorganisms, Poppy incurs a lower risk of the bowel bacteria translocating into her blood stream if fed intravenously via the central line. I am informed that, although feeding through the gastrointestinal system boosts the immune system and prevents ulceration, the human body adapts to critical illnesses by diverting blood away from the gut and skin to vital organs like the brain, lungs and heart for self-preservation, impairing absorption.

Prior to signing the bone marrow transplant consent form, we are informed that anaesthesia is not required for the infusion of some of Poppy's harvested stem cells into her central line over a few hours. The doctors remind us that each bone marrow transplant may only last a few months due to the aggressive therapies required to manage the grade 4 neuroblastoma. While we were ambitiously hoping that the bone marrow transplants would prevent the need for so many transfusions in the future, statistically the team warns that in five per cent of cases, patients called 'non-responders' experience no improvement after six months of treatment.

After the bone marrow transplant infusion, Poppy becomes extremely fatigued. Poppy's temperature is monitored closely for signs of infection, as her body's immune system integrates the infused stem cells. A major concern is that Poppy's reduced white cell count could predispose her to infections, at the same time as her low platelet count increases her risk of bruising and bleeding. Poppy has already needed so many platelet infusions, after bruising and bleeding readily on her face, limbs and gums, that I become automatically hypervigilant for the small, reddish-purple skin spots that signal critically low values.

When discussing the need for the stem cell harvests and bone marrow transplants, Dr Seth had mentioned that, although the blood product transfusions are alleviating the low red cell and platelet laboratory numbers, every transfusion carries a minor risk of infusing viruses and cancers from the donor's blood.

Even though blood banks routinely test for the viral antibodies, a donor can host a virus like hepatitis or human immunodeficiency virus (HIV) for up to two years before the antibodies tested for are produced. Therefore, since it is not economically viable to test each blood donation for viruses and cancers directly, the stem cell harvest and bone marrow transplant aim to reduce Poppy's dependence on blood products, lowering her risk of these acquired infections.

208

Chapter 13

4 February 2019

Jenny Saunderson

Aunty Beth and I relieve each other so that we can both cope with the six to eight weeks' isolation ordeal. Aunty Beth is coming in for six hours during the day to give me an opportunity to shower, visit the canteen and try to contact Suzi. Occasionally the six-hour break affords me the chance to wander outside for a walk in the sun, away from the three-metre confining isolation room. I sleep on a fold-up camp bed during the night, and often cuddle Poppy watching the television on the recliner during the day. To reduce Poppy's risk of infection, the gloomy isolation visitations remain restricted to essential services only. As Poppy sleeps for brief intervals, I take the opportunity to text Aunty Beth with reminders of any items I need her to bring in on her daily visits. I learn to indulge in brief naps in the large recliner when the opportunity arises, so that I feel more refreshed before dressing changes and treatments. I find myself interacting with friends on Facebook more when the social isolation overwhelms me as the weeks drag on.

The social isolation causes Poppy to develop a fascination with the nurse's neurological torches, after a nurse flashed a torch to check the colour of the white sclera in her eyes. Poppy borrowed the torch to playfully assess Bella's reflective eyes. One doctor even allowed Poppy to turn on the light of his otoscope after he checked her ears, so she could check his ears, albeit from a greater distance. The cheerful nursing and medical teams possess an amazing ability to distract Poppy from constantly watching the isolation room door, like a trapped animal caught in the head lights. These professionals draw on the whiteboard in the isolation room, entertaining Poppy with images of teddy bears and animals, while subliminally alerting us to the timing of the procedures planned.

When Poppy becomes tender in her right upper quadrant, with her eyes and skin developing a yellow tinge, a liver ultrasound is ordered. Poppy watches cartoons on her butterfly toddler tablet as she is positioned on her left side, with her right side uppermost and her right arm elevated, for this test. The radiologists confirm that Poppy had acquired a potentially fatal post-transplant complication called veno-occlusive disease that occurs when the veins in the liver become blocked.

Alarmingly, yet again, the treatment for this pathology requires medications that further reduce Poppy's immune system's ability to fight infections. With the liver unable to function optimally to eliminate bilirubin, the yellowish brown pigment produced from red cell breakdown, Poppy's jaundiced skin becomes swollen and pitted on pressure, signaling that fluid retention is occurring. With seven syringe drivers mounted on a bedside stand infusing drugs, we dress Poppy in button-up, pink Minnie Mouse pyjama shirts to avoid stopping any infusions.

In the confined, square, isolation enclosure, where it has been challenging so far not to tangle Poppy's lines and leads as she does crafts and drawings, her stationary posture becomes frightening. After being told that the first two to three weeks after a bone marrow transplant is when the white cells plummet is greatest, increasing the risk of bacterial infections, my anxiety spirals when Poppy begins deteriorating. The oxygen saturations probe on her finger, which uses a red light to measure the oxygen amount carried on each red blood cell as it travels through her capillaries, begins warning more frequently that it is detecting that insufficient oxygen is transferring from Poppy's lungs into her bloodstream. Poppy becomes lethargic and more breathless, despite the inhaled oxygen concentration delivery being increased.

Poppy's hands and feet become cooler to touch, indicating that her heart is no longer pumping warm blood as efficiently around her system as before. Despite the escalating crisis, it is hard not to be impressed by the professionally skilled doctors and nurses calmly responding to Poppy's deterioration, as she is transferred to the paediatric intensive care unit (PICU). The paediatric intensivists consult with the oncology, transplant and haematology teams to manage Poppy's non-invasive mechanical ventilation and complex care in a coordinated approach.

To manage this escalating respiratory distress and the critical threat of organ failure, Poppy's bedside is lit up with a wall-mounted cardiac monitor and ten syringe drivers administering medications. Poppy is breathing rapidly, with her breastbone tugging inwards with each inhalation. A non-invasive ventilator delivers oxygen via a mask strapped to Poppy's face. Toddlers can only intrinsically adjust their breathing rate, rather than their breath size, to compensate for oxygen deprivation. Therefore, the ventilator artificially enlarges the volume of breath inhaled to aerate any collapsed alveoli not receiving adequate ventilation. Using initially a continuous positive airway pressure mode (CPAP) and later bi-level positive airway pressures (BiPAP), the ventilator also increases the volume of gas remaining in Poppy's lungs between breaths, to provide a pressure gradient that will deter water migrating into her lungs.

It is during Poppy's stay in the PICU for ventilator support that I become acutely aware of the anatomical differences between children and adults. The transplant team is restrained in their use of analgesia by Poppy's compliant cartilaginous ribcage, featuring horizontal rather than curved ribs that are innately susceptible to respiratory failure.

Adding jeopardy to this mechanical design is the higher toddler metabolic rate, requiring greater oxygen delivery. In comparison to adults, toddlers also possess fewer alternative ventilation pathways in their alveoli, called Pores of Kohn, should any ventilation pathway become obstructed.

Compounding these inefficient breathing mechanics is the dilemma that toddlers' respiratory muscles fatigue readily, increasing the risk of low ventilation. Poppy's position is therefore changed frequently, so that when lying prone on her stomach, more areas of the lungs are ventilated and recruited. Even the ventilator corrugated tubing is placed on top of her blankets to prevent indentation in Poppy's skin that is trapping fluid. Since most of the time, after washing our hands, we can only tentatively cuddle Poppy or hold her hands or feet, we place Bella, Bluey and her fleecy, cartoon, bunny rugs within reach, as a comforting distraction from the multitude of alarming machines.

With a mask strapped to Poppy's face delivering oxygen and ventilator support, my despair that Suzi is still not answering her phone magnifies. I cannot imagine how angry Suzi will be when she finds out that we have done all this without notifying her. If Poppy dies, Suzi may never forgive me. When I ramp up my attempts to contact Suzi by asking a few friends to visit her address, they report that Suzi is not home, not answering their calls and the outside of her unit looks unkempt.

Fear overwhelms my spiraling stress levels. I am oblivious to being outside the PICU, sobbing loudly, until a tall, athletic man with olive complexion and curly dark hair, dressed in navy shorts and a white polo shirt, is talking to me in a calm, deep voice. I am not sure how long he has standing there or speaking to me after my last attempt to call Suzi failed. I am so overtired and distraught that he has put a hand on my upper arm, gently shaking me to get my attention, before I even acknowledge his presence.

As I look up into his concerned, dark brown eyes, the clean-shaven man is saying his name is Simon. Simon is suggesting that

I need a break from the PICU waiting room to soothe my frayed nerves. Simon, who looks like a health professional, takes me down to a table and chairs outside the canteen. With Aunty Beth inside the PICU with Poppy, I allow him to buy me a coffee as we sit in a tranquil garden area, inhaling the fragrance of the lavender flowers drifting in the cool gentle breeze.

'Sometimes, the patterns in nature, like the leaves on ferns and listening to birds, can be therapeutic,' Simon comments, attempting to engage me in conversation.

Indicating the cordless hospital phone in his hand, Simon says, 'I can see that you are very anxious at the moment. I am wondering if you would like me to see if a hospital social worker, minister of religion or a psychologist might be available to help.'

I shake my weary head, tears streaming down my face. 'I'm sorry,' I say, 'I am not meaning to be a bother. I really need to get myself together, don't I?'

After my daily ritual of washing and drying Poppy's favourite rug and cuddly toys in the ward laundry, I discover that I now lack the courage to enter the PICU again. I am terrified seeing Poppy so motionless, I am so worried about not being able to talk to Suzi, I am paranoid about Family Services trying to assume custody of Poppy, panicked about whether Poppy would survive ... so I sit like a stunned mullet, saying very little.

'Is there anything you can think of that we can do to make this crisis less stressful for you?' Simon sensitively asks.

'Not really,' I reply.

I am finding just sitting in the warm sunlight away from the PICU is relaxing me ... or perhaps it is the endorphins released from crying. I sigh, imagining what it would be like to have an eight-hour uninterrupted sleep for just one night, not worrying whether Poppy will keep breathing.

'Thank you for buying this coffee for me.'

I try to smile sincerely through my tears. Apparently, the forced smile does not spread over my face or reach my eyes enough to be convincing. I reassure him.

'Sometimes, you just have to release the unrestrained panic building and swirling inside you, I suppose.'

'Sometimes, you just need to take some time out for yourself,' Simon kindly suggests, his gentle eyes displaying empathy.

I look at my watch, knowing that I need to get back so that Aunty Beth is not driving home in the dark.

'I just hope today gets better,' I say trying to lighten this conversation. 'Thank you for bringing me outside.'

I inhale deeply, intensely wishing Poppy to improve. I know that I must make my return to the PICU while I am feeling less defeated.

'Perhaps Poppy will improve and then I will get a better sleep,' I suggest, trying to leave on a brighter note.

'I might just come by and check on you again tomorrow,' Simon offers with a genial smile. 'I think it might be a good idea if we come outside into the fresh air again. We can just have a chat about anything you want,' Simon adds sincerely, making his offer impossible to refuse.

'Okay, but tomorrow will be my shout,' I say, mustering the courage I need to return to the PICU. 'I am sure that you have had a busy day,' I say, reading Simon's photo ID which identifies him as a physiotherapist.

'What about 3 pm? Does that sound okay? We can meet down here for ten minutes, just to give you a break,' Simon insists. 'The PICU experience can induce a kind of accumulative fear that can build into a panic. When you are in there, you don't realise it is happening. You subliminally hear one alarm after another, get bad news or witness deterioration that compounds your anxiety until it gets out of control.'

'Yes, that is so true. Again, I am so very sorry. I think everything just got too much all at once. I don't really need to be burdening you with my dramas, though,' I say, sighing deeply.

'Three pm tomorrow,' Simon asserts, smiling. He escorts me back to the PICU, which he enters, using his swipe card.

The next afternoon, 3 pm as promised, I shout Simon the promised café latte.

'I am so embarrassed about yesterday's meltdown,' I confess.

'Hey, that's fine,' Simon says, 'No apology is necessary. There are few things in life more stressful than a sick child. I completely understand. It was obvious that you needed a break from the PICU.'

'Yes, I feel so powerless to help Poppy.' I swallow my coffee hastily, feeling tears welling up again. 'All the infants and toddlers in there look so terrifyingly fragile and morbidly still. It is so upsetting. I feel so useless and too emotionally drained to process everything that is happening.'

'Sometimes, as health professionals, seeing sick infants and toddlers every day, we tend to get a bit accustomed to these situations,' Simon says. 'Try to have more faith than fear, if you can. They are a brilliant team in there. Everyone tries their best, hoping to achieve favourable outcomes, even though we can never guarantee what will happen. All anyone can do in these situations is try their best. I thought Poppy looked less swollen today, actually,' Simon offers.

'Yes, I hope so. I'll gratefully accept any miracles that come our way,' I assure him. 'You must have a lot of courage to deal with this every day. Toddlers are usually so lively. It is tough to see them looking so pale, with that waxy skin, attached to those masks and machines ... so lifeless ...' I silently wipe away more tears.

'It is kind of different when it is not your own child. We divert our focus to employing the scientific interventions required for each condition, based on evidence.' Simon elaborates. 'Over time, we learn to distance ourselves, using empathy rather than sympathy to keep our emotions stable. I try to think logically about which techniques will help each child's unique situation, like less manual handling for toddlers like Poppy with low platelets to prevent bruising. It is harder for parents. They know the toddler's personality and they are often sitting there praying for twenty-four hours, with their child often in a holding pattern – or deteriorating.'

'I expected myself to deal with this better, being a nurse, but I am a crumbling mess,' I tearfully respond.

'Oh, are you on family leave?' Simon replies, intentionally diverting me from discussions about Poppy's critical illness.

'Yes, I haven't worked for about six months now. I brought Poppy to Sydney to get her constant crying sorted, not expecting this devastating diagnosis to be found. Poppy was in pain for so long, refusing fluids and feeds, and every time we stopped rocking her, she screamed. My sister and I were convinced that she was in pain, but we were unable to get anyone to take our mounting concerns seriously. So, I impulsively drove Poppy to Sydney, determined to get some investigations done when none of our soothing strategies were working.'

'That is probably why you are so distressed. First, you got an anxiety-provoking diagnosis, then the PICU admission escalates the threat, making every day and every alarm more frightening.'

'Gosh, look at the time! I'd better get back up there. Aunty Beth can't drive home in the dark. Thank you so much for your kindness and thoughtfulness yesterday,' I say, shaking Simon's hand.

'Let's catch up again tomorrow,' Simon suggests. 'I have my afternoon break at this time. We can just chat about anything. It sometimes helps to feel like you are not battling through all this crisis alone.'

I nod. 'Three pm it is, then.'

Simon and I walk back to the PICU together.

Now that he has raised my awareness that the alarms and environment could be feeding my anxiety, I am determined to do better. The next day, while Poppy is sleeping, I go to the canteen to get two coffees after Aunty Beth arrives at 10 am. On my way back in the lift to the PICU, it stops at the floor below by a bedridden patient needing a medical and nursing escort, all carrying resuscitation bags and equipment. As I step out of the lift to make room for the bed, I decide to take the stairs up to the PICU floor. On hearing a familiar, deep voice, I look over to see Simon instructing a small boy with his leg in plaster to navigate the physiotherapy practice stairs using crutches. I smile and wave when Simon looks my way as I open the squeaky stairwell door.

'The clumsy way the little boy was manipulating those crutches, he might have been safer with chop sticks,' I joke with Simon later. After being in a city with strangers for months, I begin feeling as though I have another ally besides Aunty Beth. I begin seeing Simon everywhere – in the lifts at the hospital, in the car park, even at the local supermarket.

'Are you stalking me?' Simon jests when we meet again at the canteen, a smile tugging at the corners of his mouth.

'Oh, wouldn't it be great to have that kind of energy!' I laugh.

I find myself enjoying my growing friendship with the caring Simon. His humour lightens my turbulent thoughts, helping me to relax in his company.

Aunty Beth's strategy, when she saw my spirits plummeting with Poppy's PICU admission, was to emphasise self-care, using her 'look better, feel better' mentality. Rather than existing in jeans and a T-shirt, I begin feeling slightly brighter when I use my nervous energy to focus on restoring normal routines more, like wearing makeup as if I were going to work. The 3 pm coffees with Simon also distract me briefly from the gloomy daily PICU news. Watching Simon's curly mid-length hair springing and moving, with his bubbly effervescent personality, provides a welcome brief distraction from monitors alarming and waiting eagerly during every doctor's rounds for a morsel of good news. However, while I suspect that Simon is meeting me at the canteen to monitor my stress levels, I am reluctant to comment too much on my worries, in case he is feeding information back to other health professionals.

Finally, after Poppy being critically ill and sombre for several weeks, the ultrasounds and organ function tests begin to show gradual improvement. Aunty Beth and I eventually get a cuddle of a flaccid Poppy, seriously lacking her normal, curled posture. Poppy's skin is a translucent, pale greyish colour from the accumulative effects of the bruising, anaemia and her debilitated condition. Fortunately, as Poppy responds more and more to her medications, she begins snuggling into us and communicating more. With the numbers of lines and tubes attached reducing each day, I can climb onto her bed to cuddle and comfort her as before. Finally, when Friday comes, Poppy is wheeled in her bed back in the ward isolation room. Gradually, after another month, Poppy is promoted into the general ward again, out of isolation. Teddy bears and stuffed toys tour the ward with Poppy, mounted on her intravenous pole along with her infusion pumps, as she explores the stimulating wall mounted attractions, visiting her favourite frog with the moving eyes.

Chapter 14

11 March 2019

Jenny Saunderson

Erratically, I attempt to contact Suzi, with calls still not returned. I am worried that Suzi is not coping and could be at home alone. I am also concerned that I have not had any contact from Suzi at all since she left Poppy with me, as they have both always been inseparable. I am so scared about what could have happened to Suzi that my mind is racing, catastrophising endless possibilities. I am even guilt-ridden about signing all these consents, with the nurses believing that I am Poppy's mother. I mentally remind myself that the consent form has 'Guardian' written on the line that I am signing. Unable to be in two places at the same time, I ineffectively rationalise that Suzi had requested that I look after her precious daughter, and I am. Anyway, I simply do not have the stamina to cope with looking after two people in two different locations right now.

Poppy and I are barely managing with Aunty Beth's support as it is. If I knew that Suzi would be home, I could drive the four hours home and back to get her, but Suzi is not communicating. I have continually declined the social worker assistance offered. I am too 'under-slept' and overwhelmed to be lying to anyone or fielding overly inquisitive social worker questions that could potentially escalate to custody battles. Aunty Beth supports our need to maintain this façade, as Poppy is too vulnerable for any changes in carers right now.

Poppy is cruising around the corridors in a little pink and

white car, which has large eyes where the car lights would be and a spectacular smile for the grill. Poppy is hugging the steering wheel to navigate her vehicle before periodically stopping cycling to assess the welfare of her dolly passenger. Everywhere Poppy ventures, I push a pole mounted with multiple syringe drivers to ensure her feeds and crucial medications continue.

Today is especially amazing when Poppy is finally permitted to view the outdoor hospital fairy garden in a wheelchair. As we enter the floral landscape, featuring a large bright rainbow backdrop painted across the gardener's shed wall, Poppy's spirits brighten.

'Look,' says Poppy, pointing when she is amused by a frog riding a solar-paneled motorbike over the small bridge. The concrete path is lined with fairy village cottages that include a bakery, a post office, a church and a hospital surrounded by bright coloured mushroom buildings of various sizes dispersed among the plants.

'Look,' Poppy says, entertained by yet another frog fishing on a tiny bridge built over a pond. A five-centimetre silver-grey fish is dangling off the frog's fishing pole, with another fish head visible in the fishing pouch attached to the frog's waist.

We return to the paediatric oncology unit for the radiological cancer staging tests and blood work-ups ordered, in preparation for the planned therapeutic radiation. In two days, Poppy will be allowed to go home to visit her favourite park, provided she remains separated from others.

I have just returned from trying to ring Suzi yet again when I witness the raw emotions of a distraught mother crying inconsolably, clutching her phone in the waiting room.

'Are you okay?' I ask, tentatively approaching her.

'Not really ...' she says, wiping her teary eyes.

'My name is Jenny,' I introduce myself. 'What is your name?'

'Debbie,' she sobs. Her honey-blonde hair is sticking to her flushed, sodden face. Debbie's dried, cracked hands place her phone in an old leather handbag with frayed straps. As I moved closer, attempting to comfort Debbie with a shoulder hug, she relays to me her astonishing news from the Social Services Department.

'I have just been informed that the entitlements paid to the parents of sick children is the exact same income paid for a normal infant who sleeps twenty hours a day and only wakes every four hours between feeds.' Debbie continues. 'I am financially struggling with living expenses, while neither my husband nor I are able to work while we care for our critically ill daughter. We are from Kempsey, so we have petrol costs, accommodation expenses … We need to be in Sydney to provide Gabriella with psychological, physical and social support during her chemotherapy and this extensive medical maze. We are struggling to maintain the school routines for our other children … We just cannot manage.'

Debbie's frowning face and chewed fingernails expose her turbulent emotions.

'That would be extremely stressful,' I say. 'My aunt and I have been exhausted just supporting one child!' I sympathise.

'How are we expected to afford $20,000 a month for cancer relapse prevention drugs or $500,000 for a full treatment?' inquires Debbie, tearfully wiping her eyes with tissues. 'We are struggling from pay to pay just to keep a roof over our heads. I understand that the cancer relapse prevention drugs increase survival chances by twenty-five per cent, but if the Australian Government doesn't approve and subsidise these drugs for use here in the public system, after all the chemotherapy, surgeries, radiation treatments and immune modulation therapies, our Gabriella could still die.'

Debbie looks solemnly at the cold, hospital coffee cup that remains untouched.

'Yes, our Poppy is in the same situation too. We need those drugs to be available for her in six months' time. You would think that after these brave little toddlers have conquered all these marathon treatment challenges, they would be able to access the same cancer relapse prevention drugs that are routinely available as a standard for American children, wouldn't you?'

'We are nowhere near achieving even a one-month supply of treatment,' Debbie confesses tearfully, 'even with the Neuroblastoma Association and Rare Cancers associations rallying the assistance of major companies to help. It's not as though we live in a third-world country. The Australian government needs to look after its citizens.'

Debbie adds in frustration, 'We are so exhausted just attending to Gabriella's needs around the clock and our three other children. I cannot imagine having to do all this fundraising without the help of grandparents, aunties, uncles, social media and online funding campaigns. This prolonged treatment schedule is formidable enough. Yet we find ourselves mentally drained by people asking us insensitive questions, like "What we will do with the funds if our child dies?", as though we are raising revenue to exploit our child.'

'Yes, the whole journey is physically, mentally and emotionally depleting. It is hard not to get angry when you just don't have any mental reserve to even contemplate that outcome. But the Rare Cancers Foundation website does mention that some of the pharmaceutical companies have applied for an accelerated Australian drug approval pathway to make these medicines available urgently,' I reply, optimistically.

'Yes, but how does anyone afford them if they are not subsidised?' Debbie adds, rubbing her tightened neck muscles. 'As my grandmother would say, we're so broke we've not got a feather to fly with.'

We both realise that getting these cancer relapse prevention drugs approved in Australia within the timeframe of sixty days after the immunotherapy finishes, to improve the survival of our children, remains a disheartening prospect. Even if Rare Cancer Australia and Neuroblastoma Australia are able to get the medications approved for therapeutic use in time, neither of us has the funds to pay for them.

'Yes, all the children surviving these rigorous cancer therapies need to be able access those vital cancer relapse prevention medications here,' I admit. 'It is dangerous to put immunocompromised toddlers on planes with international travelers to get them to the US to get the medications.'

'When my parents and sisters approached our federal minister, he was too busy arguing about "health being a state matter" to listen to our desperate pleas. We tried to rationalise with him that to get the subject numbers for specialised drug trials and research for children with rare cancers, the services needed to be coordinated federally. There was so much resistance that we left believing that only media support will allow us to access these drugs in Australia, in the timely manner needed for these susceptible children.'

'Yet, an accountant calculated that we only need a tenth of one per cent of the federal budget for these cancer relapse prevention drugs to be made available' I enlighten Debbie. 'If they are not affordable, what value does Australia place on a child's life or their lifelong opportunities? Personally, I don't consider we should have to bloody ask to value any child's life!'

'Yes, this experience is stressful enough without having to divert energy to fighting an impenetrable bureaucracy for access to vital drugs.'

Debbie shakes her head angrily. She and I share a fresh hospital coffee together, validating with each other how traumatic this entire experience is. We talked about innocuous subjects, too, to reduce our toxic stress levels. When the social worker arrives to notify Debbie of the additional support she has been able to muster from charities, like accommodation and uniforms for her older children for school in Sydney, I hear Jenny cry in relief as I leave to give them privacy to chat.

Witnessing this family tragedy, I am reminded that my own family leave and superannuation income protection will soon be running out. I have been constantly checking my emails and bank accounts, trying to ensure no bills are left unpaid. I have remained excessively worried about Suzi, as Aunty Beth is unable to travel alone any distance with her cardiac pain.

I am also reviewing whether I should be engaging with the social worker or police to find my sister. After Suzi previously not answering the door to the community midwives wrongly labelling her acopic, I am still hesitant to engage any services that could upset her or precipitate unwelcome custody battles.

Even when we get back to Aunty Beth's, by the time we get the washing done and ourselves sorted, Poppy is often readmitted for infections or transfusions. On the occasional day we have had free, I have washed and repacked ready for the hospital, or played with Poppy, too exhausted to go anywhere.

The next treatment break, Aunty Beth and I are determined to drive home to check on Suzi, since we have had no communication at all for over six months. We are still cautious about travelling, since the drive could potentiate Poppy's nausea, or the prolonged immobility when harnessed in the toddler capsule, along with medications like the G-CSF white cell stimulants, could aggravate Poppy's pelvic bone pain symptoms. Often Poppy cries for 'Mummy' and we have no doubt that she is longing for Suzi. We can only reassure Poppy that we have tried to ring Mummy, and that we will try to get her home to Suzi as soon as she is feeling better.

Although we are desperate to reunite Suzi and Poppy, we avoid saying Suzi's name or 'Mummy' to avoid contributing to Poppy's grief. Since we need Poppy's immune system strong, all we can do in these sad moments is distract her with play and try to travel again between each treatment break. Many hideous scenarios are playing out in my head, none of which are doing me any favours. I am actually exhausting myself considering and eliminating the endless possibilities that come to mind. Could Suzi have plummeted into a severe depression? Is she sick? I cannot imagine Suzi would have gone off with another loser, not after all those nights rocking Poppy – they were bonded.

Worried that Suzi may be depressed, I even find myself practicing how I am going to inform her about Poppy's diagnosis and all the risks involved for the treatments needed for this stage 4 aggressive neuroblastoma. I will need to inform Suzi that Poppy will need a delicate lifestyle, like avoiding contact sports after the bone radiation, and reducing her exposure to infections. Poppy will also require lifelong surveillance for her increased risk of later onset leukaemia, deafness as well as screening to ensure the neuroblastoma remains in remission.

However, *Suzi needs to pick up her bloody phone and return my calls, I think in frustration. I cannot believe I have not heard from her.*

Chapter 15

15 March 2019

Jenny Saunderson

The grass outside Suzi's place has not been mown for months, and the inside of Suzi's house is in chaos. The milk and cheese in her fridge have fungated. Caked food covered in a freckled film of black mould adheres to the dishes on the sink. Poppy has not been here for months, but there are still dirty nappies in Suzi's laundry. The combined effect of the nappies being alive with maggots and the faecal odour we inhale induce us to retch. We breathe through our mouths as we frantically use gloves to place the nappies and maggots into a tied plastic bag to discard into the rubbish bin. With a bug spray in hand, I spray the bin's infestation of maggots before placing it onto the curb, ready for the next collection day.

'You have a look around, love, and see if she's left a note,' suggests Aunty Beth.

Aunty Beth begins washing the kitchen dishes after putting a load of washing on, while I bring Poppy out of her car seat and settle her into her cot, made with clean sheets. I call my lawn service to get Suzi's lawn cut and tidied. Suzi's mail is spilling out of the mailbox onto the ground, with some of the letters dating back to last year. I can't imagine that Suzi would just leave town unless she has developed a mental illness, like severe depression from the sleep deprivation. Maybe she is with someone. Has there been foul play? My anxiety is spiralling out of control.

After we have tidied up, we venture down to the real estate

agency, worried about whether Suzi has been paying her rent. I recall that when Poppy was born, Suzi had put most of the baby bonus on her rent. Now we are informed that Suzi has had two eviction notices and is five months in arrears. Aunty Beth generously pays the agency the $5000 debt incurred, using her credit card. While I am worried desperately about my sister, I am also constrained by the need for Poppy to return to Sydney in two days for her therapeutic radiation treatment to begin.

While my first thought is that I don't have time to move Suzi's house contents over to my place, realistically I know that I cannot afford to fund or maintain both rentals, particularly when Suzi has disappeared. Rationalising the expenses, we organise with the real estate agents and a transport company to move Suzi's belongings tomorrow over to my rental and for professional cleaners to prepare the premises ready for occupancy. 'Delegate or die,' says Aunty Beth. We then purchase fold-up boxes for packing up Suzi's kitchen, furniture and clothes before our return to Sydney.

Finally, we arrive home at my place exhausted, again astonished to find no note from Suzi. With all my fridge food expired as well, Aunty Beth and I shop for enough groceries to last us for the next few days, before bathing and settling Poppy down for the night. Hoping that nothing is urgent, I sit down with a coffee to check my own mail.

'Aunty Beth, do you think we should go to the police?' I question. 'Maybe we should not be packing up her clothes, in case they need to look around.'

'Yes, I see what you mean,' says Aunty Beth. 'The problem is we don't want Family Services getting involved. Whatever has happened, this has to be greater than, say, Suzi potentially losing her phone.'

In the end, we decide that Aunty Beth will report Suzi as missing to the police in the morning, while I stay home to keep Poppy isolated and out of view.

At 8 am, with our busy day planned for coordinating the cleaners and transport drivers, Aunty Beth walks into the Bloomesville Police Station. Sergeant Timothy Baker ushers Aunty Beth into an interview room. Aunty Beth describes to the police the state of Suzi's house and shows them uncollected mail dating back over six months. Aunty Beth is dismayed to learn that, according to the police report, Jamie Johnson is still recorded on all Suzi's hospital records and her driver's licence as her next of kin.

'But Jamie Johnson had packed up and abandoned Suzi years ago,' protests Aunty Beth, keen to sway discussions away from Suzi's pregnancy and Poppy.

Sergeant Baker says, 'I am sorry to tell you that we have been looking for Suzanne Saunderson's next of kin for months. All we learnt was that Jamie Johnson had apparently left town suddenly. Regrettably, Ms Saunderson was involved in a major collision on 21 October after she drove through a red light. The front passenger in the second vehicle reported that Ms Saunderson's head had slumped forward onto the steering wheel immediately prior to the crash, as though she had fallen asleep. Ms Saunderson hit a white Hilux going through the intersection at sixty kilometres per hour. No one was injured in the Hilux. The bull bar took the full impact of the collision when Ms Saunderson swerved into the path of the oncoming vehicle.'

'Oh my God!' exclaims Aunty Beth. 'We have been trying for months to contact Suzi, but she was not answering her phone.'

The sergeant continues reading from the report on his laptop. 'Ms Saunderson was initially confused and combative before losing consciousness at the scene. Ms Saunders required intubation and mechanical ventilation by paramedics for her blunt force head injury, and four fractured ribs, sixth to tenth on the right side. Ms Saunderson was transferred to the nearest trauma centre at Newcastle Hospital, where she has been undergoing protracted rehabilitation.'

Aunty Beth explains to the police officer how Suzi had not slept due to her daughter's painful undiagnosed neuroblastoma, which had left Poppy screaming constantly for many nights. Sergeant Baker updates the police records, putting the details of Aunty Beth and me into their system. Aunty Beth describes to the initially skeptical sergeant how we have both been stranded in Sydney, prioritising the urgent back-to-back chemotherapy treatments for Suzi's very sick child and the support Poppy has required for her serious complications. Aunty Beth elaborates on our many frustrations at not being able to return home to get Suzi by informing the sergeant how difficult it has been to travel safely with Poppy.

The sergeant adds Poppy's details into the system, including the names of the treating hospital and specialists. With Suzi alive and the fear of custody battles eliminated, Aunty Beth clarifies with the sergeant how desperately we have been trying to contact Suzi to notify her of Poppy's critical illness.

'Ms Saunderson's phone was smashed in the accident. Her car was a total write-off as well,' reports Sergeant Baker.

Aunty Beth drives home, stunned about what she has learned. I am overwhelmed with guilt. My poor sister Suzi has gone through her critical injury recovery alone because of my unsubstantiated fear of losing Poppy to social workers and Family Services.

 We arrive in the rehabilitation ward to see Suzi dressed in a purple nightie, sitting beside her bed in a recliner, with a short, cream, cotton blanket draped over her legs.

Poppy, who instantly recognises her mother, races over to give her a hug.

Chapter 16

March 2019

Jenny Saunderson

With hollowed cheeks and eye sockets, Suzi looks extremely thin and weak, well below her usual fifty-seven kilograms. Suzi is receiving nutrition through a feeding tube in her abdomen. I burst into tears, unable to decide in the turmoil whether Suzi was unlucky that this happened or so blessed to have survived.

From the nursing staff, we learn that Suzi has sustained facial fractures to the middle part of her face, affecting her maxilla and nasal bones. In addition to being mechanically ventilated through a tracheostomy, Suzi had required facial surgery for the insertion of intermaxillary fixation bars and screws. We are informed that drugs were initially prescribed to stop Suzi vomiting while her jaw was wired for a month, impairing her ability to communicate. Now Suzi has progressed to recently being commenced on a soft diet, under the supervision of a speech therapist. Suzi has begun sitting out of bed daily and mobilising with the physiotherapist. We are notified that Suzi will require a minimum of two years of brain injury protocol rehabilitation with a specialised team of doctors, nurses, physiotherapists, occupational therapists, dieticians, social workers, speech therapists and pharmacists.

Suzi looks up towards us with sad, blue eyes when we call her name. A tear spills down her cheek at the sight of us all.

'Oh, Suzi,' I gush, 'we have been trying and trying to ring you every day. We've only just found out that you were in an accident.

The police had Jamie down as your next of kin.'

Shaken at the site of Suzi, Aunty Beth clarifies. 'We are so sorry, Suzi. We have been looking after Poppy. You were so right: Poppy was very sick – she was crying all the time from severe pain. Poppy needed a lot of specialised care in Sydney. Otherwise, we would have been back much sooner, darling girl.'

Suzi looks at Poppy, frowning at her loss of hair and the small feeding tube in her daughter's nose. I give my sister another hug with tears streaming down my face. Aunty Beth follows too, kissing Suzi on the cheek and gently brushing the stringy deconditioned hair off her face with arthritic fingers.

Poppy, looking up at us all, wraps her arms around to cuddle her mother's knees before placing her face in Suzi's hands, which are both rested, palms up, in her lap. Pointing to the feeding bag, Poppy says, 'Look,' recognising her mother is being tube-fed also. Since Suzi is paying attention, we apologise that our first trip needs to be brief, assuring her that we will be back with Poppy to spend more time with her, after we relocate her belongings into my unit. With Suzi still struggling to talk, feed and walk, she will not be capable of independent living anytime soon. Poppy, now holding both her mother's hands, is reluctant to leave. We gently persuade Poppy that we are leaving now for the doctor to see her mummy so that we can have more time with her when we return. As we lift Poppy up to cuddle her mother's shoulders, she stretches her hand out towards her mother's face. Suzi automatically leans forward, pretending to nibble on her toddler's plump fingers, playing a weaker version of their usual game.

We leave Suzi at the hospital at 10 am to race back to Suzi's place to let the cleaners in before the transport couriers arrive at 11 am. With the cleaners kindly offering to box up Suzi's kitchen and laundry items, Aunty Beth and I are able to focus on packing the clothes and toiletries needed for Suzi and Poppy. After following the transport drivers back to my house to store Suzi's gear, we are able to bath Poppy and return to Suzi, leaving the cleaners to finish cleaning and returning all the keys to the real estate agents.

Although Suzi was looking at us all with recognition, her poor communication skills leave us uncertain about how much Suzi can comprehend. Aunty Beth and I have organised to return to the hospital at 4 pm to talk to Suzi's doctors, to ensure it is safe for Suzi to be informed about Poppy's diagnosis and treatments. After updating us on Suzi's condition, Suzi's treating specialist, Dr Patrick Sweeney, agrees to facilitate Suzi's transfer to Sydney when a single room is available, so that she can be reunited long-term with Poppy while both continue their therapies. Dr Patrick highlights the need for Suzi's two-year rehabilitation program, as she has currently only progressed from the initial phase of controlling pain and managing the swelling associated with the head injury and facial fractures.

According to Dr Patrick, Suzi still needs to improve many basic functions, like her flexibility, muscle strength and balance. Dr Patrick states that following a head injury, Suzi's brain will take time to develop proprioception, which is how the brain locates body parts like muscles and joints to coordinate movement. While Dr Patrick anticipates that Suzi will gradually return to full activity, he considers that developing independence with daily activities like eating, dressing, mobilising and hygiene will take time. Dr Patrick mentions that Suzi will eventually be able to transition to a day care centre for six hours of daily rehabilitation as an outpatient in Sydney. I jot down 'photo albums' on my list of items to pack for Sydney, after Dr Patrick highlights the usefulness of pictures in advancing memory recall.

Aunty Beth and I question Dr Patrick on the feasibility of Suzi rehabilitating in the same hospital as Poppy in Sydney so that we can support them both. With Poppy being immunocompromised, we are glad to hear that Suzi has already been immunised for influenza. We are also relieved that Dr Patrick supports our need to transfer Suzi into a single rehabilitation room at the same Sydney hospital so that Poppy can visit frequently with less exposure to infections. It is terrific to see Suzi expressing emotion and feebly reaching out to connect with Poppy.

Poppy's face lights up again at the sight of Suzi, as she automatically runs to greet her mother with another knee hug. Poppy begins playing with the oxygen monitoring finger probe on her mother's fingers emitting a red light, recognising the device from her own surgical and PICU care. While Poppy is playing with her mother's hands, Suzi's grasping movements are notably constrained by weakness. Suzi partly smiles, in the form of a grimace, at the tiny, pale pink bunny slippers on Poppy's feet, as the cute little ears protruding from them flap up and down with walking. As Suzi contentedly watches her daughter's every move, her vivid blue eyes keep returning to Poppy's head with a puzzled expression, undoubtedly wondering what has happened to her hair.

In Dr Patrick's presence, I inform Suzi that I had taken Poppy to Sydney, where the stage 4 neuroblastoma was diagnosed. I reassure Suzi that we have been trying to contact her throughout Poppy's gruelling treatment plan, unaware that she was in hospital and that her phone was irreparably damaged. I tell Suzi that when I had reported her missing to the police, the call had ended abruptly when my battery faded. With Poppy in such dire circumstances, I had been hesitant to ring the police back again, fearing that Family Services or social workers could separate us from Poppy. I apologise to Suzi for having no idea that she had been involved in a car accident, reassuring her that all our time had been spent keeping Poppy safe. We update Suzi that, to our knowledge, most of the aggressive cancer has been surgically removed or chemically rendered innocuous with the chemotherapy.

Tears spill over Suzi's eyelids, trickling down her cheeks, indicating that she appears to comprehend the seriousness of Poppy's condition.

Aunty Beth and I apologise profusely for not returning home sooner. We describe how Poppy's numerous infections and need for transfusions of red cells and platelets have kept us both busy supporting her complex, unpredictable recovery, marred by many complications. Suzi seems to understand the logistical difficulties we have encountered attempting to travel with Poppy, given her susceptibility to the nausea from chemotherapy and the bone pain aggravated by sitting stationery in the toddler seat. Aunty Beth and I sensitively elaborate on the various predicaments we faced and risks encountered that prevented us from travelling with Poppy from Sydney after her surgery, like the unpredictable central line fracture occurring, the unplanned PICU admission and the extended bone marrow transplant isolation period.

Since we had bathed Poppy at 3.30 pm, we are able to stay at the hospital longer. Poppy is already dressed in her favourite long-sleeved pyjamas and tiny pink dressing gown, with an attached hoodie to shield her from the cool evening temperature. Excited to see her mother again, Poppy slides the draw sheet off her mother's lap, placing it over her head to play 'ghosts'. Poppy is swirling around with her arms elevated, manoeuvering up and down the clean draw sheet. Suzi's face smirks with an attempted smile at her playful daughter's antics, as Poppy squeals in delight each time Aunty Beth or I lift up the hem of the sheet.

'You were so right about that huge lump below Poppy's ribs, Suzi,' I reassure her. 'It wasn't constipation. I decided to go to Aunty Beth's after you said that you had given Poppy pain relief and it wasn't working. At the time, I did not ring you because you had left to go sleeping.'

Suzi nods as though remembering.

'I had also tried to get medical help again here but got the same fob offs that you did. I drove to Sydney to get help when Poppy was not taking her bottle and her urine was getting darker. I initially planned to come back the same day, but Poppy was hospitalised immediately. With the aggressive neuroblastoma being diagnosed at stage 4, it was safer not to delay Poppy's treatment. However, we did not imagine that we would not be able to contract you. We initially thought you were catching up on your lost sleep. I am so sorry, Suzi. I was trying to ring you every day, and of course none of my calls were answered. Friends even went to your house looking for you. No one knew where you were.'

Aunty Beth interrupts. 'We were worried that you might have been depressed, and that if we involved the police and social workers, they could take custody of Poppy. We were concerned about reigniting the previous conflicts with those health services that were engaged without your permission … all just paranoia, I suppose.'

'Thank God your instincts were right,' I reassure Suzi.

While I was suspicious about the reasons for Poppy being constantly unsettled, Suzi had instinctively known that something was wrong but had been powerless to get the appropriate help.

'We tried all the time to ring you, Suzi,' Aunty Beth reassures her, combing Suzi's light brown, oily fringe back with her stiff fingers.

The physiotherapist arrives to put Suzi back to bed. With fresh linen on the bed, Suzi is seated upright, with the head of the bed elevated to thirty degrees, to prevent aspiration of her saliva. We place Poppy on the bed with her to snuggle in for a nap. Suzi begins grunting and making grossly uncoordinated shoulder movements. Suspecting Suzi is keen to cuddle Poppy, I gently place Suzi's arm along Poppy's back to prevent it getting caught up in her feeding tube.

Aunty Beth and I sit there for three hours, watching the mother and daughter sleep together. We chat softly and get coffees from the machine, before reassuring Suzi that, now that visiting hours are over, we will return tomorrow.

Chapter 17

24 March 2019

Jenny Saunderson

On the way home, with Poppy buckled in her car seat asleep, Aunty Beth and I work out a plan for Sunday. After doing another weekly shop, Aunty Beth will remain with Suzi until she is transferred to the Sydney Hospital, before returning by bus herself.

After a final visit with Suzi, Poppy and I drive back to Sydney by car to get Poppy ready for her therapeutic radiation. Therapeutic radiation treatment delivers high energy X-rays to destroy the cancer cells that have metastasised to Poppy's pelvic bones. Even though we have been routinely warned about the risks of radiation exposure from these X-rays posing a risk of cancer later in life, it is not really as if you have a choice about which therapies you can accept. At this stage, the main goal has to be to kill the immediate known threat of the neuroblastoma, to ensure Poppy will have a future, rather than worrying about potential hazards that may occur later on. Hopefully, with more funding and progressive medical technological advances, if any of these potential conditions like leukaemia do occur, there will be safer remedies available.

Poppy requires daily anaesthetics for five days in a row for over two weeks, after which she is wheeled back to her room, positioned in bed on her side in the recovery position to sleep. Until fully awake, Poppy remains attached to transport cardiac monitoring devices, equipped with a finger probe to measure her oxygen saturation levels. Poppy's skin is becoming dry and cracked and is peeling more from the radiation therapy, even though I have been generously applying hydrating moisturisers at least three times a day as instructed. Once again, each professional emphasises how important skin integrity is as a defence to stop bacterial organisms invading the body. The nurses also reinforce that, following the chemotherapy and radiation, Poppy's immune system suppression will persist for months.

As predicted, Poppy is noticeably fatigued after these treatments. Since even simple daily activities like having a bath leave her exhausted, we try to stagger tests and procedures with two-hour intervals dedicated for rest in between them. During Poppy's hospitalisation, I call Aunty Beth on webcam while she is visiting Suzi, so that Poppy can see her mother is going okay. Although very impatient to be reunited, Poppy hopefully understands that her mummy will soon be coming to Sydney to join us. I reassure Poppy that when Mummy arrives in Sydney, we will visit her almost every day, around both their care activities. Poppy claps excitedly when Suzi looks at the camera. Poppy blows Suzi bubbles with her bubble maker, reminding her mummy that she is a 'big girl' now, mimicking the congratulatory tone we used every time potty training was productive.

Suzi looks into the phone webcam, giving the best half-smile she can manage, saying 'Bubby' to Poppy. Suzi purses her lips to blow kisses. Poppy's arms instantly rise for a pick-up, but since Suzi cannot do this at her end, I place her in my lap so they are able to continue their Face Time. Aunty Beth updates us that Suzi's transfer has finally been booked for her aeromedical retrieval to Sydney tomorrow at 10.30 am, after a delay was encountered waiting for the availability of a single room. Suzi's physiotherapists, occupational therapists, dieticians, nursing and medical professionals have written their handovers to allow a smooth transition of care.

We end the call with the knowledge that Suzi's transfer is on track, provided there are no last-minute, unplanned incidences needing the retrieval team for emergency evacuation. Aunty Beth plans to travel to Sydney the same day, so that I can pick her up from Wynyard station at 3 pm.

Chapter 18

1 April 2019

Jenny Saunderson

Poppy and I wait in the visitor's lounge in the rehabilitation ward, enthusiastic for Suzi's impending arrival. Our attention is drawn to every lift bell until Suzi appears, strapped to a gurney with a doctor, ambulance and paramedic escort carrying medical supplies, oxygen cylinders and equipment. It takes a further thirty minutes for the medical handovers to be finalised after Suzi is transferred onto a ward bed in a single room. When Poppy's arms raise enthusiastically, Suzi's male nurse nods, permitting me to lift Poppy into her mother's arms, where both promptly doze off until it is time for me to greet Aunty Beth at the Wynyard bus terminal. Poppy, after initially protesting about their separation, gives Suzi a large hug after being reassured we will be coming back after her overnight sleep. Poppy points her little finger at her mother, telling her she has to 'seep more'.

Suzi displays a lopsided smile as Poppy waves, blowing kisses, telling her mum she will be 'back moro'. We leave the rehabilitation team to finalise Suzi's admission skin assessment. The next morning, Suzi's new rehabilitation doctor instructs Aunty Beth and me to engage her in conversations that will help reignite happy memories. We place a framed photo of Poppy at her bedside and work through my phone gallery and a few albums to help Suzi integrate information from her past, like where she went to school, the names of close friends and funny events. At the mention of funny events, Aunty Beth smiles, showing Suzi a barbecue picture of our parents.

'Suzi, do you remember Carol, your mum, telling you about how your dad, Wayne, nearly threw out a tray of expensive steaks when they first met?'

Aunty Beth laughs.

Suzi shakes her head weakly but is stimulated and paying attention.'Well,' Aunty Beth continues, 'your dad had grown up on a large cattle property where they had butchered their own cattle humanely for meat. The problem was that he had never bought steaks from a supermarket. Wayne was manning the barbecue grill, when suddenly he swore and dropped the steak he had been lifting out of the meat tray with the tongs. His beetroot red face was a picture of utter disgust. When Carol went racing over, Wayne showed her the blood-soaked pads that some 'dirty bastard has put under the steaks'. Your dad mistook the blood absorbers for the feminine hygiene products he had bought for his sister after she'd had her baby. Carol was clutching the expensive steaks tightly, laughing so much she could hardly talk, while the furious Wayne was trying to throw them out. It was hilarious.'

'Oh no,' Suzi exclaimed, grinning. Suzi's appropriate responses and semi-smile indicate that while her memories were not yet organised, her comprehension was still intact.

Suzi's communication is enhanced by her expanding vocabulary that demonstrates her ability to comprehend as well as enunciate clearly. We are entertained to discover that this language capability even extends to audible swear words when Suzi's feeding tube gets caught up on the button of her nightie. Every day, Suzi is becoming more vocal, with her attempts at communication motivated by her increased contact with Poppy.

Suzi is holding Poppy's hands as they watch puppy and kitten videos. Poppy sits to the left side of Suzi's lap, away from her feeding stoma, with the recliner tipped slightly backwards to reduce her risk of falls. Aunty Beth and I sit on either side facing Suzi. Later, when Suzi returns to bed with assistance, they both have an evening nap together, if time allows, before Poppy returns to the children's ward.

In the Sydney Hospital, with familiar faces visiting daily, Suzi's strength and mobility progress daily. Suzi is walking further with the physiotherapist, Tim, who guides her posture and progress using a rollator. As Tim assists Suzi to mobilise, using the arm brackets and wheels of the rollator, Suzi's balance and ability to stand and transfer from her recliner to her bed becomes more fluid.

Every day, Suzi's eyes widen with pleasure and her mood elevates as Poppy enters her room. Suzi tracks her daughter as she plays, engaging in short conversations. The intrepid Poppy amuses herself with her little fairy houses, picnic tables and chairs. The fairy houses have roofs that looks like a flower with its petals open, tipped upside down with the stem forming a green chimney. The houses are lined with dark brown bark-like walls, with matching picnic table and chairs. Poppy has placed fairies on the tiny, pale yellow seats that look like timber logs cut across on the horizontal axis. Poppy's tiny legs fold under her in typical toddler fashion as she reaches over with her dainty little hands to move her fairies. When Simon pops into Suzi's room to say hello, he encourages Suzi to participate in Poppy's games with tasks that boost her coordination. After Poppy moves her fairies onto picnic seats, Simon tells Suzi that she needs to move the fairies as they are cold and need to be closer to their campfire, mailbox, bridge and fence. After three attempts, when Suzi's mission is accomplished, Poppy claps her hands excitedly, giggling with glee as Suzi looks up with a triumphant glance.

'I had always assumed that Poppy was your daughter,' comments Simon, looking at me.

'No, I was just written down as next of kin. Suzi was involved in a motor vehicle accident that we did not know about at the time. Suzi's phone was crushed and we could not contact her. We were persistently trying to ring Suzi, with us both stuck in Sydney.

None of our friends in Bloomesville could find Suzi either.'

'So is that why you were so distraught outside the PICU that day? Suzi's daughter was sick, and you could not tell her,' Simon says, raising his eyebrows.

'Yes, I was freaked out about everything. Poppy's diagnosis, not knowing where Suzi was ... Suzi did not even know that I had brought Poppy to Sydney. I had planned to drive home to get Suzi, but Poppy kept getting complications between her scheduled treatments. I did not mention Suzi was Poppy's mother because I was concerned about social workers and custody battles. Everything was catastrophising in my head because I'd had so little sleep,' I clarify. 'I was freaking out because I did not know where Suzi was. Poppy and Suzi were really close, and I wanted to tell Suzi Poppy's diagnosis in person rather than over the phone. When Poppy was admitted to ICU in a critical condition, Suzi did not know how sick Poppy was. So, my stress levels were extreme, creating havoc with my sleep. I couldn't relax and didn't know what to do.'

'I was apprehensive that you were on the verge of nervous exhaustion, that you were shutting off when I saw you,' Simon admits.

I look up to see Aunty Beth and Suzi both keenly observing the electric chemistry developing between Simon and me. Simon's warm chocolate eyes and magnetic smile radiate over his entire face. *He's intelligent, funny and cute, I think to myself.* I reach into my handbag to gift Simon one of the new calendars that we have had printed as a fundraiser for Poppy's new cancer relapse prevention drugs therapies.

We designed the calendars using photos of baby puppies and animals with inspiring thoughts as an initiative to fundraise the $20,000 a month that will be needed within the next six to nine months for Poppy's cancer relapse prevention treatment. Since Simon has been like a rock of support to me during this nightmare, I bought him a calendar to show my appreciation.

One of the blessings we've all experienced during our helplessness is that there are so many kind people in our sphere. From kind words to thoughtful deeds, every positive interaction seemed to energise us when we felt overpowered by emotions about Poppy's uncertain future. We wonder how we can ever thank so many amazing, compassionate people going out of their way to help the five vulnerable children in Australia presently needing these lifesaving medications to be accessible.

Chapter 19

Jenny Saunderson

For her third birthday, Poppy enjoys a chocolate layered cake covered in fairy sprinkles with three candles. After inflating the party balloons, Poppy, Aunty Beth, Suzi, Simon and I wear shiny party hats and are blowing whistles. We drink orange cordial from Poppy's tiny teacups and eat pink and white marshmallows off the tiny saucers to prevent traumatising Poppy's mucositis and to comply with Suzi's soft diet. Aunty Beth, Simon and I help Poppy unwrap her cartoon sticker books and presents. With her daughter distracted unwrapping other presents, we slip Suzi the favourite mermaid-themed outfits, handbag and a decorative soft towel she has requested for Poppy. Aunty Beth has bought Bluey pajamas the next size up from what she is currently wearing and a pink fluffy dinosaur with white protruding corrugations along its back.

Simon gives Poppy a fluffy rainbow-coloured unicorn accessorised with a matching, glittery unicorn toiletry bag. I have bought Poppy some larger sandals with soles that flash brightly with heart-shaped lights. During a brief visit to the park on our way home, I hold Poppy's hands while, in her little jade dress and flashing sandals, she negotiates her way along the aligned raised stumps that form a path.

I am seeing more of Simon that usual at the moment, as his ward rotations have shifted again. While I am conscious not to compromise Simon's professional integrity, my heart skips a beat watching him mobilise his tiny post-surgery patients in the shared corridors between the paediatric, oncology and the surgical wards. It is always a delightful surprise when I run into Simon, even though with Aunty Beth supporting Suzi and Poppy, I can no longer hang out with him for afternoon tea at the canteen. Rather than absorbing all the gloomy news as I had been, I find myself attracted to his cheerful greetings and warm personality.

Logistically, I am currently sharing a room at Aunty Beth's with Poppy's cot, to supervise her closely. This proximity allows me to change Poppy's nappies or provide topical or oral analgesia at night. Therefore, Aunty Beth has suggested that when Suzi is discharged from hospital for day rehabilitation, she should initially sleep on the other side of her king size bed, so that Suzi can also receive overnight support until she becomes more independent. Although Aunty Beth has invited us all to live with her in Sydney to access Suzi's and Poppy's long-term rehabilitation and oncology care, at the moment we are delaying this permanent relocation until our workloads lighten. Although Aunty Beth owns a very spacious, low-set, four- bedroom brick home in the beautiful tree-lined suburb of Lane Cove, we are currently too busy supporting Suzi and Poppy during their daily therapies to consider any additional workloads.

Finally, we get the relief of a weekend break from the children's ward visits before more cancer staging tests the following week. We all enjoy the slower pace of just hanging out with Suzi in her room before Poppy's immune modulation therapies begin. Poppy has a sheet over her head and is playing ghosts as Suzi tries to lift the sheet up from the back, so as not to accidently dislodge Poppy's feeding tube. When Suzi attempts to tickle her instead, Poppy erupts into laughter. We all look up to find Simon grinning in the doorway, amused by their jovial play.

'Come in,' I welcome Simon enthusiastically.

'I'm on call this weekend,' announces Simon. 'Well, don't these girls look brighter today!' Simon's hands splay apart towards both Suzi and Poppy. 'I wonder who will get to go home first,' he challenges.

'When they do get home, I hope you will visit us,' invites Aunty Beth, offering Simon her address. As Simon dutifully enters the data onto his phone, she adds, 'We are going to have a teddy bear's picnic when Mummy comes home, aren't we, Poppy?'

'Fairies and you come too,' says Poppy, pointing to Simon and each of us individually.

When Poppy is not booked in for treatments, a new challenge is set for Suzi each day before they settle down for an afternoon nap and cuddle together. Sometimes Suzi helps Poppy blow bubbles, press buttons on the toddler tablet or read short stories to Poppy, as both motivate the other's recovery.

One day, Aunty Beth is sitting waiting for the girls to wake up while I just pop out to drive down to the bank. I have just driven into the hospital grounds when I get caught in a sudden torrential downpour getting from the car park to the main building. Simon appears out of nowhere with an umbrella.

'I was just about to go home, when I saw you getting drenched,' he explains, appearing like a knight in shining armour coming to my rescue.

Simon flushes with embarrassment when I catch him staring at my drenched, white blouse now rendered practically see-through from the rain. When Simon apologises instantly, I ambitiously hope that he is developing the attraction that I am feeling, too. Simon puts his arm around my shoulders as I begin shaking with the cold.

'Oh, so you're not really sorry,' I say, beginning to flirt.

'Sorry for being caught then, maybe,' Simon jokes in a low sensuous voice as he removes his jacket to help me warm up.

'Oh well, that's different,' I banter.

I can tell by his caring mannerisms that his attention has become more passionate than a friendship. I am also surprised to find myself constantly looking around for the slim handsome physio whenever I enter the hospital.

'I would like to take you out for a meal one night,' Simon suggests. When I hesitate in answering, he adds, 'but I have seen how impossible that would be for you at the moment. Perhaps I could bring around a meal for everyone one night when you are all home'.

'That would be lovely,' I smile.

I give Simon a hug before relaxing longer into his warm embrace. I savour the closeness, acutely aware that my body is enjoying his proximity.

'I make an awesome lasagne. It would be soft enough for both Suzi and Poppy,' he boasts, smiling, as I admire his clean-shaven face and chiselled features.

'Deal. I'm not sure when, but we would all love that.'

I look up at Simon as he bends his head to capture my lips with a kiss. I hold Simon closer, possessively feeling the strength and power of his toned back muscles, with my face buried in his lean, muscular chest, before I reluctantly part.

'Ah … you've had your latte today,' I joke, recognising the pleasant taste of his recent coffee.

'You would have been invited, but you were not in sight,' Simon grins. 'I think you're an amazing person, Jenny Saunderson,' Simon whispers sincerely, maintaining eye contact.

I hug him again, my fingers tangling in his curly hair. My insides melt as contentment floods my body.

'Well, how do I respond to a compliment like that?' I ask, smiling.

I move my arms up and down his muscly back, hearing his breath catch.

'I would just like permission to use that address your Aunty gave me to see you,' Simon says.

'I would love that,' I reply with a grin, embracing Simon's warm chest in another comforting hug. Simon holds my hand as he returns to Suzi's room with me.

Simon then insists on driving Aunty Beth home and picking

her up again in the morning on his way to work, so that she is not driving in this extreme weather.

'You're such a dear,' I say, not wanting to let go of his hand. 'You are so thoughtful.'

I reluctantly relinquish his hand for them to leave. While Aunty Beth gives Suzi a farewell hug, I embrace Simon again before he leaves, feeling my attraction towards this kind-hearted man growing exponentially.

'You are so lucky to have such a wonderful family,' Simon comments. 'I really like them all.'

After Simon and I exchange phone numbers, I watch Suzi and Poppy sleep in Suzi's hospital bed with the bed rails raised. Poppy wakes up and begins running her hands over her mother's face, walking her fingers into her mother's lips. Suzi makes a sudden growling noise, accompanied by a lip-smacking noise that startles but entertains Poppy.

Watching Suzi and Poppy assuming their near normal relaxed play, I am so pleased they are finally reunited again. With Suzi awake and alert, Dr Seth visits to update her that Poppy's medical imaging results still show no detectable cancer.

Chapter 20

Simon Collins

am finding myself intrigued by Jenny Saunderson. After initially discovering her weeping outside the PICU, my first thought was to remove her from the sounds of the alarms and the sterile hospital environment. Then I found myself subconsciously preoccupied by the way Jenny's smile lighted up her cute face and expressive brown eyes, and the sway of her hips in her denim jeans. Professionally and ethically, when I thought that Jenny was Poppy's mother, I stayed at a distance, since I cannot have a relationship with someone in such a vulnerable predicament. I began feeling confused, even in a quandary, when I began looking forward to seeing Jenny during my daily hospital rounds.

In trying to calm that distressed lady, I was initially amazed by her medical knowledge and her astute observation skills, totally unaware she was a nurse. Then I was astonished at how supportive Jenny was of her sister, aunty and niece when I belatedly discovered that Poppy was not Jenny's child. Learning that Poppy is Suzi's daughter made sense.

After Suzi's transfer, Jenny appeared more relieved, although time pressured. Initially, I baulked, feeling rejected, when Jenny told me she was unable to meet for coffee. Moments later, confused that Jenny dashed off promising to catch up, I worried that Poppy had deteriorated. I realise that Jenny's exhaustive efforts are orientated towards keeping Suzi and Poppy safely bonded. I cannot help but admire Jenny's remarkable commitment as she rushes from prioritising Poppy's treatment schedules to uniting them daily for evening naps. Only when I finally saw Suzi and Poppy cuddled together did I understand why Jenny was no longer able to meet me at the canteen for afternoon coffees. It is beautiful watching the fragile Suzi and Poppy harmoniously cuddled together under the protective supervision of Jenny and her Aunty Beth. As all four members of this intriguing family present a united front, it is a pleasure to watch and integrate in their therapeutic dynamics.

Ironically, as they navigate many hurdles, more unsurmountable challenges continually arrive. The prospect of raising $20,000 a month for cancer relapse prevention drugs at the end of Poppy's gruelling treatment regimen is not something any family should have to prepare for. Almost undaunted, they do their best to achieve this unrealistic financial goal, recognising that securing Poppy's safety is the only option to be considered.

I figure the least I can do is find ways to help with cooking and fundraising. Whether it is organising the online bidding of donations, petitioning politicians, fundraising to sell calendars or preparing them some nutritious meals, hoping they might be soft enough, and not too spicy, for both Poppy and Suzi, I try to ease Jenny's responsibilities to stop her getting burnt out.

*

I knock on Suzi's door, finding them all huddled together over Jenny's laptop.

'Hi, Simon,' greets Jenny. 'I had a fantastic idea to help Suzi's memories. I am just getting Suzi into her Facebook page so that she can see what her friends have been up to since her accident.'

After a few more keystrokes, Jenny is into Suzi's page, reading out messages from friends who are missing her.

'Do you remember Ted?' Jenny asks Suzi. Suzi nods and smiles. 'Do you remember what a prankster he is?'

Suzi grins, looking over at Aunty Beth, who is leaning forward enthusiastically reading and chuckling.

Jenny giggles, unable to keep reading. Beth is chuckling too. Jenny tries again.

'Ted, Angela's husband, came off night shift. He says he heard the crunching of Angie's car on the driveway, then groceries being unloaded at the door before the key was inserted. Well, apparently, Ted was feeling frisky, so he stripped off his pyjama shorts and draped himself naked over the kitchen table with a rose between his teeth and a proud erection on display. Then he hears someone shout, "Ted, what the hell do you think you're doing!" Ted looks up to see his horrified mother-in-law! Ted is the only person we know who could get himself in the predicaments he does.'

Looking up at me, Jenny elaborates. 'In the past, Ted has been known to have a few too many drinks at the club with the boys. Last time, he gatecrashed the wedding party at the venue across the road from the club, getting some more free drinks on his way home. He ended up being escorted off the premises by security. Do you remember, Suzi?' questions Jenny, still amused.

Suzi nods, and Jenny laughs musically as though she hasn't a care in the world. Jenny then scrolls through the pictures to show Aunty Beth and me a picture of Angie and her stocky husband, Ted, dressed in a large, yellow, feathered chicken suit.

Chapter 20

Jenny Saunderson

Poppy is readmitted for her next six months of immunotherapy cycles that weaponises her own immune system to recognise and destroy cancer cells. Immunotherapy uses laboratory-made antibodies that are injected into Poppy's blood to attach to very specific cancer cells in the body. The immunotherapy agents achieve this by recognising that neuroblastoma cells have a large amount of a surface substance called GD2. The antibodies attracted to these GD2 surface substances use this cancer detection capability to identify and destroy cancer cells. Once again, we are alerted to the many potential side effects, which range from severe nerve pain to a loss of blood vessel wall integrity capable of producing swelling, shortness of breath, low blood pressure, allergic reactions, eye and vision problems, gastrointestinal symptoms, itching or low white cell counts. Most days, I stay with Poppy for her treatments as Aunty Beth supports Suzi.

One month later, with Aunty Beth's kind offer of permanent accommodation and Suzi's consent, we relocate to Sydney. Poppy, Aunty Beth and I travel back to Bloomesville for a weekend to pack up all Suzi and my belongings for the transport truck to courier back to Aunty Beth's house. The removal company has stacked the boxes and furniture temporarily in Aunty Beth's garage. We inform Suzi that if we both leave on Friday, Aunty Beth and I can both be back Monday for Poppy's next treatments and that when Suzi arrives at Aunty Beth's on her day rehabilitation program, we can spend more time with her. Simon, who is on call again over the weekend, has offered to check daily on Suzi during his rounds. This mutual long-term decision helps everyone, as Suzi and Poppy can readily access their consultants, health resources and their specialised needs, and Aunty Beth won't be getting older on her own.

During our four-hour journey home, Aunty Beth shocks me. After gently introducing Simon into our conversation, Aunty Beth furtively gives permission for Simon to stay overnight, if I wish.

'You deserve to have a social life, too, Jenny,' Aunty Beth says, as a blush heats up my face and neck at the unexpected personal detour our conversation has taken.

'Thank you, Aunty Beth. Simon and I are still just getting acquainted, at this stage … but I certainly am fond of him.'

'I just don't want you to miss out on a catch like Simon because you are focused on Suzi and Poppy's wellbeing,' Aunty Beth clarifies.

'Simon has been so supportive. He has this mature inner strength that just seems to ground me.'

'It's his hairy legs that fascinate Poppy. She loves raking her tiny, plump fingers through that coarse hair,' Aunty Beth laughs.

'Yes, there's that, too,' I admit, smiling coyly. 'An added bonus. Poppy was quite mesmerised by Simon's hairy legs, wasn't she?' I chuckle.

'And his "noodle" head hair,' smirks Aunty Beth.

'Honestly, Aunty Beth, I don't know how I would have coped without all the support you have given us. You have always been amazing. I am so grateful for all your assistance. I am sure I would have totally unravelled without you.'

'You're most welcome, my dear,' Aunty Beth says, her soft hands squeezing mine.

'All of us moving in must seem like a friendly home invasion,' I say, jokingly.

'No, it feels like I got a wonderful family to care for,' my optimistic Aunty replies.

'Well, you should know that you are truly loved and appreciated,' I emphasise.

'Don't worry if it gets a bit chaotic until Suzi is more independent. We will muddle through,' the determined Aunty Beth responds.

'I hope I can always take everything in my stride like you do,' I say, thinking how much she truly inspires me to calmly plod along every day.

'I just break every big task down into baby steps, and take one step at a time, every day. That is all any of us can do in unpredictable situations, to make progress. Otherwise, sometimes, like with all those treatments, the big picture can be overpowering.'

'Well, let me say, you have always been a blessing.'

Life gets easier with us all living in Sydney, with Aunty Beth's ongoing love, support and humour. After not doing any paid work for over nine months, I formerly resign from my employment. I electively keep my nursing registration current until Suzi's rehabilitation is finalised. After my superannuation income protection expired, I am temporarily receiving a carer's pension to facilitate the recovery of both Suzi and Poppy.

Aunty Beth invites Simon over for Suzi's coming home party. I feel my face and neck heat up again when Aunty Beth reminds me that Simon is welcome to stay in the room that Poppy and I share when we are ready to take our relationship to the next level. Aunty Beth, ever the practical thinker, knows that is probably the only way we can currently make any relationship work.

*

For Halloween, the glass windows that permit a view of the paediatric oncology corridors are decorated with coloured paper witches, orange pumpkins and large, low-hanging, black spiders anchored from the ceilings. Poppy erupts in giggles, spontaneously reaching up to catch and swing the spiders. The nurses' station is decorated in a realistic looking spider's web that engages the ill children in play and fantasy, away from their symptoms.

The day Suzi is discharged for day therapies, Poppy paints a huge rainbow, using erasable paints, over the window that looks out onto Aunty Beth's garden. Aunty Beth and I are not allowed to flush Poppy's last poo in her potty as she insists on showing her Mummy her 'big girl' achievement. How can we deny such a simple request from those melting blue eyes? So, Poppy's end product sits in the loo covered by a large paper bag until Suzi arrives. Poppy is wearing a long-sleeved T-shirt featuring a light pink teddy bear, pale pink shorts, soft woollen sock slippers and a pink beanie with teddy bear ears.

All the fairy cottages, picnic settings and mushrooms are arranged on synthetic grass, with green mossy shrubs separating the various fairy families. Poppy has all her teddy bears scattered around the tinted glass-enclosed patio and on the coffee table in celebration. Poppy waits in the garden for Mummy to arrive, after insisting on an early bath to have more playtime. Poppy watches eagerly for Suzi's arrival after setting up her tea party set in the fridge. The tiny saucers contain quarter slices of fairy bread and the little cups are filled with cheese cubes. Simon arrives, carrying a home-baked lasagne made with spinach, grated carrots and zucchini. After dinner, Poppy hops on her padded bunny rabbit rocker, holding the rabbit ears to impress her Mummy with her elevated big girl status.

After a brief afternoon tea, both Suzi and Poppy snuggle in Aunty Beth's bed with pillow borders, totally exhausted. Over the coming months, Simon has not only lightened our workloads, but he has become such a vital part of our emerging family. Simon's persistent support during Suzi's recovery has been accelerating her rehabilitation progress. We are also appreciating Simon's brilliant culinary skills, which range from tantalising seafood pizzas to tacos loaded with grated veggies.

*

Aunty Beth, Poppy, Suzi, Simon and I are decorating the solarium to welcome in our first Sydney Christmas together. Poppy, dressed in her red and green Christmas tree jumpsuit, has been lifted up to place a giant gold star and angel on the branches at the top of the ornamental tree, which is decorated with tinsel, baubles, snowflakes and fairy lights. Aunty Beth, wearing her reindeer T-shirt and Santa hat, is singing 'Jingle Bells' with Poppy. Suzi, Simon and I are wearing Christmas T-shirts decorated with angels, holly and images of presents. Poppy dances with Suzi and Aunty Beth, trying to catch the party balloons balls that Simon periodically bats towards them. Suzi is coordinating her arm movements well enough to catch most of the balloons.

Simon and I have bought Suzi a new mobile phone for Christmas, now that her fine motor skills have improved. We have also purchased two gift vouchers for Aunty Beth and Suzi to go to the hairdresser's salon during Suzi's short holiday break from rehabilitation. I've bought Simon a rock-climbing adventure that I am hoping we can watch and video as a novelty experience.

In a private moment in our shared bedroom, Simon gifts me a small, adorned, red and gold box tied with gold ribbons. As I unwrap the present, I discover the most beautiful eighteen-carat gold ring with a parti sapphire in a claw setting. My heart fills with joy as I press my lips against Simon's, embracing him in a tight hug.

'This is the only ring I could find that comes anywhere near showing you how much you mean to me,' Simon says.

'Simon, it is so gorgeous,' I say, melting into him.

'Aunty Beth helped me with the size,' Simon adds, 'so it should fit.'

'It is adorable,' I say, still admiring it in the jeweller's box.

'I love you so much,' Simon adds, kissing me enthusiastically. 'Our relationship feels so right. I enjoy every minute I spend with you. I am hoping you would like to wear this ... as an engagement ring?' Simon tentatively asks, pointing to my left-hand ring finger.

Feeling my eyes tear up with love, 'Yes, I would love that. I do believe you are to be my forever person.'

I hug and kiss my handsome fiancé, thinking life can't get better than this.

'What would our perfect wedding for you look like?' Simon enquires, beaming after his successful proposition.

'Aunty Beth, Suzi, Poppy and I all walking down the aisle to you,' I reply. I really can't help but love this kind charming partner of mine. 'It might be two years away, though; is that okay'?

'Absolutely.' Simon smiles. 'As long as we are together, I'm not concerned about the length of our engagement.'

My relationship is Simon is so strong and happy that I am hoping that one day Suzi can enjoy a loving, stable, mature relationship like this with her soulmate.

*

With four months to go until we need the cancer relapse prevention drugs, Simon has been crucial in boosting our fundraising efforts, raising public awareness of rare cancers and petitioning federal politicians.

As the crucial time to begin these cancer treatments approaches, we are extremely conscious of how vital they are to increase her survival chances by twenty-five per cent. If just one cancer cell survives, without these vital medications, Poppy's chance of survival drops to five to six per cent if she does not remain in remission. Yet we have not even raised $18,000 for Poppy's medication, not even one month's supply.

Regardless of your political persuasion, every child and adult in these dire circumstances deserve an ability to access essential medical treatments in a timely manner. Without these crucial lifesaving treatments, unnecessary patient suffering and the preventable loss of innocent lives is unforgivable. There can be no excuse for funding only third-world health care measures in affluent Western societies where all lives should matter. While most health professionals avoid wasting scarce resources because they are budget-conscious, many are disillusioned that science and research are not driving medical and nursing models of care, but accountants are.

There can be no excuse for bureaucratic inertia, when salvageable toddler and children's lives are at risk.